Past Tenses

Past Tennis

Past Tenses

Essays on writing, autobiography and history

Carolyn Steedman

R Rivers Oram Press
O London

First published in 1992 by
Rivers Oram Press
144 Hemingford Road, London N1 1DE

Published in the USA by
Paul and Company
Post Office Box 442, Concord, MA 01742

Set in Plantin
and printed in Great Britain
by T.J. Press (Padstow) Ltd, Padstow, Cornwall

Designed by Lesley Stewart

British Library Cataloguing in Publication Data

A catalogue record for this book is available from the British Library

ISBN 1-85489-032 8

ISBN 1-85489-021 2 (paperback)

History . . . still, in different hands, *teaches* or *shows* us most kinds of knowable past and almost every kind of imaginable future.

Raymond Williams, *Keywords*, Fontana, 1988, p. 148

History is what hurts.

Frederic Jameson, *The Political Unconscious*,
Methuen, 1981, p. 102

Contents

Acknowledgements

Jeffrey Weeks suggested this, and Liz Fidlon said yes, so I thank them first of all. (Perhaps, after all, I really can say, 'Two booksellers, my particular friends'.) Next I must thank those who read this in draft, and who cut me down to size: Tom Swallow and Karl Miller for their reading of my reading of *Pamela*. I am grateful for their help, and for all their plain speaking. I thank Jonathan Rée in particular, who in one fell read made one-hundred-and-fifty thousand words into a mere eighty, and who for this book, shall be named the Good Reader of Aarhus.

I wish to thank the following for permission to republish these essays: Routledge for 'True Romances' published in Raphael Samuel (ed.), *Patriotism: the making and unmaking of English national identity*, vol. 1 (1989); Routledge and *Feminist Review* for 'The Tidy House', *Feminist Review*, vol. 6 (1980) and 'Prisonhouses', *Feminist Review*, vol. 20 (Summer 1985); Routledge & Kegan Paul for 'Amarjit's Song' published in Carolyn Steedman, Cathy Urwin and Valerie Walkerdine (eds), *Language, Gender and Chilhood* (1985); *London Review of Books* for 'Horsemen' published in vol. 10, no. 3 (February 1988); Virago Press for 'Landscape for a Good Woman' published in Liz Heron (ed.), *Truth Dare or Promise* (1985).

Preface

The articles, chapters from published collections, reviews and talks that make up this selection of essays were all written between 1980 and 1990. I have shortened some of the published pieces where arguments overlap; and I have been quite unable to prevent myself from making some sentences better than they were before. I work anyway, by producing endless drafts. This seems to me not to be the kind of carefulness that people sometimes praise in an accusatory kind of way, but rather, a well-developed and highly practical method of avoiding the agony of writing: of finding out (dragging out of the viscera) what it is, *what it is you mean*, and then still being left with the job of saying it. If you draft, that process never needs to be endured; and one morning, after many minutely altered versions, it is suddenly *there*, a pile of paper on the table, achieved without mudwrestling the words; and you are happily left with a theory that writing is itself a process of cognition, a way of meaning. So I took the opportunity to make a final draft of some of the chapters in this book. Where I have cut more than a few words, I have indicated the omission by ellipses, thus . . . .

Once, when *Landscape for a Good Woman* (the closest thing to being popular I have ever written) had just been published, I did one of those literary gigs that the ICA has made a model for intellectual life in provincial places, with two quite famous writers — novelists — on the topic of women's writing, particularly autobiographical writing. One of the women took me to task afterwards about my dogged insistence on the platform, that I was *not a writer*. I meant something quite simple by the insistence — it wasn't the denial of my identity at all — I meant that I didn't earn my living by writing as my two co-panellists did, couldn't describe myself in that way on my passport, or to the Inland Revenue. I worked then, as I do now, at a job that requires me to write and publish: research and its description and dissemination is a contractual obligation placed on those who work in Universities: each academic a Colette, locked in a room and forced to write, the University Funding Council playing the part for each, of his or her own Willy. Some of the essays in this book concern the relationship between writers and readers in historical contexts, and it seems to me important here to write a prolegomenon that is an anti-romance, that will not allow one reader for one moment to think that the words exist solely out of some compulsive need for them to be said. Material circumstances produce prose, audiences are configured on economic bases which determine the relationship between readers and writers, and between the words on the page and what actually gets read. . . . (Of course, having made that point, it is only correct to acknowledge that the compulsion does exist, and that I am fortunate to take part in a system of wage-labour that allows me to write in the way I want to write, on topics I want to deal with: that allows me to write at all).

What the reader has then, is a thing called 'my work' (meaning my academic work), which is indeed, my commodity, and my invented piece of cultural capital. But not all of it: this is a selection, not a collection. The pieces that follow have been selected because all of them are about writing, in one way or other, as the Introduction explains.

Introduction

Two booksellers, my particular friends, entreated me to write for them a little volume of letters, in a common style, on such subjects as might be of use to those country readers who were unable to indite for themselves. Will it be any harm, said I, in a piece you want to be written so low, if we should instruct them how they should think & act in common cases, as well as indite? They were the more urgent with me to begin the little volume, for this hint. I set about it, & in the progress of it, writing two or three letters to instruct handsome girls, who were obliged to go out to service, as we phrase it, how to avoid the snares that might be laid against their virtue; the above story recurred to my thought; and hence sprung Pamela.

> Samuel Richardson to Johannes Stinstra, 2 June, 1753, in Wilhelm C. Slattery (ed.) *The Richardson-Stinstra Correspondence*, Southern Illinois University Press, London and Amsterdam, 1969, p.28

And it was out of that burden of emotion that there had come to the writer, as release, as an idyll, the ship story, the antique-quayside story, suggested by 'The Enigma of Arrival'; an idea that came innocently, without the writer suspecting how much of his life, how many aspects of his life, that remote story (still just an idea for a story) carried. But that is why certain stories or incidents suggest themselves to writers, or make an impression on them; that is why writers can appear to have obsessions.

> V.S. Naipaul, *The Enigma of Arrival*, Penguin, London 1987, p.96

For a very long time now, I have wanted to write something about Samuel Richardson's novel of 1740. I teach *Pamela*, the account – told in letters – of a fifteen-year-old servant girl's resistance of her young master's advances, his attempts at her seduction and (for Richardson does not mince the meaning of what he depicts) her rape; of her resistance to the point where, reading Pamela's account of all that has passed (and there is no other account: the whole of *Pamela* is Pamela's letters and journal), he proposes marriage to her instead. Teaching the book, I do of course, always have to have something to say about it; but those are formal and required observations, not entirely related to my private brooding on the text, which provides me now with the clearest agenda for thinking about the way some stories simply come and take you, occupy you, make you work out again and again what it is they mean, and the meaning of your own obsession with them. For a start, *Pamela* is a story of class and gender, and a journey of class transition. It provides me with a continued astonishment that an accurate description of *what it was like, what it was going to be like*, not just for a fictional teenager of the 1740s, but for me, now, was penned by a middle-aged London printer two and a half centuries ago. At times of great social transition (where the final turns of feudalism into capitalism wreak havoc with individual lives, shape psychic structures, alter the very body's meaning) people will think things that they do not yet know about, write what they cannot yet think. So it was with Samuel Richardson. It is a commonplace of biographical criticism that Pamela is Richardson's own self, his invented means of exploring his journey through the class structure of early 18th century England, and of asserting his own experience against all the condescending voices that mocked him (and his lower class heroine, once he had written her).[1] What remains unexamined is why, if this is the case, Richardson embodied arguments about himself (arguments that were both psychological and political) in the figure of a young girl, of the poorer sort. Certainly Pamela is the first thoroughly written example of the new version of an old, old history that Nancy Armstrong gives us in her *Desire and Domestic Fiction*. Here, she rehearses the familiar story of the production by Protestantism and Capitalism of the modern individual, but also shows us how that first modern individual was a woman rather than the figure we are used to reading about in this tale: was Domestic Woman rather than Economic Man.[2] *Pamela* is of course, central to Armstrong's argument. But what remains for exploration is the way in which a particular man — Samuel Richardson — was able (was only able) to describe his own individuality, his own sense of interiority, through the figure of a girl, of the poorer sort.

The grand themes that are to be found in *Pamela* (the body's possession, the stewardship of land and property, the abuse of social power and of wealth) are dealt with again by Richardson, in the tragic mode, in *Clarissa* (1747-8). There, Clarissa heroically evades Lovelace's possession of her body through rape, by first unconsciousness, and then by death. There is nothing so grand in *Pamela*. She may faint at the point of penetration, and in what has rightly been called one of the most unerotic scenes in English literature, turn grandeur of theme into the fumbling of domestic farce.[3] What remains erotically charged in *Clarissa*, which is her death, is due to her social standing and her class position. We can never laugh at Clarissa as we can at Pamela, though our laughter at one is perhaps more terrible in implication than our tragic response to the other, for *Pamela* does two things by the conjunction of august theme and farce: it tells us plain that these grand issues (bodily integrity, habeas corpus, land tenure, ownership, occupancy and exploitation) affect the poorer sort in every aspect of their existence, but that their story of resistance and accommodation simply cannot be told as tragedy.

I read *Pamela* for the first time after I had written 'Landscape for a Good Woman' (pp.21-40 below) and the book of the same title. I read Richardson's text then as a confirmation of my own understandings of the creation of psychic structure in historical circumstances. Each new reading continues to work in that way still, affirming that you never do understand something once and for all, even though you may write the understandings down. In fact, each act of reading and writing shows you that the moment of insight, the sudden, shocking comprehension, must be worked for again and again: that nothing ever is known, once and for all.

Pamela then, carries these meanings for me. But it is also a text about writing, and how we might describe the act of writing in both social and psychological terms. It is a text about learning and education, specifically about the embodiment of the skills of literacy and a store of cultural capital in women who teach. That the Pamela who teaches is both of 'the poorer sort' and a *girl* makes her personification of these ideas and principles a means to primary historical reconstruction. *Pamela* teaches as a text (it is part conduct-book: a very thorough description of how to live and how to feel in particular social circumstances); and Pamela herself teaches lessons of sensibility as well as giving instruction in reading and writing.

These preoccupations of Richardson provide a neat thematic summary of much of the work reproduced in this book. As I shall argue in more detail later in this Introduction, *Pamela* allows reflection on the very process of writing itself, and on the development of ideas in written language. Finally, and above all, Richardson's text provides an agenda for thinking about the processes involved in making reconstructions of the past, in the writing of history. Many of the articles and papers reproduced here, evolved into the books I have published, but trajectories of thought are reshaped now by the collection together of fragmented pieces of writing. The organisation of texts, the arrangement and ordering of the documents (like Pamela's letters) is itself an act of interpretation: nothing can remain as it was, for the very act of reconstruction alters the account of the past, and thus the past itself. Margaret Doody describes very well how perpetual motion is held in statis by *Pamela* (it is I think, tribute to the fertility of Richardson's text that it produces such elegant and moving commentry in its critics). She discusses the way in which the text doesn't 'end', how 'Richardson defies the conventions of "an ending" by running right past it'; and she comments that when you close the book (in this case, the paperback edition of the original first and second volumes)

everything is growing and changing and developing — like the seeds of the beans Pamela planted or the seed of the child which is growing in Mr B.'s wife at the end of the novel. No process comes to an end, because consciousness doesn't come to an end, nor the natural world whose impulses it shares . . .[4]

It is something like this that I mean: that even the past is changed by the act of reconstructing it in *Pamela*; by the reader's reading of it: that nothing stays the same. At the very least, *Pamela* allows me to say things about the essays that follow, their origins and evolution, the perpetual argument about the past that they contain, that I would not otherwise be able to say.

What I want to write about is: Pamela's being all words, and the sad — but written — knowledge that in the end, Richardson can do nothing with the marvellous, funny, agitated girl, who gets what she wants (what she thinks she wants: what is the only thing *to* want, given the historical circumstances out of which she is created); whose creator dims the light, pulls her indoors, stops listing the *things* that make her earlier world (cups, coins, ink, earth, beans, paper, seeds, shifts, petticoats); dresses her as a doll, limbs stiff, sauciness gone: in her Exalted Condition.

But the desire to say something — each elegant insight — is always pre-empted. There is Jocelyn Harris's fine delineation of Pamela as the embodiment of protest and Protestantism, of Locke's 'Fundamental, sacred and unalterable Law of Self-Preservation'; Pamela, always and absolutely *her own Self*, and of course, utterly subversive as a figure embodying these political principles because she is of the poorer sort, and a girl.[5] Margaret Doody has written better than anyone else about Pamela's funniness, about this 'comical girl' whose existence allows me, even at this great distance from her time and circumstance, to allow the reader to mock me because I mock myself at the finesse of my own sensibility, to see myself as laughable as the girl who compares the result to her hands of doing a bit of washing-up with what the Protestant martyr experienced, putting a finger in the flames.[6] The point is, that all we laugh at in Pamela is contained within the narrative she gives us of herself.

Terry Eagleton, in his account of Richardson's more dignified and lauded *Clarissa* has come as close as anyone has so far, to outlining *how it happens*, how a figure in a text (and at this moment, it is of Pamela that he speaks) might become 'a whole cultural event . . . the occasion or organising principle of a multimedia affair'. He sketches the extraordinary reaction to the appearance and reading of *Pamela* in 1740, and writes that

> The literary text is not merely to be read: it is to be dramatised, displayed, wielded as a cultural totem, ransacked for moral propaganda or swooned over as love story. preached from the pulpit and quoted in salons. Pamela . . . [is] public property subject to strategic uses, lynchpin of an entire ideological formation.[7]

Later, he remarks that *Clarissa* embodies a 'true' history (a history like Pamela's, but in a different key, of 'women's oppression at the hands of 18th century patriarchy'), not particularly more fictitious than the history written by Burke and Gibbon; that it is certainly the case that Clarissa Harlowe 'never existed', but not important that this is the case. She is, he says, 'as it were, real enough to be going on with'.[8]

There are the commentaries of Doody and Harris and Eagleton; two years ago, describing a pedagogy of startling virtuosity, a teacher from a college of business and design in Manhattan gave an account of the way in which he made this text matter to students of fashion and textile, who were 'visually rather than verbally gifted'. Florian Stuber writes:

> *Pamela* was in many ways a perfect choice for FIT [Fashion Institute of Technology] students . . . Since they were students with vocations, many living away from home for the first time, I thought they might recognise themselves in Pamela, a working woman away from her parents, a woman who had become 'a little expert at (her) Needle', and who, like many of them, both designed and made her own clothes. I thought that Pamela's situation at the opening of the novel would immediately interest women who planned to enter the business world, who would have to face the possibility of sexual harassment on the job; I thought, too, that many would appreciate the chance to discuss seriously the issues of love, marriage, and family raised in the rest of the book since their

professional goals did not preclude these more personal hopes. Finally since this was a course in Composition, I thought it good to present my students with a model of a woman who was a writer, who took pleasure and pride in writing, who wrote at length and who wrote well, and whose writing had real effects on people in her world and outside it.[9]

Not only pre-empted, but jealous too; for I have never made *Pamela* matter in this way, to students who are theoretically much closer to the concerns of the text than are Stuber's, undergraduates who are going to teach, spend years in those places that are the site of the production of the vast majority of writing in society — in schools; students who need a sophisticated knowledge of the kind of popular forms that feed *Pamela*, and of the relationship of autobiographical writing to the development of the self. They will as teachers, possess a cultural capital that it is their job to transmit; the same social and class ambivalence will attach to their doing so as it did to Pamela, for they are understood to be only the footsoldiers of intellectual endeavour, purveying a cheap knowledge to cheap people. In fact, Pamela herself, in the enclosed space of Volumes III and IV, keeps her domestic school, instructing her husband's illegitimate daughter along with her own little brood, by the means of stories and a highly ambivalent relationship with John Locke's *Some Thoughts Concerning Education*. The last two volumes of *Pamela* (*Pamela Two*) are not published in paperback, so practically and for teaching purposes they cannot matter in the way that the first part (*Pamela One*) does, where Pamela's very self, her body, the figure she makes in the text *is* the valuable skill of literacy, and where her abilities on this score (as on so many others) are vastly superior to those of the clumsy young gentleman she is to marry. All words, nothing but words; we do not need to know about the letters in her bodice, sewn into her petticoat, to understand that she is a body of words, though it adds much delight when it becomes clear that it is the body of words that finally makes Mr B. see Pamela plain, through his desire to possess them (read them, take them); and know that he loves her.

Pamela is an instructress then, the first in a long line of

domestic figures in fictional settings who will, with increasing seriousness as the century passes, teach the reader about the organisation of household space, and the furnishings of a subjectivity. She is both commodity and cultural capital; she mediates a set of cultural principles as yet (in the 1740s) unborn, in the sense that they are not quite understood by and therefore not quite articulated by Richardson. She is made by these cultural principles; the words she writes embody them. She is the body Mr B. cannot have, and that he then achieves; to a darkening of the light.

I can write these things about *Pamela* then, though they have been said before, and my words are only transliteration of the extraordinarily pleasurable observations of others. Pamela, a girl whose seduction would 'hurt no family', whose attempted rape is 'only what all young gentlemen will do', dares to set the highest price upon herself, to refuse 'to be his property'. She talks of these attempts upon her person as her potential undoing; and 'Mighty piece of undone!' sneers Mrs Jewkes, her jailer in the Lincolnshire property where she has been taken after her abduction. But it is Pamela's pen that first records the evidence that allows us to make the charge of outrageous and laughable pretention. Who *does* she think she is? There is no other discussion in English literature that I know of that chorus of small, sneering voices that accompany those who rise above their station, make their escape from among the poorer sort; the voices that whisper malevolently through the years: Who the hell does she think she is?[10]

And Richardson gives me even more, for he actually allows his character to reflect on these matters. Pamela is given Locke's *Some Thoughts Concerning Education* as a present and a reward by her husband, when she is delivered of her first born, a boy. She has difficulty with this manual of child care and education, for it promulgates a very different socialisation from the one she has received, being intended for the guidance of gentry parents of boy children: 'I think that a Prince, a Nobleman, and an ordinary Gentleman's Son, should have different ways of Breeding . . .', said Locke.[11] Dissatisfied with it, Pamela pens her own, in a series of letters to her husband. One of her sticking places is with Locke's strictures against false modesty in the socialisation of upper-class boys — 'sheepish bashfulness', he called it; and commented that 'there is often in People, especially in children, a clownish shamefacedness before strangers, or others above them'. He argued that little boys should be taught 'Assurance', 'not to think meanly' of themselves; 'we ought', he wrote 'to think so well of ourselves as to perform these actions which are incumbent upon us, and expected of us, without discomposure or disorder'.[12]

Pamela cannot take this. Writing of herself (of the character that her creator has allowed his character to see) rather than her baby, she says:

> I would beg leave to observe, that however discommodious a bashful temper is . . . yet in my humble opinion . . . is always to be preferred to an undistinguishing and hardy confidence . . . . A mind that never doubts itself must be a stranger to its own infirmities; and suspecting none, is impetuous, over-bearing and incorrigible . . .[13]

Well, the comical girl of Volumes I and II would never have put it like that; but she is now the matron of the conduct books, and bound to speak in these terms. The part of her former self that remains though, is an understanding of how class circumstances, the socialisation of children within different classes of society, shape psychic structure.

This has been a mighty round-about way of saying that to publish a selection of essays is a pretentious thing to do (I'd like to have the kind of safe disclaimer that Richardson had; I want to begin by saying that 'two booksellers, my particular friends, entreated me to write for them a little volume . . .'); but without *Pamela* I could not have simultaneously made the point that whilst structures of feeling, which are made in specific class and historical circumstances, are both damaging and constraining, fettering the mind and the spirit, they are also cherished possessions, matters of pride and defiance; your own self. And not bad ones these: the inculcated humility keeps you one step ahead, to ask, 'who the hell does she think she is?' just that moment before the others do: to control the story.

In introducing this book, and discussing its organisation, I want to distinguish between theme (with which I shall deal first of all) and structure, for the one does not exactly match the other. A central preoccupation of this book, and one that runs through all its four sections, is the relationship of written and public histories to personal pasts. I want to suggest however, through 'Landscape for a Good Woman', 'History and Autobiography' and all of the chapters of Part IV, that the path of reinsertion offered by the new history of the 1970s and 1980s (people's history, labour history, oral history, women's history) in fact only offers an endless repetition — a useful, and indeed, politically necessary repetition, as all those lost and abandoned and forgotten stories are added — but not the place where the interesting questions lie. I think that my book *Landscape for a Good Woman*, which was written after and out of the piece of the same title reprinted below, often has been read as an act of that kind of reinsertion, a kind of mending of labour history and people's history, by the addition of the working-class woman's part, the child's story. It certainly was intended to confront the theories we live by, with the experience of class and (to a lesser extent) the experience of gender. But history (as in Auden's 'Homage to Clio') turns her blank face to reinsertion: whoever is there, it is still the same old story.[14] It is not that it cannot be done, for the story is rewritten on a daily basis: women, children, new categories of working people enter her train constantly; and she does not care. I have never been angry with history, in the way that philosophy has made me mad, many Marxisms and post-structuralisms and feminisms have driven me to fury, for I have always assumed that even though the historical tale is about a King, a Queen, a battle, a reform act, plagues, earthquakes, enclosures — that I am somewhere there, in the story. It seems probable that history cannot work as either cognition or narrative without the assumption on the part of the writer and the reader of it that there is somewhere the great story, that contains everything there is and ever has been — 'visits home, heartbeats, a first kiss, the jump of an electron from one orbital position to another', as well as the desolate battlefield, the ruined village — from which the smaller story, the one before your eyes now, has simply been extracted.[15] So anger or irritation at the absences in written history seem to me not to be the point at all. Rather, now, the task is to recognise the form and function of historical narrative, work out what kind of cultural form it shows itself to be, as a way of thought and a means of cognition. I think that the contemplation of these questions leads us to another form — cultural form and narrative form — that behaves epistemologically much like history: leads us to the idea of childhood.

I am interested in the way in which the modern idea of history (an account of the past to be told out of the accretions of documentary evidence) grew to pre-eminence at the same time as the modern idea of childhood, both of them in the middle and later years of the last century. There is a general familiarity with the idea of each and every individual's childhood as the buried past, the place that is *there*, within us, but never to be obtained. This understanding of the individual human subject was examined and expressed in many forms of writing in the 19th century, from the scientific treatise to slush fiction, though it was growth-studies — the popularised physiology of the mid-century — that put new formulations of human insideness — of having an inside, a space within: an interiority — on the cultural agenda. This is to say (and it is the account of Margaret McMillan's work below, that shows this most clearly) that it was through descriptions of a child's body, and the way in which that description was written into common-or-garden political programmes of the turn of the century, that this notion of human insideness was conveyed to a very large number of people living in the society. But before this — for the preceding two centuries — 'childhood' had collected around itself a similar range of cultural meanings, and these are explored in both Part II and Part III of this book.

I take childhood to be a *form*: an imaginative structure that allows the individual to make exploration of the self and gives the means to relate that understanding to larger social organisations. Its specific literary expression is the late 19th century 'childhood'; but since that period it has shaped a very wide range of writing, and in late 20th century society is a taken-for-granted means of understanding the human subject, of locating it in time and chronology, and 'explaining' it. It has something (but by no means everything) to do with real children, and the material circumstances of the last three hundred years, that histories of childhood can describe.

The first task then, seems to be a historical exploration of the common origin of the idea of history, and the idea of childhood. But once this is done, the next important investigation must be into the contradiction and dichotomy that their juxtaposition suggests. History offers the fantasy that *it may be found*: that out of all the bits and pieces left behind, the past may be reconstructed, conjured before the eyes: found. Childhood — the idea of childhood — on the other hand, may tell us that the search is futile (though it can be necessary and is sometimes compulsive); tells us that the lost object is not to be found, for the very search for the past in each of us changes the past as we go along, so that the lost thing is not the same now, as it was before. The reader must see the chapters entitled 'The Watercress Seller' (Part IV), and 'Written Children' (Part III) as notes towards this larger project, rather than as completed arguments.

When I want to mock myself, I make a wry observation about the way in which I sometimes look up from the page and reflect on the fact, that in the past few years, I have not done much more than produce long, and elaborate and historical footnotes to Raymond Williams's accounts of 'culture' in *Culture and Society*, *Marxism and Literature*, and *Keywords*. I have, for instance, published a book which describes the development and use of 19th century cultural theory within British socialism, and the reorganisation of some of its key components around the figure of the child and the idea of childhood, in the period 1890–1920. (Some of these arguments are rehearsed in the essay 'The Written Child: Margaret McMillan, Marigold and Mignon'). I am thus able, at the end of *Childhood, Culture and Class* to suggest that Williams's radical philology was missing something: that an explosion of growth studies from the middle years of the century and a consequent theorisation of those social subjects who demonstrate and embody growth, may align a late 19th century understanding of 'culture' with an older one, with the earlier meaning that Williams outlines in *Keywords*, of the actual material improvement and cultivation of bodies and minds in society.[16] There are those blank pages at the end of the 1983 edition of *Keywords* for your own notes, the sign, as Williams wrote 'that the inquiry remains open'; but my notes of contribution to the definition of terms are three-hundred pages long. . . .

My other argument with Williams's work is to be found in the essays entitled 'Prisonhouses' (Part I), 'Amarjit's Song' (Part II), and 'The Mother Made Conscious' (Part IV). There is a history of subjectivity (of the kinds of subjectivity that people have felt obliged to make for themselves in different historical circumstances) that can connect subjectivity to the idea of culture. Both of these ideas have often been organised around women, particularly the figure of the teacher. I return often to the passages in *Marxism and Literature* where Williams describes first, the notion of 'civilising', as a bringing of men within social organisation; then, how the aim of civilsation was expressed by the word 'civil', as orderly, educated, polite; and finally, how 'civilisation' and 'culture' were in the late 18th century, interchangeable terms, how their eventual divergence came through the attack on 'civilisation' as superficial, the attack on all things artificial as distinct from those in a natural state. Williams then argues that the attack on 'artificiality', made through into the 19th century, was 'the basis of one important alternative sense of "culture" — as a process of "inner" or "spiritual" as distinct from "external" development'.[17]

I am still astonished that an accurate description of an actual historical process can take place without any reference to its material components: to what actually happened. For this development, located by Williams in the history of the last three hundred years, is inexplicable without some knowledge of the history of women and children (the idea of women and children) in European society. 'The primary effect of this alternative sense of the term "culture" ', says Williams, 'was to associate it with religion, art, *the family and personal life* . . .' Indeed, in those five words lies occluded a whole history; and yet without the history, Williams is still able to say that through these processes, 'culture' came to be related to 'the imagination': to the 'inner life, in its most accesible, secular forms'. I think that the history of teaching in English society (which is to some extent a history of the women who became teachers) is one component of the account that remains unspoken in Williams's work. The school was the place where a society placed the burdens of creativity and imagination on children (from about 1930 onwards; this is a variation of the story of educational progressivism that figures in these essays), and the burden of culture on women. The disdain and suspicion with which items of culture have been bestowed on upper working-class girls training to be teachers, and the baffled denial with which they have offered these commodities to children, are part of the long shift in social organisation and meaning that Williams describes in his various writings on culture.

These then are the main themes of this book; but what it turns out to be *about*, as a book, is writing. The term 'writing' must be taken to mean: written language and its relationship to spoken language; a psychological process (an individual act of cognition) that is at exactly the same time a social form: 'writing in society'. 'Writing' connotes form and function. That is to say, as an idea it must continually draw our attention to the way in which, as a material process and a technology, it places constraints on us (is not the same as speech-written-down; is not a transcription of spoken language). As an idea, writing must continually spell out both restraint and permission, must draw our attention to the literary forms available to people in different historical epochs, forms that sometimes restrain the writing of the self, sometimes permit it.

Because it seems to me that all the essays in this book are more or less about these topics, I have sectionlised it in the following way: Part I concerns questions of self and writing, the way in which, through writing (autobiographical writing in this case) the self is written out of, and into its historical context. In part II, I have put together those essays and articles that deal with children learning to write, children actually writing, and children using other people's written language for their own purposes — which are always developmental and always social, both at the same time. Part III, which deals with adults' writing, raises questions about writing as a process of concealment and revelation in the work of respectively, a woman of working-class origin writing a 'childhood' in the 1920s, Margaret McMillan using the sentimentalised child-figure in major pieces of her journalism to construct both a political programme and a depiction of herself, and an ex-soldier and policeman writing his memoirs in the early 1880s. Part IV is about the historian writing. 'Forms of History' and 'The Watercress Seller' propose a series of questions about historical narrative, the grandeur of history as a written form (and thus its desirability), and the historian's transferential relationship to the past. (The historian writing about the history of pedagogy in a class society, and a history of women in classrooms in 'The Mother Made Conscious' here is also the ghost of the self I wrote in 'Prisonhouses', in Part I of the book).

Through analysing the children's narrative 'The Tidy House' (which was actually produced in 1976, and which I started to work on in 1980) I learned most of what I know about writing as a form of cognition and a means of representation. Ten years later, I still found the description of written language available from cognitive psychology and developmental linguistics the most useful approach to the Radical Soldier's Tale, to the text produced by John Pearman, the radical, republican, free-thinking policeman and soldier, some time in the early 1880s. I know John Pearman as a writer better than anyone else in the world; I know the nooks and crannies of his 'Memoir', each altered punctuation mark; once, I counted and classified every spelling error he made. The children's text of 1970s and the working-class autobiography of a century before are both evidence for a (as yet unwritten) history of literary forms and figures, and the uses made of them. Both of them show, I think, that concomitant with a history of writing in society must be the development of a theory of reading, that shows *how it happens*: how texts come to matter, how forms and figures get used, transmuted, changed. I very badly indeed want historians to take as a serious object of study, forms and figures, and their constant re-shaping, so that one day soon, we might be in a position to describe the relationship between the history of forms and the history of societies. If however, we are to begin work on this most urgent of historical tasks, of describing how writing and reading happen in societies, and how texts and figures come to

operate in this way, then (to return to an earlier discussion) I
think that it will be Pamela Andrews, rather than Clarissa
Harlowe, who will be the first to show us all of her vulgar and
practical historicity, and allow us to theorise by it.[18]

What happened to the letters? A veritable corpus, too
many pages at the end to sew into bodices and linings. They
become a corpus after they have been pressed to Pamela's
body, to be sent out — we know this much — to relatives-in-
law, perused and pondered over: letters of conduct and
feeling. The final volume ends with Pamela's dreadful nursery
tales, told for the edification of her children and Miss
Goodwin, Mr B.'s illegitimate child. Four exemplary figures
feature in these stories, Coquetilla, Prudiana, Profusiana and
Prudentia, through whose tedious biographies proper female
modes of behaviour are expounded. Though little Miss
Goodwin is able to burst out at the end with literary insight: 'O madam! madam! . . . PRUDENTIA IS YOU! — Is You
indeed! — It *can* be nobody else! — O teach me good Heaven!
to follow *your* example, and I shall be a SECOND PRUDENTIA!',
what the reader notices is, that of all four fictional girls,
Prudentia is the only one who doesn't have a story at all, only a
list of virtues. This is the place then, where Pamela's own story
(for she certainly had one) and her own self, is negated by
Richardson, and we can see the hundreds and hundreds of
letters implode, even as Pamela signs her name for the last
time and sends the sorry little tales off to Lady Grereby.[19] It is
indeed, all very sad stuff, at the end. For those who make it to
the end of Volume IV then, speculation about the fate of the
letters becomes irrelevant, for Pamela no longer exists.

Richardson recommended writing to his female acquaintances (his was the famous and touching observation that 'the
pen is almost as pretty an implement in a woman's fingers, as a
needle'[20]), on the grounds that through writing, they would
surprise themselves into thoughts they knew not (yet) they
had. Writing is this form of cognition and of self-revelation, of
course; but it acts, at exactly the same time, as the mask of
meaning, holds meaning behind itself, waiting ready for later
scrutiny. The piece of writing that has caused me excessive
self-scrutiny and recrimination over the years is 'Amarjit's
Song', reproduced in Part II. This was the first thing I

wrote, in 1979, after quite a long period of refusing to write anything at all, and it was the most changed of all the pieces, between the time of writing and publication. It started out as a much shorter account of the incident that is still here described, its sentimentality quite naked and aggressive. Later, when I read Margaret McMillan's heart-wrenching socio-fictions of working-class childhood, that she published in the labour press between 1895 and 1910, I recognised what kind of political form I had been working within in the very private piece of 1979. Much later, in his 'Kindergarten' of 1985, Franco Moretti theorised 'moving' fiction for and about children — again, fiction from the turn-of-the century — and discussed what it is in certain pieces of writing that make the reader cry.[21] The first version of 'Amarjit's Song' certainly made me cry, which must have been part of its purpose; but by the time it came to be published, the 'moving' story was embedded in what is a much more interesting discussion of the role of speech–play in second language acquisition. Anyway, the published piece got the only really bad review I've ever had, taking me to task over the sections concerning Punjabi children and their understanding of the dowry system. My nervousness at the topics I was dealing with are signalled by my very many strange moves into the passive tense in 'Amarjit's Song', and are I suppose, to do with my refusal of the structuring facts of racism in this child's life, and my removal of her ethnicity in favour of her class position. I was edgy on this score — it is clear now — but would still want to argue that the most useful way of understanding the events described here is through the historical circumstances that placed the child in a particular pedagogic position. It still seems to me that the history of education in a class society has a good deal of explanatory power in Amarjit's case.

What I really do regret, and it is a more general regret than over 'Amarjit's Song', is that I seem incapable of saying anything at all (in this case, something reasonably important about child-language development, bi-lingualism, and the use made of particular texts by readers) without messing with some other story, some other person's narrative: without, in these particular pages, right now, using *Pamela* as my front. Of course, I do know that what you find in that imagined room which is Pamela's letter-store, the closet of the human heart, are always all the other books that shape your words, long-forgotten, always present. The letter-closet is also the facsimile of history, and historical writing, suggests why it is you might want it, more than any other story: because it is the grandest narrative of all, offers the chimera of the letters, bundles and bundles of them, letters that contain everything there is, all the story, everything that has ever been said, so that the book before you — in Pamela's case, which is why she is so important a fantasy — *is* the documentary evidence for the story, and the story itself. So Pamela's story is also about the pretension of the historical enterprise: about that enterprise as a fantasy of power (owning it all, *having* the past), and about its desirability as a fantasy, which is why the letters and documents are made indistinguishable sometimes from the pretty things (petticoats, plackets, bodices, linings — now silk, now linsey) that hide and hold them, and which are indeed, as close as it is possible to get to the body in question.

Autobiographies

1

Autobiographies

1 Landscape for a Good Woman[1]

When I was three, before my sister was born, I had a dream. It remains quite clear across the years, the topography absolutely plain, so precise in details of dress that I can use them to place the dream in historical time. We were in a street, the street so wide and the houses so distant across the other side that it might not have been a street at all; and the houses lay low with gaps between them so that the sky filled a large part of the picture. Here, at the front, on this side of the wide road, a woman hurried along, having crossed from the houses behind. The perspective of the dream must have shifted several times, for I saw her once as if from above, moving through a kind of square, or crossing place, and then again from the fixed point of the dream where I stood watching her, left forefront.

She wore the New Look, a coat of beige gabardine which fell in two swaying graceful pleats from her waist at the back (the swaying must have come from very high heels, but I didn't notice her shoes), a hat tipped forward from hair swept up. She hurried, something jerky about her movements, a titupping, agitated walk, glancing around at me as she moved across the foreground. Several times she turned, and came some way back towards me, admonishing, shaking her finger. Encouraging me to follow in this way perhaps, but moving too fast for me to believe that she wanted me to do that, she entered a revolving door of dark polished wood, mahogany and glass, and started to go round and round, looking out at me at she turned. I wish I knew what she was doing, and what she wanted me to do.

This book (Liz Heron [ed.], *Truth, Dare or Promise*, 1985) is about childhood, a time when only the surroundings show, and nothing is explained. It is also about a period of recent history, the 1950s, and about the way in which those years shaped individual lives and collective ideas. But children do not possess a *social* analysis of what is happening to them, or around them, so the landscape and the pictures it presents have to remain a background, taking on meaning later, from different circumstances. Understanding of the dream built up in layers, over a long period of time. Its strange lowered vista, for instance (which now reminds the adult more than anything else of George Herriman's *Krazy Kat*, where buildings disappear and reappear from frame to frame[2]) is an obvious representation of London in the late Forties and Fifties: all the houses had gaps in between, because of the bombs, and the sky came closer to the ground than seemed right. I understood what I had seen in the dream when I learned the words 'gabardine' and 'mahogany'; and I was born in the year of the New Look, understood by 1951 and the birth of my sister, that dresses needing twenty yards for a skirt were items as expensive as children — more expensive really, because after 1948 babies came relatively cheap, on tides of free milk and orange juice, but good cloth in any quantity was hard to find for a very long time.

Detail like this provides retrospective labelling, but it is not evidence about a historical period. The only *evidence* from that dream is the feeling of childhood — all childhoods, probably: the puzzlement of the child watching from the pavement, wondering what's going on, what they, the adults are up to, what they want from you, and what they expect you to do.

Worked upon and reinterpreted, the landscape becomes a historical landscape, but only through continual and active reworking. 'The essence of the historical process,' says Tamara Hareven in *Family Time and Industrial Time*,

is the meeting between an individual's or a group's life history and the historical moment. People's responses to the historical conditions they encounter are shaped both by the point in their lives at which they encounter those conditions and by the equipment they bring with them from earlier life experiences.[3]

But children possess very little of that equipment, and in the process of acquiring it, the baggage is continually reorganised and reinterpreted. Memory simply can't resurrect those years, because it is memory itself that shapes them, long after the historical time has passed. So to present the decade through the filter of my parents' story, and my growing awareness of the odd typicality of my childhood, is the result of a decision to see the 1950s as a political moment when hope was promised, and then deferred. We rework past time to give current events meaning, and that reworking provides an understanding that the child at the time can't possess: it's only in the last few months that I've come to understand who the woman in the New Look coat was.

Now, later, I see the time of my childhood as a point between two worlds, an older 'during the War', 'before the War', 'in the Depression', 'then'; and the place we inhabit now. The War was so palpable a presence in the first five years of my life that I still find it hard to believe that I didn't live through it. There were bombsites everywhere, prefabs on waste land, most things still rationed, my mother tearing up the ration book over my sister's pram outside the Library in the High Street when meat came off points in the summer of 1951, a gesture that still fills me with the desire to do something so defiant and final; and then looking across the street at a woman wearing a full-skirted dress, and then down at the Forties straight-skirted navy blue suit she was still wearing, and longing, irritatedly, for the New Look, and then at us, the two living barriers to twenty yards of cloth. Back home, she said, she'd be able to get it from the side door of the mill, but not here; not with you two . . . I was three in 1950, only twelve when the decade ended, just a child, a repository for other people's history; and my mother gave me her version long before my father did.

By the time my father could sit down with me in a pub, slightly drunk, tell me and my friends about Real Life, crack a joke about a Pakistani that silenced a whole table once, and talk about the farm labourer's — his grandfather's — journey up from Eye in Suffolk working on the building of the Great North Western railway to Rawtenstall on the Lancashire-Yorkshire border, I was doing history at Sussex, and knew more than he did about the date and timing of journeys like that. My father, old but gritty, glamorous in the eyes of the Class of '68, a South London wide boy with an authentic background, described his grandfather's funeral, about 1912, when a whole other family, wife, children, grandchildren, turned up out of the blue from somewhere further down the line where they'd been established on the navvy's journey north. (This was a circumstance paralleled at his own funeral, when the friends and relations of the woman he'd been living with for part of the week since the early 1960s, stole the show from us, the pathetic huddle of the family of his middle years.) My mother's story, on the other hand, was told to me much earlier, in bits and pieces throughout the Fifties, and it wasn't delivered to entertain but rather to teach me lessons. There was a child, an eleven-year-old from a farm seven miles south of Coventry, sent off to be a maid-of-all-work in a parsonage in Burnley. She had her tin trunk and she cried, waiting on the platform with her family seeing her off, for the through-train to Manchester. They'd sent her fare, the people in Burnley: 'but think how she felt, such a little girl, she was only eleven, with nothing but her little tin box. Oh she did cry.' I cry now over accounts of childhood like this, weeping furtively over the reports of 19th century commissions of inquiry into child labour, abandoning myself to the luxuriance of grief in libraries, tears staining the page where Mayhew's little water-cress girl tells her story. The lesson was, of course, that I must never, ever cry for myself, for I was a lucky little girl; my tears should be for all the strong, brave women who gave me life. This story, which embodied fierce resentment against the unfairness of things, was carried through seventy years and three generations, and all of them, all the good women, dissolved into the figure of my mother, who was, as she told us *a good mother*. She didn't go out drinking or dancing; didn't do as one mother she'd known (in a story of maternal neglect that I remember feeling was over the top at the time) and tie a piece of string round my big toe, dangle it through the window and down the front of the house, so that the drunken mother, returning from her carousing, could tug at it, wake the child, get the front door opened and send it down to the shop for a basin of pie and peas. I still put myself to sleep by thinking about *not* lying on a cold pavement covered with newspapers. She must have told me once that I was lucky to have a warm bed to lie in at night.

What she did, in fact, the eleven-year-old who cried on Coventry station, was hate being a servant. She got out as soon as she could, and found work in the weaving sheds — 'she was a good weaver; six looms under her by the time she was sixteen' — marry, produce nine children, eight of whom emigrated to the cotton mills of Massachusetts before the First World War; managed, 'never went before the Guardians'.[4] It was much, much later that I learned from *One Hand Tied Behind Us* that four was the usual number of looms for a Lancashire weaver. Burnley weavers were not well organised, and my great-grandmother had six not because she was a good weaver but because she was exploited.[5] In 1916, when her daughter Carrie's husband was killed at the Somme, she managed that too, looking after the three-year-old, my mother, so that Carrie could go on working at the mill.

But long before the narrative fell into place, before I could dress the eleven-year-old of my imagination in the clothing of the 1870s, I knew perfectly well what that child had done, and how she had felt. She cried, because tears are cheap; and then she'd stopped, and got by, because nobody gives you anything in this world. What was given to her, passed on to all of us, was a powerful and terrible endurance, the self-destructive defiance of those doing the best they can with what life hands out to them.

From a cotton town my mother had a heightened awareness of fabric and weave, and I can date events by the clothes I wore as a child, and the material they were made of. Post-War children had few clothes, because of rationing; but not only scarcity, rather names like barathea, worsted, gabardine, twill, jersey . . . fix them in my mind. The dream of the New Look has to have taken place during or after the summer of 1950, because in it I wore one of my two summer dresses, one of green and one of blue gingham, that were made that year and lasted me, with letting down, until I went to school. Sometime during 1950, I think before the summer, before the dresses were made, I was taken north to Burnley and into the sheds. My mother was visiting someone who worked there whom she'd known as a child. The woman smiled and nodded at me through the noise that made a surrounding silence. Later, my mother told me they had to lip read: they couldn't hear each other speak for the noise of the looms. But I didn't notice the noise. She wore high platform-soled black shoes that I still believe I heard click on the bright polished floor as she walked between her looms. When I hear the word 'tending' I think always of that confident attentiveness to the needs of the machines, the control over work that was unceasing, with half a mind and hands engaged but the looms always demanding attention. When I worked as a primary school teacher I sometimes retrieved that feeling with a particular clarity, walking between the tables on the hard floor, all the little looms working, but needing my constant adjustment. The woman wore a dress that seemed very short when I recalled the picture through the next few years: broad shoulders, a straight skirt that hung the way it did — I know now — because it had some rayon in it. No New Look here in Burnley either. The post-War years were full of women longing for a full skirt and unable to make it. I wanted to walk like that, a short skirt, high heels, bright red lipstick, in charge of all that machinery.

It is extremely difficult for me to think of women as people who do not work. Their work moreover, is visible and comprehensible: they can explain to, or show children what it is they do and how — unlike men, whose processes of getting money are mysterious and hidden from view. There has been a recent reassessment of the traditional picture of the enforced flight from the labour force to domesticity on the part of women just after the War, and far from a flight, large-scale recruitment to the new industries in the early 1950s now seems to present a more historically accurate picture. It is probable that the memory of most children of our generation is of women as workers. I had no awareness of the supposed stereotypical mother of that era — lipsticked and aproned, waiting at the door — and I don't think I ever encountered a picture of her, in books, comics or film, until the early 1960s.

As a teenage worker my mother had broken a recently established pattern. When she left school in 1927 she hadn't gone into the sheds. She lied to me, though, when I asked about the age of eight what she'd done: she said she'd worked in an office, done clerical work. Ten years later, on a visit to Burnley and practising the skills of the oral historian, I talked to my grandmother, and she, puzzled, told me that Edna had never worked in any office, had in fact been apprenticed to a dry cleaning firm that did tailoring and mending. On the same visit, the first since my early childhood, I found a reference written by a local doctor for my mother, who about 1930 applied for a job as a ward maid at the local asylum, confirming that she was clean, strong, honest and intelligent. I wept over that of course, for a world where some people might doubt her — my — cleanliness. I didn't care much about the honesty, and I knew I was strong; but there are people everywhere waiting for you to slip up, to show signs of dirtiness and stupidity, so that they can send you back where you belong.

She didn't finish her apprenticeship — I deduce that, rather than know it — sometime, it must have been in 1934, came south, worked in Woolworths on the Edgware Road, spent the War years in Roehampton, a ward maid again, at the hospital where they mended fighter pilots' ruined faces. Now I can feel the deliberate vagueness in her accounts of those years: 'Where did you meet Daddy?' Oh, at a dance, at home.' There were no photographs. Who came to London first? I wish now I'd asked that question. He worked on the buses when he arrived, showed me a canopy in front of a hotel that he'd brought down on his first solo drive. He was too old to be called up (a lost generation of men who were too young for the first War, too old for the second). There's a photograph of him standing in front of the cabbages that he'd grown for victory wearing his Home Guard uniform. But what did he *do*? Too late now to find out.

During the post-War housing shortage, my father got an office job with a property company, and the flat that went with it. I was born in March 1947, at the peak of the Bulge: more babies born that month than ever before or after, and carried through the terrible winter of 1946–47. We moved to Streatham Hill in June 1951, to an estate owned by the same company, later to be taken over by Lambeth Council. A few years later, my father got what he wanted, which was to be in charge of the company's boiler maintenance. On his death certificate it says 'heating engineer'.

In the 1950s my mother took in lodgers. Streatham Hill Theatre (now a bingo hall) was on the pre-West End circuit, and we had chorus girls staying with us for weeks at a time. I was woken up in the night sometimes, the spare bed in my room being made up for someone they'd met down the Club, the other lodger's room already occupied. I like the idea of being the daughter of a theatrical landlady, but this enterprise provided my most startling and problematic memories. Did the girl from Aberdeen really say 'Och, no, not on the table!' as my father flattened a bluebottle with his hand, and did he *really* put down a newspaper on the same table to eat his breakfast? I feel a fraud, a bit-part player in a soft and southern version of *The Road to Wigan Pier*.

I remember incidents like these, I think, because I was about seven, the age at which children start to notice social detail and social distinction, but also more partcularly because the long lesson in hatred for my father had begun, which in the early stages was in the traditional mode, to be found in the opening chapters of *Sons and Lovers* and Lawrence's description of the inculcated dislike of Mr Morrell: of female loathing for coarse male habits. The newspaper on the table is problematic for me because it was problematic for my mother, a symbol of all she'd hoped to escape and all she'd landed herself in. (It was at this time, I think, that she told me that her own mother, means-tested in the late Twenties had won the sympathy of the relieving officer, who ignored the presence of the saleable piano because she kept a clean house, with a cloth on the table.)

Now, thirty years later, I feel a great regret for the father of my first four years, who took me out, and who probably loved me, irresponsibly ('it's alright for him; he doesn't have to look after you'), and wish I could tell him now, even though he was, in my sister's words, a sod, that I'm sorry for my years of rejection and dislike. But we had to choose, early on, which side we belonged to, and children have to come down on the side that brings the food home and gets it to the table. By 1955 I was beginning to hate him — because *he* was to blame, for the lack of money, for my mother's terrible dissatisfaction with the way things were working out.

The new consumer goods came into the household slowly — because of *him*. We had the first fridge in our section of the street (he got it cheap — contacts) but were late to get a television. The vacuum cleaner was welcomed at first because it meant no longer having to do the stairs with a stiff brush. But in fact it added to my Saturday work because I was expected to clean more with the new machine. I enjoy shocking people by describing how goods were introduced into households under the guise of gifts for children: the fridge in the house of the children we played with over the road was given to the youngest as a birthday present — the last thing an eight-year-old wants. My mother laughed at this, scornfully; but in fact she gave us Christmas and birthday presents of clothes and shoes, and the record player came into the house in this way, as my eleventh birthday present. But I wasn't allowed to take it with me when I left; it wasn't really mine at all.

I remember walking up the hill from school with my mother after an open day, and asking her what class we were; or rather, I asked her if we were middle class, and she was evasive. She was smiling a pleased smile; and working things out, I think it must have been the afternoon (the only time she visited my primary school) she was told I'd be going into the eleven-plus class and so (because everyone in the class passed the exam) would be going to grammar school. I was working out well, an investment with the promise of paying out. I answered my own question, and said that I thought we must be middle class, and reflected very precisely in that moment on my mother's black waisted coat with the astrakhan collar, and her high-heeled black suede shoes, her lipstick. She *looked* so much better than the fat, spreading South London mothers around us, that I thought we had to be middle class.

The coat and the lipstick came from her own work. 'If you want something, you have to go out and work for it. Nobody gives you anything; nothing comes free in this world.' About 1956 or 1957 she got an evening job in one of the espresso bars opening along the High Road, making sandwiches and frying eggs. She saved up enough money to take a manicuring course and in 1958 got her diploma, thus achieving a certified skill for the first time in her forty-five years. When I registered her death I was surprised to find myself giving this as her trade, because learned history implies that only the traditional ones — tailoring, weaving, joining, welding — are real. She always worked in good places, in the West End; the hands she did were in *Vogue* once. She came home with stories and imitations of her 'ladies'. When I was about twelve she told me how she'd 'flung' a sixpenny piece back at a titled woman who'd given it to her as a tip: 'If you can't afford any more than that Madam, I suggest you keep it.' Wonderful! — like tearing up the ration books. From her job, supported by the magazines she brought home, and her older skill of tailoring and dressmaking, we learned how the goods of the earth might be appropriated, with a certain voice, the cut and fall of a skirt, a good winter coat; with leather shoes too, but above all by clothes, the best boundary between you and a cold world.

We weren't, I now realise by doing the sums, badly off. My father paid the rent, all the bills, gave us our pocket money, and a fixed sum of £7 a week housekeeping money — quite a lot in the late 1950s — went on being handed over every Friday until his death, even when estrangement was obvious, and he was living part of the time with someone else. My mother must have made quite big money in tips, for the records of her savings, no longer a secret, show quite fabulous sums being stored away in the early Sixties. Poverty hovered as a belief. It existed in stories of the Thirties, in a family history. Even now when a bank statement comes in that shows I'm overdrawn, or the gas bill for the central heating seems enormous, my mind turns to quite inappropriate strategies, like boiling down the ends of soap, and lighting fires with candle ends and spills of screwed-up newspaper to save buying wood. I think about these things because they were domestic economies that we practised in the 1950s. We believed we were poor because we children were expensive items, and all the arrangements had been made for us. 'If it wasn't for you two,' my mother told us, 'I could be off somewhere else.' After going out manicuring she started spending Sunday afternoons in bed and we couldn't stay in the house nor play on the doorstep for fear of disturbing her. The house was full of her terrible tiredness, her terrible resentment; and I knew it was all my fault.

When I came across Kathleen Woodward's *Jipping Street*[6] I read it with the shocked amazement of one who had never seen what she knew written down before. Kathleen Woodward's mother of the 1890s was the one I knew: mothers were people who told you how long they were in labour with you, how much it hurt, how hard it was to have you ('twenty hours with you,' my mother frequently reminded me) and who told you to accept the impossible contradiction of being both desired and being a burden, and not to complain. This ungiving endurance is admired by working-class boys who grow up to write about their mothers' flinty courage. But the daughter's silence on this matter is a measure of the price you have to pay for survival. I don't think the baggage will ever lighten, for me or my sister. We were born, and had no choice in the matter; but we were burdens, expensive, never grateful enough. There was nothing we could do to pay back the debt of our existence. 'Never have children, dear,' she said. 'They ruin your life.'

Later, in 1977, after my father's death, we found out that they were never married, that we were illegitimate. In 1934 my father left his wife and two-year-old daughter in the North, and came to London. He and my mother had been together for at least ten years when I was born, and we think now that I was her hostage to fortune, the factor that might persuade him to get a divorce and marry her. But the ploy failed.

Just before my mother's death, playing around with the photographs on the bedroom mantelpiece, my niece discovered an old photograph underneath one taken of me at the age of three. A woman holds a tiny baby. It's the early 1930s, a picture of the halfsister, left behind. But I think I knew about her and her mother long before I looked them both in the face, or heard about their existence; knew that the half-understood adult conversations around me, the quarrels about 'her', the litany of 'she', 'she', 'she' from behind closed doors made the figure in the New Look coat, hurrying away, wearing the clothes my mother wanted to wear, angry with me yet nervously inviting me to follow, caught finally in the revolving door. We have proper birth certificates, because my mother must have told a simple lie to the Registrar, a discovery about the verisimilitude of documents that worries me a lot as a historian.

In 1954 *The Pirates of Penzance* was playing at the Streatham Hill Theatre, and we had one of the baritones as a lodger instead of the usual girls. He was different from them, didn't eat in the kitchen with us, but had my mother bake him potatoes and grate carrots that he ate in the isolation of the dining room. He converted my mother to Food Reform, and when she made a salad of grated vegetables for Christmas dinner in 1955, my father walked out, and I wish he'd taken us with him.

I've talked to other people whose mothers came to naturopathy in the Fifties, and it's been explained as a way of eating posh for those who didn't know about Continental food. I think that it did have a lot to do with the status that being different conferred, for in spite of the austerity of our childhood, we believed that we were better than other people, the food we ate being a mark of this, because our mother told us so — so successfully that even now I have to work hard at actually seeing the deprivations. But more than difference, our diet was to do with the desperate need, wrenched from restricted circumstances, to be in charge of the body. Food Reform promised an end to sickness if certain procedures were followed, a promise that was not, of course, fulfilled. I spent a childhood afraid to fall ill, because being ill meant my mother had to stay off work, and lose money.

But more than this, I think a precise though unconscious costing of our childhood lay behind our eating habits. Brussels sprouts, baked potatoes, grated cheese, the variation of vegetables in the summer, a tin of vegetarian steak pudding on Sundays and a piece of fruit afterwards is a monotonous but healthy diet, and I can't think of many cheaper ways to feed two children and feel you're doing your best for them at the same time. My mother brought the food home at night, buying it each day when she got off the bus from work. My sister's job was to meet her at the bus stop with the wheel basket so she didn't have to carry it up the road. We ate a day's supply at a time, so there was never anything much in the house overnight except bread for breakfast and the staples that were bought on Saturday. When I started to think about these things I was in a position to interpret this way of living and eating as a variation on the spending patterns of poverty described in Booth's and Rowntree's surveys; but now I think it was the cheapness of it that propelled the practice. We were a finely balanced investment, threatening constantly to topple over into the realms of demand and expenditure. I don't think though, that until we left home, we ever cost more to feed and clothe than that £7 handed over each week.

Now, I see the pattern of our nourishment laid down like our usefulness, by an old set of rules. At six I was old enough to go on errands, at seven to go further to pay the rent and the rates, and make the long, dreary trip to the Co-op for the divi. By eight, I was old enough to clean the house and do the weekend shopping. At eleven it was understood that I washed the breakfast things and scrubbed the kitchen floor before I started my homework. At fifteen, when I could legally go out to work, I got a Saturday job, which paid for my clothes (except for my school uniform, which was part of the deal, somehow). I think that until I drop I will clean wherever I happen to be on Saturday morning. I take a furtive and secret pride in the fact that I can do all these things, that I am physically strong, can lift and carry things that defeat other women, wonder with some scorn what it must be like to have to learn to clean a house when adult, not have the ability laid down as part of the growing self. Like going to sleep by contrasting a bed with a pavement, I sometimes find myself thinking that if the worse comes to the worst, I can always earn a living by my hands; I can scrub, clean, cook and sew; all you have in the end is your labour.

I was a better investment than my sister, because I passed the eleven-plus, went to grammar school, would get a good job (university was later seen to offer the same arena of advantages), marry a man who would, she said, buy 'me a house, and you a house. There's no virtue in poverty.' The dreary curtailment of our childhood was, we discovered after my mother's death, the result of the most fantastic saving — for a house, a dream house that was never bought. When I was about seventeen I learned that V.S Naipaul wrote *A House for Mr Biswas* in Streatham Hill.[7] I think of the poetic neatness of the novel about the compulsive, enduring desire for a house of one's own being composed only a few streets away from the place where someone with infinitely fewer resources tried to mobilise the same dream. It was at least an important dream, a literary dream, that dictated the pattern of our days.

It seems now a joyless childhood. My sister reminds me of our isolation, the neighbours who fed us meat and sweets, the tea parties we went out to, but which we were never allowed to return. I remember the awful depression of Sunday afternoons, my mother with a migraine in the front bedroom, the house an absolute stillness. But I don't *remember* the oddness; it's a reconstruction. What I recall is what I read, and my playing Annie Oakley by myself all summer afternoon at the recreation gound, running up and down the hill in my brown gingham dress, wearing a cowboy hat and carrying a rifle. Saturday morning pictures provided confirming images of women who not only worked hard, earned a living, but who carried a gun into the bargain.

The essence of being a good child is taking on the perspective of those who are more powerful than you, and I was good in this way as my sister never was. A house up the road, Sunday afternoon about 1958, plates of roast lamb offered. My sister ate, but I refused, not out of sacrifice nor because I was resisting temptation (I firmly believed that eating meat would make me ill, as my mother said), but because I knew — though this formulation is the adult's rather than the ten-year-old's — that the price of the meal was condemnation of my mother's oddness, and I wasn't having that. If people give you things, they should give freely, extracting nothing in return. I was a very upright child. At eight, I had my first migraine (I could not please her; I might as well join her; they stopped soon after I left home), and I started to get rapidly and relentlessly short-sighted. I literally stopped seeing for a very long time.

School taught me how to read early, and I found out for

myself how to do it fast. I read all the time, rapidly and voraciously. You couldn't join the Library until you were seven, and before that I read my Hans Christian Andersen back to front when I'd read it twenty times from start to finish. Kay was the name that I was called at home, my middle name, one of my father's names, and I knew that Kay, the boy in 'The Snow Queen' was me, who had a lump of ice in her heart. I knew that one day I might be asked to walk on the edge of knives like the Little Mermaid, and was afraid that I might not be able to bear the pain. Foxe's *Booke of Martyres* was in the old Library, a one-volume edition for 19th century children with coloured illustrations and the text pruned to a litany of death by flame. My imagination was furnished with the passionate martyrdom of the Protestant North.

I see now the relentless laying down of guilt, and I feel a faint surprise that I must interpret it in that way. My sister, younger than me, with children of her own and perhaps thereby with a clearer measure of what we lacked, reminds me of a mother who never played with us, whose eruptions from irritation into violence were the most terrifying of experiences, and she *is* there, the figure of nightmares, though I do find it difficult to think about in this way. My mind turns instead to the communality of this experience, of all those post-War babies competently handled but generally left alone, down the bottom of the garden in their pram, in the fresh air and out of the way. Expectations of childhood and ways of treating babies changed rapidly in the 1950s, and perhaps the difference in perception between me and my sister is no more than four years' difference in age, and a reflection of a change in expectation on the part of children themselves, learned from the altered practice of the adults around them. Against this learned account, I have to weigh what it felt like at the time, and the message of the history that was delivered up to me in small doses: that not being hungry and having a bed to sleep in at night, we had a good childhood, were better than other people, were *lucky* little girls.

My mother had wanted to marry a King. That was the best of my father's stories, told in the pub in the 1960s, of how difficult it had been to live with her in 1936, during the Abdication months. Mrs Simpson was no prettier than her, no more clever than her, no better than her. It wasn't fair that a King should give up his throne for her, and not for the weaver's daughter. From a traditional Labour background, my mother rejected the politics of solidarity and communality, always voted Conservative, for the left could not embody her desire for things to be *really* fair, for a full skirt that took twenty yards of cloth, for a half-timbered cottage in the country, for the Prince who did not come. My childhood was the place where, for my mother, the fairy tales failed; and through the glass of that childhood I now see that failure as part of a longer and more enduring one.

The 1950s was a period when state intervention in childhood was highly visible. The calculated, dictated fairness that the ration book represented went on into the new decade, and when we moved from Hammersmith to Streatham Hill in 1951 there were medicine bottles of orange juice and jars of Virol to pick up from the baby clinic for my sister. This overt intervention in our lives was experienced by me as entirely beneficient, so I find it difficult to match an analysis of the welfare policies of the late Forties, which calls 'the post-war Labour government . . . the last and most glorious flowering of late Victorian liberal philanthropy',[8] which I know to be correct, with the sense of self that those policies imparted. If it had been only philanthropy, would it have felt like it did? I think I would be a very different person now if orange juice and milk and dinners at school hadn't told me, in a covert way, that I had a right to exist, was worth something.

My inheritance from those years is the belief, maintained with some difficulty, that I do have a right to the earth. I think that had I grown up with my parents only twenty years before, I would not now believe this. For I was also an episode in someone else's narrative, not my own person, my mother's child, and brought into being for a particular purpose. Being a child when the state was publicly engaged in making children healthy and literate was a support against my particular circumstances, its central benefit being that, unlike my mother, the state asked for nothing in return. Psychic structures are shaped by these huge historical labels: 'charity', 'philanthropy', 'state intervention'.

It was a considerable achievement for a society to pour so

much milk, so much orange juice, so many vitamins down the throats of its children, for the height and weight of those children to outstrip so fast the measurements of only a decade before. But the 1950s divided people from each other; large-scale benevolence maintained individualism, and reveals its basis in the philanthropy described above. The statistics of healthy and intelligent childhood were stretched out along the curve of achievement, and only some were allowed to travel through the narrow gate at the age of eleven, towards the golden city. This particular political failure of post-War welfare policies, to provide equality and not just the opportunity for individual achievement, was set in its turn against the dislocation that my mother's 1950s represent: welfarism in one country did not embody the desire people felt for the world that had shaped them.

From a current vantage point, I see my childhood as evidence that can be used. I think that it is a particularly useful way of gaining entry to ideas about childhood — what children are *for*, why to have them — that aren't written about in the official records, that is, in the textbooks of child analysis and child psychology, and in sociological depictions of childhood. This public assertion of my childhood's usefulness stands side by side with the painful personal knowledge, I think the knowledge of all of us, all my family, going as far back as the story lets us, that it would have been better if it hadn't happened that way, hadn't happened at all.

People said at the time that the War had been fought for the children, for a better future, and the 1950s represent a watershed in the historical process by which children have come to be thought of as repositories of hope, and objects of desire. Accounts like Jeremy Seabrook's, in *Working Class Childhood* see in the material affection displayed towards children of our and more recent generations, the roots of a political failure on the part of the Labour movement to confront the inculcated desires of the market place. 'Instead of the children of the working class being subjected to rigorous self-denial in preparation for a life-time in mill or mine,' he writes, 'they have been offered instead the promise of the easy and immediate gratification which, in the end, can sabotage human development and achievement just as effectively as the poverty and hunger of the past.'[9] There hovers in *Working Class Childhood* the ghostly presence of more decent and upright children, serving their time in the restriction of poverty and family solidarity: 'the old defensive culture of poverty gave working children . . . a sense of security which is denied the present generation . . .'[10]

But in this sterner, older world, the iron entered into the children's soul, and many of them had to learn that being alive ought simply to be enough, a gift that must be ultimately paid for. Under conditions of material poverty the cost of most childhoods has been most precisely reckoned, and only life has been given freely. (One of the least attractive features of *Working Class Childhood* is its denial of the evidence it presents, its interpretation of people's consciousness of grim childhoods in terms of regret and loss.) After that initial investment, no one gave me and my sister anything. The landscape of feeling that this measured upbringing inculcated in countless children has yet to be surveyed. We should start, perhaps, with the burden of being good, and the painful watchful attention towards the needs of others rather than oneself.

I carried with me the tattered remnants of this psychic structure: there is no way of not working hard, nothing in the end but an endurance that will allow me to absorb everything that comes by way of difficulty, *holding on* to the grave. This psychology must have served capitalism at least as well as a desire for the things of the market. At least Jeremy Seabrook's cut-out cardboard teenage figures of abject horror and pity know, as they sit sniffing glue and planning how to knock off a video recorder, that the world owes them something, that they have a right to the earth, an attitude at least as subversive as the endurance that is the result of being never given very much.[11]

It is a mistake, I think, to confuse the gift relationship with mindless material indulgence, for it is only by being given things that anyone ever learns that they have a place in the world. I want to reinterpret the metaphor of the Fifties, of childhood as a community's investment in the future, and find its material base in the individual circumstances that help

interpret historical developments. My sister and I were invest-
ments that did not pay off, for the income that is derived from
investment is *unearned* income: having made the initial pay-
ment, the investor need make no further effort. An older
history brought this idea forward to a new era: we were
brought up to be simply grateful for being alive, guilty at the
fact of our existence.

Two weeks before my mother's death, I went to see her. It
was the first meeting in nine years — for the day of my father's
funeral doesn't really count. The letter announcing my visit
lay unopened on the mat when she opened the door, and an
hour later I came away believing that I admired a woman who
could, under these circumstances and in some pain, treat me as
if I had just stepped round the corner for a packet of tea ten
minutes before, and talk to me about this and that, and
nothing at all. But I was really a ghost who came to call.
Talking to my sister on the phone about the visit, she insisted
that the feeling of being absent in my mother's presence was
nothing to do with the illness, was the emotional underpinning
of our childhood. We were truly *illegitimate*, our selves *not
there*. Our unconscious acknowledgement of this at the time
lay in taking up as little space as possible, not being a nuisance.
Paradoxically, this denial of the known self makes its boundaries stronger.

As I went out, past the shrouded furniture in the front
room (things made ready these twenty years past for the move
that never came) I noticed a Lowry reproduction hanging over
the mantelpiece that hadn't been there on my last visit. Why
did she go out and buy that obvious representation of a
landscape she wanted to escape, the figures moving noiselessly
under the shadow of the mill? 'They know each other,
recognise each other,' says John Berger of these figures. 'They
are not, as is sometimes said, like lost souls in limbo; they are
fellow travellers through a life which is impervious to most of
their choices . . .'[12] Perhaps she did buy that picture because it
is concerned with loneliness, with 'the contemplation of time
passing without meaning',[13] and moved then, momentarily,
hesitantly, towards all the other lost travellers.

Where is the place that you move into the landscape and
can see yourself? When I want to find myself in the dream of

the New Look, I have to reconstruct the picture, look down at my sandals and the hem of my dress, for in the dream itself I am only an eye, watching. Remembering the visit to the cotton mill, on the other hand, I can see myself watching from the polished floor; I am in the picture. To see yourself in this way is a representation of the child's move into historical time, one of the places where vision establishes the child's understanding of herself as part of the world. In its turn, this social understanding interprets the dream landscape.

When I was about nine, I grew positively hungry for poetry. I learned enormous quantities to say to myself in bed at night. The poetry book I had was Stevenson's *A Child's Garden of Verses*, and I read it obsessively, once going in to Smith's in the High Road to ask if he had written any other poems. I liked the one on the last page best, 'To Any Reader', and its imparting of the sad, elegiac information that the child seen through the pages of the book

> . . . has grown up and gone away,
> And it is but a child of air
> That lingers in the garden there.

You're nostalgic for childhood whilst it happens to you, because the dreams show you the landscape you're passing through, but you don't know yet that you want to escape.

2 History and Autobiography:
different pasts[1]

I've been asked to talk about *Landscape for a Good Woman*, the question of autobiography, and the difference between writing autobiography and writing history. I shall do that; but I also want to talk about my problem, which I think actually *is* history: why I want it, and so few of my audience do, and why I insist on their having it. Before I could write the account found in *Landscape for a Good Woman*, I had to find a history, or rather, I had to find the very stuff of historical practice: a document, a text, some trace of the past, to work on. The story of writing the book might start like this: Some years ago I came across, was transfixed by, and then edited Kathleen Woodward's *Jipping Street*.[2] It was republished in 1983, and it was in working on it that the groundwork for *Landscape for a Good Woman* was laid. *Jipping Street* was written in 1928, ostensibly a working-class autobiography, set in that most derelict and abandoned part of London and narratives of London life — in Bermondsey — in the years before the First World War.

What struck me most forcibly in its opening pages was a portrait of a working-class mother whose love towards her children was terrible and ambivalent: a mother who was a central and impossible contradiction in her daughter's life. It was with this figure in the pages of a book that I first saw my own mother plain; or: not quite like that: saw what I knew but had not before ever seen written down, about what might be born out of such an ambivalence. The second striking force of the book lay in its oddness: it didn't ring true. I didn't believe it — as history that is. I certainly believed it as psychological truth.

Working on the book, I discovered what I knew I would discover: that Kathleen Woodward was born in relatively genteel Peckham, not in abandoned Bermondsey, that Jipping Street was the landscape of her imagination, an invented way of making the writing of a 19th century 'childhood' possible for a working-class woman writing outside the conventions of working-class autobiography current in the 1920s. I think Kathleen Woodward wrote what I would call a psychic reconstruction of working-class childhood, rather than a historical account of one. When I wrote *Landscape for a Good Woman*, I was careful to avoid the censure that I gave to *Jipping Street*, very careful to convey the contemporary sense of alrightness and ordinariness of my childhood, and to locate its oddnesses in the action of memory, in the adult's reworking of past time.

I saw something in the book as well, about the refusal of reproduction in women. In *Jipping Street* there is a child — Kathleen Woodward — shrinking from sexual knowledge, and there is a relationship depicted between mother and daughter that resulted not in the daughter's wish for a child, but in the daughter's refusal to reproduce herself. I wanted to understand this refusal, was asked, a long time ago, to write a book about those brief lines in my Introduction to *Jipping Street* that deal with this topic. For a long time, I thought that I had to have a text to do this with; that one day I would find a diary in the archives, a bundle of letters, a long-out-of-print novel that would allow me to explore these questions. When Liz Heron asked me at the end of 1983, to contribute to *Truth, Dare or Promise*,[3] found that I had my text after all, only I'd written it myself. I think that for the main part in the book, I do preserve that distinction between text and commentary, memory and analysis, though it breaks down a bit in the chapter on my father. . . .

I wanted to write a drama of class, and to do so, I believed I had to engage with working-class autobiography and an emergent set of formulae about women's autobiography, in which women's stories are constructed through their relationships with other people, by a notion of dependency in women's lives, and by fathers who are representative of patriarchy. That I was clearly aware of what I was up to here, does not I think reduce the validity of what I say about my mother's power, or my father as one of patriarchy's failures (I mean that in the sense of the failure of an analytic and organising device rather than as one man's individual failure). What I had to engage with in working-class autobiography were: notions of cheerful decency, poor-honest-but-happiness: everything embodied in the titles that I evoke in the first chapter of the book. I think that it is a book that is designed to hurt, to tell them (who are '*them*'?) that they have not experienced — have not had, can't ever have — that which places you on the outside, and makes you bitter and envious enough to want to hurt in this way. I think it is ungrateful and resentful towards feminism as well, which has objectively given me so much opportunity; ungrateful in that one of my organising principles in *Landscape for a Good Woman* is the pitching of class against gender, and class is allowed to win, as the more interesting, important, and relevatory interpretive device.

All of that was prolegomenon: a way of talking about the real problem, which I believe to be history itself, and here and now and particularly, the relationship of history to autobiography. The standard histories of autobiography that we possess describe a development over the last five hundred years, of a specifically historical consciousness.[4] It is this consciousness that has provided the framework for the emergence of the autobiographical form. In many literary and critical accounts of the *genre*, it is Goethe in particular, in *Dichtung und Wahreit* who first formalised the notion of self-formation as the result of an interplay of the self and the world around the self. This recognition, of the historical dimension of all human reality, which was made about 1800 and which followed on a century or two of various autobiographical endeavours, meant that autobiography itself assumed a significant cultural function, within the lineaments of which we still operate. In accounts like these, which I am summarising in a somewhat breathtaking fashion, autobiography is to be distinguished from such *genre* as memoir and reminiscence by the status and function of experience within it. In the form of memoir for instance, it is a series of external factors that is presented as dictating the narrative course. These factors or events may be translated into inner experience, but that inner experience — lived and felt experience — is not its focus, as it is in autobiography.

And yet that history — that historical dimension of all human reality, that historical consciousness, historicity — is a problem for the daily telling of life stories. History is an irrelevance in common understanding, though historical explanation is my mode of thinking and public presentation, and perhaps of being. I say to students, to friends: 'a hundred years ago, it wasn't like that'; and I watch the shadow of polite boredom pass over their face. Or licensed for egotism, by this Conference, by this week-end, I could ask: Why do I care? Why do I want to tell my story in this particular way? And especially, why do I insist on telling a story within a historical framework, when many people, whom I respect and admire, think that I could manage just as well without? What am I hiding through my use of history? Or (to cut the self-abnegation) what am I finding? I shall start to answer my own question by considering the development of historical consciousness in children.

The historical imagination — a variant of historical consciousness — appears in children, in my experience, as part of the family romance. I am talking now about my memories of myself at about eight years of age, about many children of about that age that I taught once upon a time, and others. Children, at many times during the course of growing up, construct a fantasy, in which they are not the children of the parents who bore them, but the daughters and sons of much more romantic, glamorous and wealthy people, typically, Kings and Queens. They write fairy stories about these figures, if they know what fairy stories are (and perhaps even if they do not), tell tales, have dreams. When they draw pictures to accompany these stories, these figures of romance, these fantasy parents, are dressed in the clothing of the past. This seems to be the case as well in Victorian children's journals and diaries that I have looked at. It is very simple, at one level: you need only to have seen a picture (or a moving picture) of someone in medieval or Elizabethan dress to clothe your figures of imagination in this way. Presumably, if you had no picture of the past like this, then you would not do it.

At seven, eight, or nine, if you do this, you are I think, both playing about with the romance and, quite simply, because it *is* set in the past, which is not now, showing that you know it is not true, and that you want others at some level, to know that you know this. This is altogether something plainer and more sophisticated than the imaginings that Freud located in three and four-year-olds when he wrote 'Family Romances'.[5] A child can use the historical past, four or so years on from this time, to say that things are both not-true, and true. It is also at this age (at seven, eight or nine) in this society that history plays another role in the child's development. Using the fairy-tales and other fictions, the child has categorised narratives into true and not-true. History now delivers up its bleak message: that it was all true, that *it really did happen* that way, that very few people indeed were Kings and Queens. So the child plays out romance against that reality: the same figures, little drawings of princesses with ropes of hair, serve as both acceptance and denial.

What function does the historical past serve me in *Landscape for a Good Woman*? I am very eager to tell readers, close to the beginning of the book, that what they are about to read is not history. At the end, I want those readers to say that what I have produced *is* history; which would please me much more than anything else. The denial of history at the beginning of the book has a technical and functional purpose. I didn't do any real empirical research for the book. I didn't go to Burnley, didn't read the local press for the pre-First World War period, didn't write to Fall River, Massachusetts. I didn't check marriage registers, nor census returns, nor hospital records; didn't do anything serious about the Lancashire cotton trade, just read a few theses written by other people. I relied entirely on secondary sources, and on memory; told no lies, but never checked the truth of anything either. I want real historians to know that I know this. And anyway, I really do believe, as a result of my education and socialisation as a historian, that nothing can be said to have happened in the past until you have spent three years at it (three years at least), got on many trains, opened many bundles in the archives, stayed in many flea-bitten hotels. This is the craft-romance of historical practice, and I fall for it all the way.

But there are other reasons for saying that the book does not constitute history. One is to do with its central device, which is to claim that the life of many people in this society is not explained by the dominant forms that give expression to lived experience: novels, other literature, film, history (though we should remember the eight-year-old, telling her story with the device of the princess's farthingale, to remind ourselves of what people manage, in the cracks in between, using someone else's story). In this way then, the book refuses the path of romance. I think that people's history and oral history are romantic devices (which is not to say that they shouldn't be undertaken), and I refuse to say that my mother's story, or my father's, or mine are perfectly valid stories, existing in their own right, merely hidden from history, now revealed. I won't do this. I think that the central stories are maintained *by* the marginality of others, but that these marginal stories *will not do* to construct a future by. They will have to be abandoned, for they were made out of multiple poverties and real deprivations. So I have to refuse the label history to what I say about Burnley in the 1920s, about the possible way my mother was brought up, about the more certain descriptions of my own childhood — not because I don't present perfectly true and useful historical information here, but rather because my rhetorical framework would collapse if I said that this was history: the central story.

I don't ever promise that this is really how it was. It is at this point that I remember most clearly an eight-year-old in a crowded post-War South London classroom, writing a life of Queen Victoria in three volumes (three LCC exercise books): the holly pinned to the little princess's collar to make her sit up straight at meal times, the moment of destiny on the stairs when the men in frock coats fell at her feet. This story I write (dip pen, a good round hand: it's 1955) is me, but also, exactly at the same time, not-me. It will go on operating like that, the historical past will, as acceptance and denial.

I know that there is no 'really how it was' at all. But knowing about all the pretensions of the historical enterprise that seeks to conjure the past before our eyes, as it really was, does not stop me from wanting what all of history's readers want: the thing we cannot have, which is past time: the past 'as it really was'. The child in the 1950s South London classroom knew (she might be able to articulate this, if you asked her the right question) that the point isn't what happened, nor how the young Victoria sat at the table, nor the hurried drive through the dark to announce ascension to the throne; the point is what the child does with that history.

Later, the child will learn the fine and delightful constraints of this particular literary endeavour — the writing of history. She will learn the pleasures of the plot shaped according to what the documents forbid, or authorise, but which they never contain in themselves. She will learn what massive authority this appeal to the evidence will give her as a story-teller. So when, thirty years on, she denies that what she is doing is writing history, then she is actually relinquishing the arena of her own authority; she does want you to know that. It is also of course, the rhetoric of denial. The way to show this is to proceed by making a contrast, between the telling of life-stories and the telling of history.

Stories come to an end when there is no more to be said, that is to say, when the listener as much as the teller knows that there is no going back on what has already been delivered up, when it's too late to change what has been said, when you can see that this point you have reached, this end, was implicit in the beginning, was there all along.[6] Then, the story ends. In the autobiography, or in the telling of a life story in a pub, there is in operation a simple variant of this narrative rule. The person there, leaning up against the bar, or in another place, writing a book, is the embodiment of the something completed. That end, that finished place, is the human being, a body in time and space, telling a story that brings you (wherever the teller actually ends the story) to this place, here and now; this end. And written autobiography has to end in the figure of the writer (which is why you have to see that the good woman is me). I am talking about the simple physicality of writing, nothing more than that: that the story is told by someone here, now, in time. And of course, I do know that life goes on after the writing, that other tales will be told, and that there is a more permanent ending.

I wonder perhaps, if the historians who proffer a total history, and who dream of delivering up the past as it really was, do not in fact, aspire to the autobiographer's position: the all-seeing eye, the certainty of memory, of having been there, of telling a story that is completed in the figure of he or she who does the telling. But in fact, history writing represents a distinct cognitive process precisely because it is constructed around the understanding that things are not over, that the story isn't finished: that there is no end. In fact, in their day-to-day practice, historians do know and acknowledge that the story they tell isn't over, doesn't have an end. Closures have to be made, in order to finish arguments and books; but the story can't be finished because there is always the possibility that some new piece of evidence will alter the argument and the account. Historians have as their stated objective exhaustiveness (finding out again and again, more and more about some thing, event or person), and they proceed upon the path of refutation by pointing to exceptions and to the possibility of exception. The practice of historical inquiry and historical writing is a recognition of temporariness and impermanence, and in this way is a quite different literary form from that of autobiography, which presents momentarily a completeness, a completeness which lies in the figure of the writer or the teller, in the here and now, saying: that's how it was; or, that's how I believe it to have been.

By drawing these distinctions between the telling or writing of autobiography and the practice of history, I do not want to deny important similarities. History and autobiography work in the same way *as narrative*: they use the same linguistic structure, and they are both fictions, in that they present variations and manipulations of current time to the reader. These similarities are the matter of a different paper, and the topic of a different Conference. Rather, what I want to do instead, by looking at the distinctions between the two, is point to the psychological functions that autobiography and history serve — for the writer and the teller, for the listener and the reader. What I have dwelt on so far, is the *end*, the sense of completeness that a life story allows, whenever it is told, which I have suggested that history does not really allow; and the way in which the historical past, in my example, used by children, might allow them to explore possibility and denial, both at the same time. The telling of a life story is a *confirmation* of that self that stands there telling the story. History, on the other hand, might offer the chance of denying it.

I see now, that in writing *Landscape for a Good Woman*, I was most profoundly pulled between these two understandings, of autobiography and history, though I do not think I could have been clear about this at the time. The autobiographical part of the book happened — or at least, I believe that it happened, which might come to the same thing in the end. And I do not want it to have been that way. I think I hoped that history might rescue me from that bleak knowledge — that it would have been better if it hadn't happened that way; hadn't happened at all.

I need to pursue the bleakness just a bit further. I used a contrast in the book, between history and case-history. History, I argued, was to do with time. In doing and writing history, I said, the historian goes back through time, finds something, considers it, looks at it this way, and then that: gives it meaning. Then, with these bundles of meaning, the journey is taken again, forward this time. Things are put in order, and it is the order that they are put in that gives them historical meaning. They are held together in a particular configuration that explains them: a causal configuration. This causal configuration is dependent upon a general understanding of time moving forward. In the book, I contrasted this chronological configuration with a *timeless* configuration, a mode of story-telling in which time does not shape the narrative: that of psycho-analytic case-study. I said that the book was constructed on this model, and that the form of narrative that Freud invented allows the dream, the wish, the fantasy, to be presented as evidence. The case-study is not concerned with what really happened, it is not told in the order of historical time; chronology makes few demands on it.

Now, this seems fine as far as it goes, and indeed, this rhetoric did allow me to present a dream as the shaping device of the book, to present my reconstruction of my mother's desire as evidence; and all the rest of it. It was useful then, this distinction. What I notice now, however, is how very little I actually said about history. I did not, for instance, explore the question of chronology, did not acknowledge that history does not have to be told in that linear fashion; that the historian can move about amid the order of things, present ends before beginnings, write thematically among the dates. But despite this, is still ends up as a story to do with time and causal connection, because that knowledge of chronology and time, that 'basic historicity' is there already, in the head of the reader. I could write it backwards indeed, and you would still know that it happened forward.

Is this what the historiographers mean, when they write of our 'basic historicity', the sense of history, historical consciousness? Historical consciousness then, is only an elaboration of what the eight-year-old knows, about a communality, a community of cognition. It is for the potentialities of that community offered by historical consciousness I suppose, that I want what I have written to be called history, and not autobiography.

3 Prisonhouses[1]

Those who live in retirement, whose lives have fallen amid the
seclusion of schools and other walled-in and guarded
dwellings, are liable to be suddenly and for a long while
dropped out of the memory of their friends, the denizens of a
freer world . . . there falls a stilly pause, a wordless silence, a
long blank of oblivion. Unbroken always is this blank, alike
entire and unexplained. The letter, the message once frequent,
are cut off, the visit, formerly periodical, ceases to occur; the
book, paper or other token that indicates rememberance,
comes no more.

Always there are excellent reasons for these lapses if the
hermit but knew them. Though he is stagnant in his cell, his
connections without are working in the very vortex of life. . . .
The hermit — if he be a sensible hermit — will swallow his
own thoughts, and lock up his own emotions during these
weeks of inward winter . . .

> Charlotte Bronte, *Villette* (1853), Penguin,
> Harmondsworth, 1979, p. 348

Great numbers of women have taught for a century and a half
now — teaching became a woman's job, both statistically and
by reputation, some time before the First World War — and,
rare for work performed by women, they have written about it.
They write, but they reveal very little about it as a process of
labour, a job of work. Lucy Snowe in *Villette* performs a still-
recognisable miracle of classroom control and this is recorded,
but not the detail of daily routine that makes up the work for
which she says she feels a passion. We know she is good at

51

it: she says so; but we do not see how. Her lover buys her a school, neatly equipped, commodiously arranged; he has advertisements printed for her. It is a recognition of her passion, his declaration that he *sees* the passion, and thereby sees Lucy Snowe. But the schoolroom, the place where this no one will become a someone, is the uninscribed conclusion to the novel, not its scene of action.

The narrator of Ruth Adam's *I'm Not Complaining* turns her back on the grimy blur of Standard II, gazes down from the Board School window at Depression-time Nottinghamshire, thinks her own thoughts: love, gossip, wretchedness; the company of women in the staffroom.[2] Five hundred miles away in a Glasgow Infants' Department, Jeanetta Bowie watches her children with a pawky wisdom, the feminised irony of the Lad o'Pairts. The bairns are the subject of funny stories in the staffroom, and their toothless, decaying parents are bit-part players in the Comedy of Life.[3]

Sylvia Ashton Warner said what she did. Out of the myriad lives lived out in classrooms, minutes, days, weeks, multifoliate activity, enforced stillness, a universe of human relations, there emerges an image: a Maori child holds in his hand a small piece of card on which his teacher has written 'car'. It is his word; he clutches it; a word in the hand is worth a thousand in the reading primer. It connects with his unconscious, and with infinity. Soon, he learns to read.[4]

I was a teacher. I never wanted to be, and now that I've stopped, I never will be again, but for several years it took my heart. I entered a place of darkness, a long tunnel of days: retreat from the world. I want to explain, to tell what it is I know. Teaching young children must always be, in some way or other, a retreat from general social life and from fully adult relationships, a way of becoming Lucy Snowe's dormouse, rolled up in the prisonhouse, the schoolroom. The woman who teaches (ignore the generic 'he' in Charlotte Bronte's description) must know

> that Destiny designed him to imitate on occasion the
> dormouse . . . make a tidy ball of himself, creep into a hole of
> life's wall, and submit to the drift which blows in and blocks
> him up, preserving him in ice for a season . . .[5]

I loved my children and worked hard for them, lay awake at night worrying about them, spent my Sundays making workcards, tape recording stories for them to listen to, planning the week ahead. My back ached as I pinned their paintings to the wall, wrote the labels with a felt-tip pen, a good round hand, knowing even then the irony with which I would recall in later years the beacon light of the martyr's classroom shining into the winter's evening, the cleaner's broom moving through the corridor of the deserted schoolhouse.

Simone de Beauvoir calls the having of children the swiftest route to a woman's slavery.[6] I know that you do not need to bear children in order to have them. As in most primary school classrooms, they rarely left me. We stayed together in one room most of the day long. Shabby, depressed, disturbed social priority children learned to read under my care: the efficacy of affection. I admired their stoicism under disaster; I lost my temper with them: they longed for my approval again. I could silence a room with a glance. I was good at jokes, the raised eyebrow, the smile, the delicate commentary on the absurdity of things that is the beginning of irony in eight-year-olds. We laughed a lot, cried a lot, wept over all the sad stories. An on-going show of human variety: what the old people forget as they rehearse their infant rebellion for the oral historian, is that classrooms are places of gossip, places for the observation of infinite change: new shoes, new haircuts, a pair of gold ear-rings for pierced ears; passion, tears, love, despair.[7] No one goes into a classroom in the morning without the faint anticipation of something happening, that something made more eventful by the smallness of the stage, and its remoteness from the real theatre of life.

My days were passed in the most extraordinary watchfulness: the management of time and space. I never interrupted a child, though I struck a few. I took it all, the nightmare insoluble adult conflict, the hard lives, hard times that produced the children's passion washing over me. I didn't sleep properly in seven years. When I left the class of children of whom I had grown the fondest of all, I wrote a poem (all the bad, abandoned poems) in which the children jumped and played in the windy yard, the girls' skirts caught in the frozen triangle of a child's wax crayoning, hair flying stiffshaped, the shouting very distant like that of a water-erased dream. It was a poem about love: all our bondage is bought by the soft pressure of fingers, the child's arms slipped unthinkingly around the adult's waist, the head resting, momentarily, listening to a heart-beat, the darkening November afternoon outside.

Or: there is the other way. She moves from her desk to the window, looks down at the yard, the gates, the streets, the fields beyond; smooths an eyebrow with a finger, corrects the setting of a belt. She thinks of: not being here, of love, a houseful of furniture, of marriage, the meeting of bodies, a new winter coat. The children's murmur rises behind her; she turns to quiet them, and they bow their heads to their books in obedience. It is a crenellated Board School in Deptford in the 1890s, Glasgow in the 1930s, now, anywhere. In an Italian nursery school she is shown sitting at her desk thinking over her own affairs, smoothing her hair: real life, marriage, this time next year — as she gazes out over the heads of the children.[8] At the window she stands, looking out. She is a woman liberated, a woman who has escaped all our fate: she is a woman who is not a mother, a woman who does not care: *a woman who has refused to mother*.

There was no other way to write this: only the ironies of self-dramatisation available for narration; and indeed the story itself could only achieve the status of ironic proposition after I had found a history that allowed me to understand the place where I had stood for so many years. To present a summary of that history now is to perform a deliberate act of disjuncture, to suddenly turn a story into another piece of historical or literary evidence, to add to examples of earlier ones.

The daily detail of teaching and my experience of it directed all my reading, all my research, furnished my imagination, helped me to see the classrooms of the recent past. But the history I am about to present seems to mask what went into its making. What follows then, is framed by two problems, which are not disconnected from each other. The first is to do with the kind of concealment that the writing of history involves, the way in which, as a narrative form, it does not reveal the pictures the historian sets up in her head to think by:

> This concealment, this silence, envelops — the choice of which subjects to treat, which questions to ask, and which not to; the process of reasoning by which the historian arrives at the positions she or he holds; and the structures within the text by means of which the answers are presented to the reader. . . . The result of this concealment, which makes the historian appear the invisible servant of his materials, is to endow him with massive authority over the reader.[9]

It is important to at least attempt the writing of a history that at some point reveals the processes of its production.

The second problem is the history of education which, like much educational writing in general, treats its field of inquiry as separate from general social and political life, and which remains largely institutional in focus.[10] To write any kind of history of women in classrooms means an encounter with that kind of history, an encounter in which the first priority must be to shift the perspective, see the prisonhouse in the light of history and politics, infinitely connected with the world outside, whose artifact it is.

There have been explanations advanced for the peculiarities of educational history, and for its tendency to present evidence about classrooms and teaching as disconnected from wider historical issues. It has been suggested that this closing of frontiers between education and other disciplines has served to increase its mystique and status for practitioners whose own intellectual history is different from and, within a class system, bound to be seen as inferior to that acquired within the traditional academic disciplines.[11] The effect of this enclosure on the history of education is quite simple, and quite deadening. Information about pedagogic change, or about changes in the background of recruits to the job are used as facts that do one thing: illuminate the development of an institutional form. Thus: in the early years of the 19th century the majority of teachers of infants were male; as compulsory state education advanced, more and more women were recruited to the ranks of the profession — in the 1870s, the numbers of men and women teaching in elementary schools were roughly equal, and by 1914, in a striking reversal of earlier figures, women made up 70 per cent of the teaching force. So is progress towards the present illuminated.

Yet it has recently become clear that the job changed from being a predominantly masculine one not only because of the obvious economic reckoning of various local authorities faced with recruiting teachers on a large scale, but also because of certain societal shifts in the idea of family government, and the decreasing status of the father as a patriarch.[12] In the early 19th century overt reasons for selecting men as instructors of infants had to do with assumptions about the ordering and disciplining of families, with the practice of judicious tenderness that such domestic practice helped acquaint men with, and that was seen as so vital an experience for the successful management of large numbers of small children.[13] Towards the end of the century women could be seen to occupy this position of authoritative watchfulness.

A sociological perspective like this, however cursorily it employs historical evidence, immediately makes the educational outline more interesting. But there are perhaps even more radical and interesting things to be done with the outline. The last ten years have seen the development of wide-ranging work on the subject of mothering. Psycho-analysis has been wedded to sociology to produce an account of how the need and desire to mother is reproduced in little girls.[14] Serious attempts have been made to outline the particular thought processes that result from mothering small children.[15] Several accounts, by using content analyses of books and magazines of advice to mothers show how very recent a historical development our ordinary, everyday, common-sense understanding of mothering actually is.[16]

The features of this everyday understanding are: a belief in the efficacy and importance of attention to the child and a responsiveness to her needs; a belief in the practice of child-care as the responsibility of natural mothers; and a belief in the psychological effectiveness of love. The central and overriding feature is a conviction about the importance of a significant other, that is, the consistent presence in the child's life of a reliable and loved adult.[17] Particularly important and pervasive is this last belief: it has crossed class barriers, and Ann Oakley found many working-class mothers in the early 1970s defining themselves as good by virtue of their constant presence in their children's lives.[18]

Yet this ideal, of constant attention to children, is a very recent historical development, its origins probably no older than the period immediately before and after the Second World War. The 'good' 19th century mother was a guide and exemplar to her children, but in order to be good, only her intermittent presence was required. Child-care manuals, women's magazines and the like did not emphasise the effects of mother-child separation until the 1940s, and it seems that the pervasive beliefs about mothering that are being questioned today are no more than forty years old.

The arena for this development of ideas about mothering is the middle-class home (and indeed, most modern investigations of mothering and the reproduction of mothering are restricted to the same milieu). And yet the children of those 19th century mothers who, in Marilyn Helterline's account in 'The Emergence of Modern Motherhood', acted as distant moral exemplars to their children, who saw them once a day for half-an-hour before dinner, who enjoyed the occasional romp with them in the garden, were looked after by other women, who washed them and fed them, and in whose company they passed the night. Up on the nursery floor the quality of attentive watchfulness was developed, and the fourteen-year-old nursemaid could truly say that she never left the children — because it was in the terms of her employment to be with them in this way. It may be that the lineaments of modern good mothering were developed by women who were not the natural mothers of children in their care, and because they were paid to do so. In this light, it is illuminating to look at the schoolroom as an arena for this kind of development, as a place where attention, empathy, watchfulness and enforced companionship were the dimensions of a job of work and became the natural-seeming components of a relationship. The classroom may be one of the places where the proper relationship between mothers and children has been culturally established.

This kind of relationship obviously existed long before it became a matter of recommendation in the magazines and manuals of the 1940s and 1950s, and it is for this reason that the infant and elementary school classroom (now the primary school classroom) is of such importance, and why the secondary school and the relationships there constructed remain outside the scope of this argument. In secondary schools children receive an education that is subject-based, and they encounter several teachers in the course of a day. Though *Villette* provides the epigraph for this article, it is in fact a novel about a seminary for young ladies — a kind of secondary school — and the relationship between Lucy Snowe and her pupils that it describes cannot be used as evidence.

The essential feature of the primary school on the other hand, is that one woman (sometimes a man) stays in the same room all day long with the same group of children. They will leave her occasionally, perhaps for a music lesson or to go swimming, but essentially their teacher is responsible for them throughout the school day, and generally, she works alone. The outline of an educational history that can be called the feminisation of a trade, can be turned right round, and we can see that in classrooms, as in the middle-class nurseries of the 19th century, the understood and prescribed psychological dimensions of modern good mothering have been forged — and forged by waged women, by working women — by nurses, nannies and primary school teachers. . . .

Two factors need to be highlighted in the continued transmission of and developments within the idea of teaching as a kind of mothering. Administrative changes and the development of a system of secondary education in the years before the Second World War began to make the elementary/primary school classroom a more enclosed and separate place. For increasing numbers of children it became a stage on the route to further schooling, not a system that fed them directly to the labour market. This growing separation between primary and secondary education was formalised in the Education Act of 1944; and the 1940s and 1950s saw publicity given to new ideas of motherhood that, in some cases, drew analogies between the attention and empathy that both mothers and teachers in schools could provide for children. . . .[19]

I didn't know this history when I entered that enclosed place, the primary classroom. I didn't know about a set of pedagogic expectations that covertly and mildly — and *never* using this vocabulary — hoped that I might become a mother. And yet I became one, not knowing exactly what it was that was happening until it was too late, until I was caught, by the pressure of fingers, looks and glances. In the story I tell now, *Villette* provides a romantic substructure: my narrative is about another place, almost another country, where I hide myself from view, like Lucy Snowe am unseen, roll myself into the dormouse ball, yet expend vast passion in the classroom. (The streets outside shine with rain; I am alone; I almost don't understand what it is they speak, like the blur of voices in the streets of Villette). The romantic vision is allowed to women who teach; and *Villette* itself is the romantic transmutation of Charlotte Bronte's loathing for the work of the prisonhouse, expressed fifteen years before the novel was completed, in the school at Roe Head:

> I had been toiling for nearly an hour with Miss Lister, Miss Marriott and Ellen Cook to teach them a distinction between an article and a substantive. The parsing lesson was completed, a dead silence had succeeded it in the school-room and I sat sinking from irritation and weariness into a kind of lethargy. The thought came over me am I to spend all the best part of my life in this wretched bondage forcibly suppressing my rage at the idleness apathy and hyberbolical and most assinine stupidity of those fat-headed oafs and on compulsion assuming an air of kindness patience and assiduity? Must I from day to day sit chained to this chair prisoned within these four bare walls, whilst these glorious summer suns are burning in heaven and the year is revolving in its richest glow, and declaring at the close of each summer's day, that the time I am losing, will never come again? Stung to the heart with this reflection I started up and mechanically walked to the window . . . an uncertain sound of sweetness came on a dying gale from the south, I looked in that direction — Huddersfield and the hills beyond all bathed in blue mist, the woods of Hopton and Heaton Lodge were clouding the water-edge and the Calder silent but bright was shooting among them like a silver arrow . . . I shut the window and went back to my seat . . . just then a Dolt came up with a lesson. I thought I should have vomited . . . [20]

My recovery of this history, in which disgust and disdain are the hidden counterpoint to identification, empathy and love, and my writing of that history were part of my long process of detachment from teaching, a way of leaving, of getting out. In fact, a quite different historical narrative carried me to the primary classroom. Like this: in the town of X, in the year 197-, a child was killed, a slow death at the hands of a parent. I, through the exigencies of life, found myself in that city, looking for work. . . . In the early 1970s it was as easy to get a job teaching if you had a degree as it was to find work filling supermarket shelves, and I walked into the Education Offices, and went out on supply.

In the city, a committee of inquiry investigated the circumstances of the child's death. I went and sat in the gallery on the days when schools didn't need me. One morning — Fate led me, I had been meant to arrive at this place — I was sent to the school where the child had been in intermittent attendence at the time of death. From the high building the crumbling, stained houses ran in lines over the horizon. I came home in this place of poverty. I had been a historian of the 19th century, had never really spoken to a child under ten. There was a sudden new vision: the denizens of ragged schools sat here in this 20th century classroom, tired workers educated by their union, Keir Hardie scratching his letters on a slate deep in the mine, the Little Watercress Girl intently telling her story to Henry Mayhew. I fell in love; they were my children; I couldn't ever leave them.

I don't care any more about sounding pretentious, so now I tell people who ask at parties why I did it for such a very long time, that it did seem a way of being a socialist in everyday life. I believed immensely in their intelligence, thought I could give them peace and quiet, a space of rest from the impossible lives that many of them had to lead. No one cared — indeed, no one knew — what social and political theories informed my practice: I only looked like a good teacher, doing what all the text books said I should. I think of great fondness now of my little socialist republic, that intensity of use of time and space, the pleasures of its working, my clear-sighted refusal of all the liberal notions of false democracy that the official pedagogy of child-centredness provided me with. What mattered was that they believed that I knew they could do it: learn, learn to read, defy the world's definition of them as deprived, pitiful, social priority children. And I kept the door shut, and the children quiet.

I didn't know what was happening to me. My body died during those years, the little fingers that caught my hand, the warmth of a child leaning and reading her book to me prevented all other meeting of bodies . . . I never left them: they occupied the night-times, all my dreams. I was very tired, bone-achingly tired all the time. I was unknowingly, covertly, expected to become a mother, and I unknowingly became one, pausing only in the cracks of the dark night to ask: what is happening to me? Simone de Beauvoir tells you how to avoid servitude: she tells you not to live with men, to work, to attain financial independence; but above all she says, women should not have children, women *should refuse to mother*. Children make you retreat behind the glass, lose yourself in the loving mutual gaze. The sensuality of their presence prevents the larger pleasures: the company of children keeps you a child.

Now, look, up on the balcony over the playground, a woman watches. In the room behind the boxes are packed, she is leaving, the walls are bare of the children's drawings. She turns, goes back for a moment through the door, removes her gaze. The stiff skirts swing into folds, a rope turns and the children run and jump, the volume of their voices rises: released, the children go on playing.[21]

The Child,
the World,
and the Text

4 The Tidy House[1]

I ain't a child and I shan't be a woman till I'm twenty, but I'm past eight, I am. I don't know nothing about what I earns in a year, I only knows how many pennies goes to a shilling, and two ha'pence goes to a penny. I knows too how many fardens goes to tuppence — eight.

Street trader in watercresses, 1850

■ Introduction: the narrative

This is an account of three working-class eight-year-old girls writing a story. They wrote the story during one week of the summer term in a Social Priority primary school classroom, four years ago.[2] The children's first and second drafts were kept, as were the typed and edited versions that were bound and displayed, in three volumes, for other children in the class to use. Drawings and illustrations were also kept, and altogether, the writing produced by the children amounted to about seventeen hundred words. For one day during the week in question, a friend, a lecturer from a local training college who was in the process of collecting material for a course on child language, had a tape recorder running continuously on the table where the three girls were working. There are some four hours of recorded conversation on these tapes, conversation between us and the children, and between the children themselves, to accompany the other material. There is a hum of voices in the background, a boy bends down to sing into the microphone, a bell rings, someone comes to the door. There is a class lesson about triangles, a plaster is put on a bleeding finger by one of the three girls; all is suddenly lost in clatter as the rest of the class go out to play. Taping under these conditions, some conversation has been lost. But where we talked to the three girls, and where they — infrequently, only from necessity — talked to each other about their work, there is a remarkable clarity. Later, these tapes were transcribed.

It was a very hot summer, the summer of 1976. The doors and windows of the classroom stood open to the acres of stained cement houses stretching to the parched hills up behind the rubbish tip. The clatter of the girls' platform soles measured out the time as they moved about the classroom. The heavy air divided us, as it heightened sudden sound and movement. It is sound and movement that form memories of that week, as well as the pieces of paper, the drawings, the words that trickle like sand from the tape recorder now.

Evidence from that week has been carried around, preserved, as if it bore the seeds of a new life, a way of explaining, a means of understanding. Yet the children's story — their 'Tidy House' — is difficult material to interpret, partly because it is so totally without guile. There are no dragons for translation here, no princess sits weeping in her high tower, enchantment is not employed. The Tidy House is the house that the three writers will live in one day, the streets that their characters walk to the shops through are the streets of their own decaying urban housing estate, the pattern of life described is one they know they will inhabit, the small children they create (a uniformly irritating, maddening crew) are the children they know they will have, and that their own parents think them to be. In 'The Tidy House', absolutely no one is forgiven.

The first part of the three-part story was written by Carla. Her extraordinarily accurate ear for conversation was now, at the end of her eighth year, being directly employed. The confidence and verve of her opening passage arrested me when it was first put into my hands, and still has that power, after several years and many readings.

One day a girl and a boy said
Is it Springtime?
Yes, I think so; why?
Because we've got visitors.
Who?
Jamie and Jason. Here they come.
Hello our Toby. I haven't seen you for a long time.
Polkadot's outside and the sunflowers are bigger than us.

(Carla, 'The Tidy House')

Two married couples meet here in the back garden of a council house, and they are the central characters of the story. Jo and Mark, whose Tidy House it is, are childless. The couple who visit, Jamie and Jason, have a small son called Carl.[3] The plot is simple: it is concerned with the getting and regretting of children.

The childless wife Jo spoils the maddening Carl, her friend's little boy, is criticised by his mother Jamie, and gets a child to prove that she does know how to bring up children. 'She's up in competition, see?' said Carla. With grim satisfaction, the three writers have Jo produce boy twins, Simon and Scott. They called the last part of their story 'The Tidy House That Is No More a Tidy House', for obvious reasons:

They saw Simon and Scott. They were one and a half, but Carl kept on pushing the twins over and making them cry. So Jamie had to sit him on her lap until it was time for the twins to go to bed, then she would put him down. So it went on like that . . .

(Melissa, 'The Tidy House')

Jamie, Carl's mother, produces another boy during the course of the story, and he, as he grows up, fights continually with his brother Carl. All the children produced in the story are boys. Jamie though, longs for a girl:

She wanted a girl because she had thought up a name, the name was Jeannie. Jamie adored that name, she thought it was lovely . . .

(Melissa, 'The Tidy House')

The extraordinary dark nights of whispering and fumbling in

the getting of children, overheard by an eight-year-old girl
through the thin walls of her 1930s council house bedroom,
were translated into this:

> What time is it?
> Eleven o'clock at night.
> Oh no! Let's get a bed.
> OK. Night sweetheart. See you in the morning.
> Turn the light off Mark.
> I'm going to — Sorry.
> Alright.
> I want to get a sleep.
> Don't worry, you'll get a sleep in time.
> Don't let us, really, this time of night.
> Shall I wait till the morning?
> Oh stop it.
> Morning
> Don't speak.
> No you.
> No.
> Why don't you?
> Look it's all over.
> Thank you Mark.
> Mark kissed Jo. Jo kissed Mark.
>
> (Carla, 'The Tidy House')

The other two girls, who became co-authors after the first
section of part one was written, always sought to make
concrete the scenes that Carla constructed entirely by the use
of dialogue. They made a collage picture of the Tidy House,
and described it in this way:

> In the back garden there are lots of sunflowers. They're
> bigger than Jo and Mark. They also have rose bushes.
> They've got a dog called Toby. He is black with a white
> chest. They've got a rabbit called Polkadot. It's white and
> black. Now, outside their house it is brown on the walls and
> has blue curtains on the right side and brown cord on the left.
> On the top right side is fancy coloured curtains, and in the
> top left corners is brown.
>
> (Melissa, 'The Tidy House'.)

In the same way, Melissa tried to make visible the bedroom scene that Carla wrote at the beginning of part one. She drew a picture for the cover of the second book, the bedroom of the Tidy House. There are hearts everywhere, making the shape of the lamps, the pattern on the rug, the frame of a picture on the wall, the outline of the flowers in the vase. Carla was scathing of this visual interpretation of night's desires:

Carla: Miss, never seen heart flowers.
Teacher: (Pointing to a circle covered with hearts) That's the rug, is it?
Melissa: No, that's a nest of babies.
Teacher: Oh. (Pauses in astonishment) A nest of babies! Of course, in every bedroom a nest of babies!
              Lindie: Course there is! (Quotes) 'What is the mother without them.'
Teacher: (To Melissa) But your mum hasn't got a *nest* of children, only two . . .
Melissa: No, not a nest; but she's got this big bed, and she's got all these cuddly toys around it. She's got a teddy that big . . .

For all three children, the writing of 'The Tidy House' was a way of trying to understand life's mysteries. The girls knew quite well how babies were conceived and born, and they knew quite well that I knew they knew. The nest of babies was at once a serious physical metaphor, and a serious statement of their feelings about the closed bedroom door, the parental and private place. The doctor's advice to Jo (childless wife at the beginning of the story) to 'try harder' in order to conceive a child, was dealt with in a scene at once furtive and ribald, that Carla and Lindie, who both made attempts at it, knew was dirty enough to necessitate the literary euphemism of the dash, to replace the unsayable, unwritable word. But this was not really what interested them. Procreation was only a means to the emotional relationship between parent and child. Forced to distance themselves from the untidiness, roughness and lack of consideration that is socially disapproved off in little girls, they bestowed these attributes upon the small boys of their story. To write of themselves, they had to see themselves as grown women, bearing unbearable children. Yet when they

wrote of the boy children they had created for the story, they
spoke not precisely of themselves, but rather of how they knew
they were perceived by their parents.

The child Carl (small son of the visitors in the opening
scene), caught in an irritated and depressing relationship with
his mother, was drawn from life. Six months before 'The Tidy
House' was started, Carla wrote:

> On Saturday my aunt and uncle and my cousin Carl come up
> my house. On Sunday all of us had some ice-cream, but Carl
> would not eat it. After my mum cleared up, Carl wanted some
> ice-cream, but there was none left, and he started to cry. He
> was after biscuits all the time. He ate a whole tin of biscuits.
>
> (Carla, diary entry)

From that plain account developed an acute fictional observation of the emotional politics of family life:

> Jamie came over to Jo's house.
> Hello. Happy anniversary.
> Oh, you silly thing — Hang on, the doorbell is ringing.
> A boy said, Is my mummy here?
> Yes. Jamie, here is Carl.
> Go home. I won't be a minute.
> No, I want to stay here.
> All right. Stand still and shut up.
> Jamie smacked Carl. Carl started to cry.
> Then Mark and Jason came home.
> What's this then?
> Carl ran up and Jason picked him up and stopped him from
> crying.
> He gave Carl 10p to get an ice-cream when the ice-cream van
> came round.
> Jo said: Let's have some tea.
> Carl said: Can I have a cup of tea? Please, please, aunty Jo.
> No.
> So Carl started to cry.
> Shut up.
> Jason took Carl over his Nan's . . .
>
> (Carla, 'The Tidy House')

The child Carl cries a good deal. A thin, persistent whine fills
the pages of 'The Tidy House':

. . . he didn't want to go home. He started to cry.

> (Melissa, 'The Tidy House')

Carl came in with an ice-cream. He was crying.
What's the matter?
He dropped his ice-cream.

> (Carla, 'The Tidy House')

He started to cry.
Stop it now, boys don't cry and not on their birthday, do
they?

> (Carla, 'The Tidy House')

That made Carl get in a temper and he started to shout and
Jamie gave him a hard smack which made Carl cry all the way
home.

> (Melissa, 'The Tidy House')

On Carl's fourth birthday, after three crying bouts, his mother
remarkes in heartfelt tones, 'Tomorrow he goes to school,
thank God'. (Carla, 'The Tidy House')
The three children were almost entirely without sympathy
for their creation, as their recorded commentary revealed:

Melissa: He's babyish, isn't he?
Teacher: Do you think he suspects that his mum's glad to
get him off to school?
Lindie: Well, in the story she *said* she's quite glad to get
rid of him.
Carla: She probably *is*.
Lindie: His dad pampered him.
All: Yeah.
Melissa: He's spoiled. By his nan and grandad . . .

They soften towards Carl on only one occasion, when he
receives a small car as a birthday present:

It was a small car. It was small as a matchbox. Carl was
overjoyed. He fell in love with it. He was playing every day
with it. Jamie had trouble in getting him to school. She had
to let him take it with him.

> (Melissa, 'The Tidy House')

They watch Carl's appealing and childish antics with an indulgent but wary eye:

> After dinner they went to Jo and Mark's house and had a cup of tea up there and a bit of cake and they sang happy birthday to him, and he got all shy and covered his eyes up and hid behind the chair, and when it was over, Jo put a candle on Carl's bit of cake and he blew the candle out and they had a good time up Jo's house . . .
>
> (Melissa, 'The Tidy House')

The three authors of 'The Tidy House' kept their distance from Carl's pretty tricks, partly because they knew what treachery lay in the relationship forged by them. Dealing with Darren, the boy that they had Jamie bear in part three of the story instead of the longed-for girl, Lindie wrote:

> The baby was called Darren and he was lovely. When he was four he and Carl were always fighting, but Darren never got the blame and Carl was always sent to bed. Carl hated him because he was not spoiled any more. Darren was lucky, 'though I'm not,' thought Carl.
>
> (Lindie, 'The Tidy House')

At the end of Carl's first day at school, in part two of 'The Tidy House', he refuses to go home (having earlier refused to enter the classroom), and his mother has to carry him screaming out of the building. 'Big lump', remarked Lindie disparagingly, but Carla reached swiftly the heart of the matter, the point of having constructed the scene they were discussing: 'My mum would love us if we didn't want to come home from school.' Carla remembered quite clearly how pleased her own mother had been, four years before, to 'to get [her] off to school . . . get rid of [her].'. . . We asked Carla how many of her own sisters were still under school age:

Teacher: Who's still at home?
Carla: Jeannie.
Teacher: How old's she?
Carla: Three.

Teacher: What will your mum do, when she's off to school?
Carla: Go out I suppose. Go out and get rid of us. That
          what she says she's gonna do. And she's not gonna
          come back and she's gonna leave my dad, do all the
          work, and he's got to go up and down to school . . .

Later, when two of the children were asked why one of their characters, Mark, husband of the childless Jo, did not want children, Carla replied, 'Probably hates kids', and Lindie continued 'I think all mums do, don't they?' It is mothers who matter, whose bed is the nest of babies, who make decisions and persuade and cajole and negotiate children into life:

Carla: [Jo] met Mark, and they decided to get married.
          And she wanted a baby from the beginning —
Lindie: But he wouldn't let her —
Carla: And then he sort of liked the idea . . .

Through a discussion of their narrative, all three children remembered their first day at school, the admonition that they hand on to their own characters: 'Don't cry; if you cry you'll get bad luck . . .' Later, they moved to the sociology of their families. Divorces were counted, half-brothers and sisters were listed, the number of children in a family compared. Fathers were dismissed in a short list of variations. They could be flirted with and made ally in a battle with a brother. They could be absences — 'comes in at eleven, goes out again' — and their sudden and violent anger at the spending of money was related to the daily mystery of their absence and the unknown process that gets cash and brings it home. Parental approval was understood to be most clearly expressed in the spending of this money on the children. Lindie was felt by the others to be the most favoured child:

Carla: She does have presents. Her mum and her dad
          spoils her when it's her birthday . . .
Lindie: Yeah, I know. I get — I get . . .
Carla: She gets gold chain necklaces.
Lindie: Last Easter me and my brother got two whole bags
          of Easter eggs . . .

What informed the writing of the three children, was the tension that lay at the root of their existence. They knew that their parents' situation was one of poverty, and that the presence of children only increased that poverty. 'If you never had no children,' said Carla towards the end, 'you'd be well off, wouldn't you. You'd have plenty of money.' They knew that children were longed for, materially desired, but that their presence was irritation, regret and resentment. They knew, in some clear and uncomplicated way, that it would have been better had they never been born. But their situation, and the plot that they constructed out of it, was complex. Carla knew quite well how to prevent children being conceived. She knew that women didn't produce babies as long as they remembered to 'take their pills'. But that wasn't the point: 'they can't help it [having babies] can they?' 'The Tidy House' was about this sort of compulsion and necessity. The children's task was urgent: they needed to understand what set of social beliefs had brought them into being.

How can a reader set about understanding a narrative like 'The Tidy House'? There are two sets of problems to consider when we as adults come to read the writings of children. The first concerns the obvious difficulties that children, as yet imperfectly in command of written language, encounter. Our reaction to spelling mistakes, to errors in syntax, to the distortions of imagery that arise from a child's incomplete comprehension of the world, is often expressed as a sentimental delight in her misapprehension. But in fact, adult delight in charming childish error is as irrelevant to an understanding of children's writing as a delight in a little girl's pretty lisping is to an understanding of her development of spoken language. The second set of problems is to do with the *use* young children make of language, both spoken and written, and the part it plays in their growth and development. It is concerned with real distinctions between the intentions of adults and children when they come to write (or paint, or draw). The next two sections of this chapter attempt to explore our reactions as adults to the reading of children's writing. If we are not overwhelmed by the *obvious* differences between child and adult writing, then we will be in a position to understand what function the child's writing is actually performing for the writer.

It is easy to construct a dreadful sentimentality of intention around the words of children, especially their written words. That there is a willing public for the view that children are naive versions of our better self, is attested to in the sales of books like *Mr God, This Is Anna* and *Children's Letters to God*. The obvious difficulties encountered by children when they come to write, create in their turn, problems for adult readers when they come to consider the work of children. Children may be hampered by poor writing skills, and by an inability to spell, though truly, in the history of child writing, not many have been hindered in this way, except when adult strictures upon handwriting and spelling have made their task impossible. The reaction of adult readers to such errors poses a much greater problem. When the adolescent Opal Whitely translated the scraps of her childhood diary into *The Journal of an Understanding Heart*,[4] she was careful to leave many artless and saleable spelling mistakes in her new text: 'the mama where I live says I am a new sance [sic] I think it is something that grown ups don't like to have around'. Later editors have continued to find such errors 'charming' — the editorial equivalent of chucking little girls under the chin to see them smile.[5] This sentimental reaction stands in the way of interpreting the purposes of children when they write. By concentrating on the surface differences between child and adult writing, readers can, in a warm and naive affection for the deficiencies of child writing, actually trivialise an important means of growth.

Children with extremely limited reading and writing skills can nevertheless use written words in a deliberate and highly structured way. I remember a story written by a nine-year-old boy with a reading age of barely six, who had been profoundly influenced by the tale *Tripple-Trapple*, disguised his own child- and wife-battering father as the devil — the iron pot of the tale — and his mother and sisters as rabbits (echoes of a gentler stimulus than *Tripple-Trapple*).[6] With these simple figures he recounted assault, kidnapping, a desperate fear of rejection, and hope of rescue. In the end, the black iron pot was shot to pieces by a man with a gun, the man who had by then come to live with his mother.

The child who wrote this story could never have *said* what were the limitations placed on his life by others, could not, in any clear way have *thought* about his family pathology. He manipulated the symbols of his fears as seriously and as intentionally as children play, and the words provided the means to reflection, to speculation: the route to conscious thought.

To use written words in this way, children need to be operating at some level of literary competence. They need to have some understanding of conventional orthography and its relationship to the phonological and lexical bases of the language. The child needs to know what it means to write, and that what she has written can be read. She needs to be able to read and write just well enough to operate independently. That we as readers put a wider interpretation on the activity of writing than this, and know that her functioning is (for the time being) minimal, is not the point at all.

When children's writing is to be read by adults or other children, then child writers need editors. In both cases, an editor of children's writing needs an acquaintance with the categories of verbal and written linguistic error that children of that age commonly make, and some knowledge of local dialect. The purposes of the edition for adults and children, are different though. When children's writing is corrected in school, this is done partly so that other children can use it as reading material, and so that conventional orthography and syntactic structure can be emphasised. This method is also used to help the child writer to spell and structure written language. But the editor who corrects surface errors in child writing (and editing here emphatically does not mean cutting) for an adult audience, is performing far more of a translator's role. Ideally, adult readers should have access to both the child's unedited text and a sympathetic and revealing edition of that text. In this way, the reader can be helped over a concentration on the obvious and superficial features of the text and gain easier access to its purpose and meaning.

Children often need to be asked what they mean by their writing. I typed the final version of part one of 'The Tidy

House' from Carla's draft, and spent a whimsical few minutes interpreting 'polkadots'. . . . (see above, p. 67) as some version of sunspots dancing in the garden around the burgeoning sunflowers. I was told next morning that Polkadot was a rabbit; and I think that Melissa was prompted to write her strictly factual guide to the Tidy House as a prophylactic against such romanticism. Yet an editor cannot always seek a child's opinion. I decided to put the conversation between Carla's characters on the page without quotation marks, because she used what they were saying to control and structure events in a way that Lindie and Melissa did not. She rarely indicated in her text who was speaking, and in some sense, this device was deliberately used, for she knew what quotation marks were, and could employ them to some extent. There is meaning here in this manner of writing that is more useful to adults in interpreting children's perceptions of the world than it was to the child who wrote the words. Indeed, for this aspect of Carla's text to have become pedagogically useful to her it would have been best to have put in the speech marks, returned to her typed and punctuated text, and have helped her to learn from it.

We read children's writing for more than the means to pedagogy, or to the fleeting and indulgent smile. We need to read it as well for evidence of individual psychologies created in particular social circumstances, and the fact that some child writing offers better evidence than others, delineates the second and more difficult problem in reading it. Carla had a fine ear for dialogue. Developed, encouraged, well-taught, Carla could come later in life to write very well indeed. Some children do write better than others, and their success and effectiveness depends not on a fast and legible joined hand, nor on a mastery of the spelling system, nor on an ability to maintain continuity over involved linguistic structures (though all these features are of enormous usefulness to young writers, and need to be taught). Their success and effectiveness depends rather on their ability to *know* the symbols they are manipulating, to have some understanding of, some control over, their meaning. Our difficulties as readers of children's work must not confuse our appreciation of their writing with the function it actually serves for children.

In their written words, children may manipulate and rearrange the symbols of their social circumstances. But if words are the means by which they can act and become powerful, the world itself remains obdurate. Indeed, children do not write to act upon and change the world (though they may, by writing, reveal that they wish the world were different: things not as they are), and a consideration of the precise usefulness of written language to children must take us a long way from conventional ideas derived from adult literary and fictional production. Children do not have an audience in mind when they write, nor a set of assumptions that they share with that audience, about the ability of literature to bring about altered states of mind. Children's writing is useful to the children who produce it in a way that it is not useful to the adults who read it (which is not to say all that it is not useful in other ways). Like a child's first spoken language, written language enables her to do what she would not otherwise be able to do.

Early language development gives young children access to a symbolic representation of the world, a system that they can manipulate and change and restructure, in an attempt to take hold of its meaning. The errors in English tense structure that most who have anything to do with young children have noticed, are the clearest example of children's use and abandonment of theories within a symbolic structure. For instance: the most common verbs in English have irregular past tenses ('I went', 'she saw'), yet young children generalise the rule for '-ed' endings, and use constructions like 'ranned' and 'rided', which they have never heard from adults. They do this out of their own reflection on a language system, and it is a helpful, though not altogether satisfactory analogy to see child language — children's use of rules and meanings — as a kind of foreign language that can be studied and understood in its own right, and that must not be confused with our own. It may well be that access to written language allows children to construct and discard theories, and to reflect on form and meaning in much the same way as access to spoken language does.

If this is the case, it becomes clear that it is particularly important not to *equate* child writing (and child art in general) with adult art. As long as we do not see child writing (or drawing, or painting) as the same *order* of production as adult art, then we are free to use it as a window onto child development, free to know that it is not significant that some pieces of work are more appealing, seem better than others. In this way, we can view child writing as a means of growth available to all children, work wrought by its own internal rules, as we see a child's first sentences having structure and validity in their own right, and not just as some imperfect version of adult production.

Of course, the second and most difficult problem still remains: some children do write better than others. It is not enough simply to agree with Berger's point about the difference between child and adult art (in this case, painting): 'A work of art must be born of conscious intention and striving: and the spectator . . . must be able to infer this. A child paints simply to grow up . . . .The adult paints in order to create something outside himself in order to add to and . . . alter life'.[7] There are two reasons for going beyond this important distinction. First, there lies within it the adult desire for a state of innocence in children, and the consequent route to our sentimentality: Berger calls children's paintings 'almost natural objects', and likens them 'to a flower'. Second, by seeing in child art only an absence of the intention that informs adult art, it gives us no way of exploring what children are actually up to when they manipulate the symbols of their world in drawings or (words). But when we do understand how children can use the symbolic representation of written language to change and manipulate their experience, then we are free to see that questions of ability, of talent, of writing well, are *our* problems and questions, not the problems of the child writer, and that to create in us these impulses to literary appreciation was nowhere near her intention. Knowing this, it is then possible to talk about 'The Tidy House' as a rare piece of child writing, to acknowledge that it is powerful, and revealing, and important.

The tension in child writing that we may then perceive — the knowledge that children grow up, that this symbolic representation is of its very nature transitory, that in the end nearly all of us stop saying that 'Goldilocks woked up and ranned away' — will then help us to understand that a child who has chosen to rearrange the pieces of her life, not with a doll, nor a skipping game, nor a smashed tower of bricks, but as *words*, has chosen to rearrange them in a highly deliberate way. Then her writing can be seen as serious, as intentional, and as purposeful as play. Then we, in our different way, through the glass of distance and forgetfulness, half-remembering our own lost childhood, can ask at last, what understanding of social circumstances it was that prompted the writing of 'The Tidy House'.

'The Tidy House' is then, unlike much of the writing that children produce in order to think about their condition. Nobody here is represented as a dragon, nor a monster; no dreadful possibility wears the clothing of a witch. It does not follow the conventional three-part pattern of the folk fairy-tale — assault on a given situation, striving, resolution — that many children use as a model for their story writing. Much of the secret and self-exploratory writing produced by girls and women in the past has been in journal form, and by far the largest category of writing that children in contemporary British primary schools are asked to produce, is autobiographical in this way. But 'The Tidy House' does not proceed step by step through the simple past-tense listing of events that is the feature of school diary writing. By constructing a story with no matter what bare bones of their daily life, the children were able to move away from an account of their immediate social reality, to an investigation of what would be the pattern of their future.

By her use of conversation to direct the narrative, Carla did actually bring the story of 'The Tidy House' directly into the present. It is not so much as if her characters — talking, shouting, quarreling, smacking — provide an allegory of her own life, or of what she knew her life and the life of other working-class girls would be, but rather, it is as if they stand as constant, formless and insistent commentatotors on what already *is*. The characters are never described; we know nothing of what they wear, nor the colour of their hair, nor what they hand over to each other as anniversary gifts. What the children chose to make visually substantial was the Tidy House itself, and the rooms within it.

The writing of children, bearing direct testimony to their daily life, as 'The Tidy House' does, is rarely to be found. It is rarer still from the 19th century, yet there are diaries extant, written by children, from this time.[8] In all those 19th century journals that I have read, I have not found any conversation reported in dialogue (in fact, even indirect reporting of speech is extremely rare). The past tense accounting of upper-class girls' journal writing confirmed their social world both as it was, and as it was meant to be; all conflict, all interchange impaled by the chronological listing of events.[9]

This kind of personal autobiographical narration confirms two things for the writer: that the events really took place, and that she was a witness to them.[10] Fiction-writing, on the other hand, offers much greater scope for the selection, reversal and denial of events. It was as a *story* that Carla, Lindie and Melissa recounted the events of 'The Tidy House'. Their account does, of course, contain many elements of personal autobiographical narration: the third-person of the children's recounting of imaginary events could theoretically — and very easily — be replaced by 'I'. By actually performing this manipulation of the children's text we can see that in the following extract from Melissa's narrative, the character Jamie's voice could become that of her child-inventor's — could become Melissa's voice — and she could talk of herself and the child-character Carl as 'we', thus producing prose much like the dairy entries of the Victorian schoolroom:

> After dinner, *they* went up Jo and Mark's house, and had a cup of tea up there . . . and sang happy birthday to him. *He* got all shy and covered his eyes up . . .

But much of the children's text was not constructed in this conventional way; it was written rather in the timeless present of dialogue, and we cannot perform a similar trick upon it:

> Is it Springtime?
> I think so. Why?
>
> What time is it?

11 o'clock at night . . .'[11]

These passages cannot be related to autobiographical narrative by replacing the third person with the first: there is no 'he', 'she' or 'they' to replace. It is similarly impossible to recast the present-tense dialogue of 'The Tidy House' in the past tense. The children's text is a *dramatisation* of the circumstances they describe, not to be confused with the narration of a particular event. For the children, the text asserted that they were *not* there, were *not* witnesses. It is as if, projected onto a screen, the events of the story take place *out there*, out of real time; and the children briefly watch them, involved and fascinated, considering them and perhaps denying that this will be their future, that they will have children they don't really want, and spend their days in irritation and regret. In some clear though unconscious way, the children who wrote 'The Tidy House' knew what function writing could serve the writer, and its possibilities for objectifying, denying and transmuting experience.

The voices that the 19th century journals transmit are overwhelmingly female voices, for journal keeping was viewed as a suitable pedagogic device for the instruction of small girls. All these female voices are middle class, and to look for continuity in working-class girls' perceptions of their society, and their future place in it, it is necessary to look to those 19th century social investigators who spoke to children, and who took some pains to record their words directly. It is important to do this, not just for the making of neat historical connections, but because within a historical period when many currently dominant theories of childhood were created, the metaphors that poor children have used to comment on their own socialisation and in order to think about their future as women, have remained remarkably consistent.

The tension between the physical desire for babies — the looks, the glances, their pretty ways — and the weariness and burden of their presence that informs every page of 'The Tidy House', is present in the words of the little girls that Henry Mayhew spoke to on the streets of London a century and a half ago. It is important to remember that these children's spoken words, like the written words of 'The Tidy House' were extracted by means of a relationship within which the children felt permitted to speak and write. For the transcribed words of the Victorian street children, the relationship was swiftly made, and soon over. For the middle-class investigator, the relationship with the children he spoke to was partly built on his fascinated repulsion from their wild hair and broken boots.[12] Mayhew felt as well though, the charm of his subjects' smiles, the prettiness of their frowns.[13] A genteel paedophilia, soon to set many middle-class gentlemen taking photographs of appealing little girls in tumbled clothing,[14] may possibly have shaped part of Mayhew's response to the small girls he spoke with. But whatever propelled his warmth, the children felt it, and talked to him not only out of deference and in expectation of the coin to be handed over when the shorthand notebook was shut. The importance of this testimony then, when linked with 'The Tidy House' is to show that whilst the material conditions for a childhood of poverty may alter to some degree, children's reactions to such circumstances follow a distinct pattern. Little girls take part in the process of their own socialisation, as they have done in the recent past.

Carla, Lindie and Melissa displayed a reluctance to speculate on their story. We talked to the children about their writing, but that conversation, easy on the surface, familiar, friendly, is empty really. Some essential point was not grasped, there was something we did not understand. Was it that, like Mayhew, speaking to the watercress seller whose words open this article, we found ourselves undone in the face of experience without knowledge, adulthood without a history, a world measured out by restrictions and limitations? 'I did not know how to talk with her', said Mayhew of that 19th-century eight-year-old. 'At first I treated her as a child, speaking on childish subjects, [but she] was indeed in thoughts and manner, a woman . . .'[15]

The girls' discussion of 'The Tidy House', even when it centred on aspects of the narrative not yet composed, was couched in the present and past tenses:

Teacher: What did Jo do before she got married?
Carla: Dunno.
Lindie: She's a typist. My aunt used to be a typist.

Result was confused with intention:

> Melissa: We thought . . . um, that, er . . . Jamie would have
> a boy, and Carl and the boy — the little boy —
> always used to have fights. And then . . . and
> then . . .
> Teacher: Why do all these people have these babies?
> Melissa: Then Carl won't be pampered then, will he?

Their story was not a means of talking about the future, for
there was no future. Their lives had already been lived. Yet
within this sad certitude — the modern reader turns away,
conventional developmental psychology cannot let us see the
writers as anything but children, their obsession seems unchild-
like, a kind of neurosis — the writers of 'The Tidy House'
acted upon the story of their life, and the symbol for the
greatest restriction, the baby, became the arena for the greatest
play of imaginative freedom.

Babies played the largest role in the imagination of the
Victorian street-traders too. The girls of the 1850s
remembered a baby fed and cared for, a badly missed little
sister, the heart-trapping smiles of infancy, feeding a baby —
the only work they didn't call work:

> I had to take care of a baby for my aunt. No, it wasn't heavy
> — it was only two months old; but I minded it for ever such
> a long time, till it could walk. It was a very nice little baby,
> not a pretty one; but if I touched it under the chin, it would
> laugh.
> (Watercress seller, 8 years, Mayhew (1851), pp.151–3)

> I hadn't to do any work, only just clean the room and nuss
> the child. It was a nice little thing.
> (Crossing sweeper, 13 years, Mayhew (1861–2), p. 506)

> I never had no doll, but I misses little sister — she's only two
> years old.
> (Watercress seller, 8 years, Mayhew (1851), p. 151–3)

These ties of affection and responsibility are made early in life,
as the writers of 'The Tidy House' knew. But what they wrote
there is not simply a sad account of the way in which working-

class girls become working-class women. It is not just an account of the tension in which girl children find themselves, between the dichotomy of being born, and at the same time, being able to bear a child. 'The Tidy House' had a context in the other writing that the children produced. Carla especially, frequently touched on its themes in her writing. In one narrative, finished a month before 'The Tidy House' was started, she dealt at greater length with the possibilities of action for women. In the story 'Jack Got the Sack', all the children are girls:

Jack, Jack, got the sack.
'Oh Jack, go to work please, to get some money for the children'
'Oh, all right'.
'Bye'.

Jack came back soon, at half past two.
Jack got the sack.
'Jack, you've got the sack'.
'I've got the sack'.
'What are we going to do now?'
'Don't ask me.'

Jack went to every place he could think of.
He got back home at five o'clock.
'I can't get a job now.'

Jeannie his wife said: 'I don't care.
Just get a job, Jack. We'll starve to death'.

They had a row, and Jeannie left Jack.
The girls came too.
Oh how sad Jeannie was.

She got a job as a barmaid.
It was good money at £20 a week.
Jeannie bought Lindie a bike to ride and Melissa a doll
and their friend Lisa a dog.
They were happy for ever after.

(Carla, 'Jack Got the Sack')

Another story written after 'The Tidy House' was completed, was the only one in which, during that school year, Carla used any image, any figure. 'Flower Lady' was the only writing she produced that did not follow her own life on parallel tracks of commentary:

> One day, Flower Lady went for a walk. She was sad because she had no friends. She sang a sweet song, and it went like this: 'No friends, no meat, no food to eat; at least I've got to have some wheat'.
>
> That's what she sang, going along the road. Flower Lady lived in a den with chairs and tables, happily.
>
> One evening, when it was very dark, Flower Lady sang the sweetest song she'd ever made. It went like this: 'My name is Flower Lady. You may like me. May be you like me better than a bee, and I love trees and bumble bees'.
>
> Then she went to bed and had a dream about songs and laughter.
>
> O, what a night.
>
> (Carla, 'Flower Lady')

Perhaps she remembered here a grandfather, who had died the previous autumn. He had been living rough, not allowed into the Tidy House by his daughter, Carla's mother. His body had been found in a little den that he had constructed on some waste land. Carla, entering the classroom, her face incoherent with tears, writing what she could not say:

> My granded is dead, he's about 60 or 61, he is going to be buried on Tuesday at ten o'clock. It makes you feel funny when a cat dies, and two grandads dead, actually two cats died, one cat we had is in the shop, it had diarrhoea, so one dog and forty three pigeons, four went to the poodle parlour, my Nan had one . . .
>
> (Carla, diary entry)

If her grandfather provided the feeling image of freedom discernible in her story, then memories of him afforded the elegiac self-containment of the song that Flower Lady sang. Image and desire move across children's writing like dreams, as they name imaginary children after their friends, make boy children repositories of all that is disapproved of in themselves, and heap indulgence on their more favoured creations as they long for such indulgence to be extended to them.

It is often the case, as we have seen, that this imagery seems dull and stark, a fantasy constructed out of the workaday, the dull, the uneventful. I think we found it harder to see that Carla's face only really became animated when she spoke of clothes, the unbearableness of flat-heeled sandals (in a summer of platform soles), the appropriate garb for a funeral . . . than did Mayhew to hear how the watercress seller describe how she kept herself clothed:

> Carla: She had to go [to a funeral] all in blue, she never had no black shoes. Don't wear black anyway, do you?
>
> Second
> Teacher: No. I went to a funeral the other day, and there was nobody in black.
>
> Carla: Dark blue's next to black, because my mum bought a dark blue top and a dark blue skirt and it came to twenty quid. And my dad went mad — just over a funeral.

> All my money, I puts into a club and draws it out to buy clothes with. It's better than spending it on sweet stuff for them that has a living to earn.
>
> (Watercress seller, Mayhew (1851), p.152)

Conventional developmental psycholgy has taught us to expect more than this from children. Within the context of contemporary theories of childhood, children confound us when they speak, as the watercress seller did, and as the writers of 'The Tidy House' do, not of childhood, nor of adulthood, but of some serious preparation for the latter, of some attitudes and beliefs wrought out of material so threadbare and poverty-stricken that they seem no more able to keep a soul warm than did the watercress seller's shawl her body.

What we are left with in this case, are some children's words, and we need some way of interpreting them that is both helpful and uncondescending. When there are no dragons, no frogs to kiss, then we must look at the words, and the linguistic

and social structures that support the words. The three girls'
ability to think about the circumstances of their lives, to
speculate and reflect, was rooted in the very restrictions that
prompted the writing of 'The Tidy House'. The long hours
spent in adult female company, the walks to the shops, up and
down to the nursery school, visits, cups of tea — 'stand still
and shut up' — all that listening, gave the children access to a
symbolic form of this life, that they could manipulate and
change, in written words.

The way in which little girls are taught to be aware of how
they look to others, to set themselves at a distance from their
own charm and pretty ways,[16] can, under certain circumstances, be translated into that most fundamental impulse to
creation: the knowledge that whilst we are as we know
ourselves, we are also most profoundly as others see us. The
children knew that whilst it was their fathers who created
many of the conditions of restriction in their life, it was their
mothers who fashioned the chains — those who told them to
stand still and shut up, who longed for them only in order to
dress them up and because girls' names are so pretty. But out
of these circumstances, they were able to find the possibility of
power for women.

The long hours of listening had already, long ago, played
their part in making the girls' preference for staying in,
negotiating the world in an indirect way:

Teacher: What's going to happen to all these people?
Melissa: We're going to have another book. Four books.
Lindie: We're going to try four books. So at playtime, can
just we three stay in and do the next one?
Teacher: Yes, I think so.

Power had been derived from that listening. The rhythms and
cadences of spoken language had been translated and con-
tracted by Carla into the strongly alliterative way in which she
wrote. The structure of her particular narratives, propelled not
by what people did, nor by what happened next, but *by what
they said to each other*, offers an insight into child development
— restricted, altered, made meaningful by precise social and
historical circumstances.

The testimony of the three authors of 'The Tidy House' rests not just on the enabling interest of a friendly adult (the Victorian street children, briefly, had that), but more importantly, on their ability to write. Reflecting on language, they were able to reflect on their own circumstances in a way that the Victorian working-class girls could not. What Mayhew noticed in the children he spoke to was their inability to see themselves through other people's eyes;[17] but what the children who wrote 'The Tidy House' were able to understand was that they existed in other people's image of them, as well as in their experience of themselves. Knowing this, they could assess their relationship with the world, and find it wanting.

The very narrative of 'The Tidy House' is a way of placing events in time, of moving the meaningful symbols into new order. The order may seem to us dull and sad, so that we move away, like Mayhew did, in despair and confusion, from children who have seen so clearly where they are bound to go. Yet the circumstances of restriction carry within them the means to change: little girls, should the circumstances permit, can work together, and using the very abilities that female socialisation has taught them — quietness, the ability to listen, and to see themselves as they are seen by others — can think about their lives, and deal in terms of change.

> My sister is the youngest
> I am the eldest.
> My mum works in town
> With all my family
> And leaves my little sister
> In the arm of me.
>
> (Carla, a poem)

5 Amarjit's Song[1]

Introduction

Several years ago I was working in a primary school in a provincial city — a northern city, a working town — that year without a class, a 'remedial teacher', a teacher for 'language development'. About half the children in the school spoke English and a second or third language, and under these circumstances I saw Amarjit, a 9-year-old Punjabi girl, every day, when she came to my room as part of a small group of children who received extra help with reading and writing. We thought vaguely that she had problems, difficulties with reading (staffing levels were still generous then; I doubt that anyone now could afford to think that she had a problem). She was in fact, a child in the process of becoming bilingual. Terminology has moved on in the last few years, and in some cases is more helpful than it was then. Four years ago [this was written in 1984] Amarjit was, in the jargon, 'a second language learner', a label that confirmed her as being in possession of some irritating and elusive inadequacy. Born here, speaking the local dialect, she was a child who didn't need to be taught to speak English, but who failed in some mysterious way to write English adequately, to measure up to the norm on reading tests, to demonstrate the requisite quality of imagination and the proper degree of promise.

It has become clearer over the years since the incidents described in this chapter took place that this reaction of mild

irritation and exasperation shown towards the written produc-
tions of a child like Amarjit, and towards the inadequacies of
her reading aloud, was a heightened version of a much more
general attitude towards the intellectual efforts of working-
class children in schools. Part of the purpose of this chapter is
to outline the history of this attitude, and to find Amarjit's
place within it, a place that has to be read in terms of race and
ethnicity, but which race and ethnicity and attitudes towards
them, cannot entirely explain.

But more than this, this chapter is designed to show that
Amarjit was not the passive inheritor of her own history, nor
of the pedagogical narrative designed to explain her position
within it. She confronted that history: used it, exploited it;
entered into it her own experience. What happened was that
the child used a reading book she had borrowed from school to
make up a song. That is what the following pages are about: a
child's artifact made out of the materials she had to hand — a
reading primer in a second language, set in the mythic
European past, and her voice.

An act of transformation like this can be seen as an act of
play, in the same way as reading and writing are play, a way of
manipulating the symbols of a social and emotional world, and
of abstracting meaning from a particular reality. Children will
do this where they find themselves, and with what is available
to them at the time, in school, out of school; in the brief respite
from picking stones from a windswept Cambridgeshire field in
the 1860s.[2] Play is a way of understanding the world without
becoming involved in it, a means of 'assimilating reality to the
ego without the need for accommodation.'[3] The particular
value of what Amarjit did lies only in there being evidence of
the process, in the text that she made her song from, and in a
recording of her voice.

But there may be more to it than this. Amarjit's song was a
production of dislocation (a working-class child, whose family
came from a rural Punjabi background, an industrial city,
working England of the late 1970s); but at the same time it
represents a journey through dislocation to a powerful synthesis. For us as adults, it can serve to reveal the historical
circumstances that the child found herself in, and in this way
help us read the undrawn map of our own displacement. And

perhaps the song served something of this function for Amarjit herself, allowed her to know the topography of her disjuncture, to use an act of play to discover a social and political world and to work out what it implied for her future. What Amarjit thought she was doing when she made up her song was to practise her reading; but what this chapter is concerned with are the *effects* of this conscious effort, and the place where the by-products of her invented method of reading aloud permitted her to examine and accommodate the meaning of both a linguistic system and a social structure.

I was impressed by the child's song, and made a tape of it which I played — foolishly I know now — at morning assembly. Some children laughed. Neither they nor their teachers thought very much of Amarjit's production. That's the story.

■ March 1979: Amarjit's Song

The reading group to which Amarjit belonged arrived one Friday morning, and she produced from her folder the book she had taken home the day before. It was *The Green Man and the Golden Bird*, a book in the 'Hummingbird' series by Sheila McCullagh.[4] 'I like this book. I really like this book,' said Amarjit. 'I love this book. I don't read my reading book. I sing it in bed at night.'

The part of the text that she had chosen for her song describes the children's — Colin's and Redigan's — mother in the story, buying a caged golden bird in the market. Her daughter begs her to let it go: 'The song is so sad I can't bear to listen to it. The bird wants to get out and fly away.' 'Don't be silly', replies the mother. 'That bird cost me a lot of money.' Amarjit had quite simply set the words to music of her own composing. She sustained the melody over a considerable portion of the book, and with some skill dealt with the difficulties of incorporating the irregular rhythms of prose in regular melody. The tune is sad, distant; it reminded me at the time of some Northumbrian folksongs.

Amarjit seemed quite clear about which musical tradition she was operating in. When I had recorded the song, I asked her if I could take the tape home to ask a musician I knew if there were any influences from Indian music on the song. She said I needn't bother, because it was English, she knew it was English. But I did take the tape home, and the tune was notated. It was apparent at the time that Amarjit must have used a good deal of implicit and intuitive knowledge of Punjabi and English in the composing of her song, and that she had used a written text, and her translation of it into musical composition, to practise the language she was acquiring, just as nine years before her infant babbling had been her practice in her first language, Punjabi. She chose as well a familiar place of safety for her enterprise: children's chosen environment for reading seems to be their bed, and earlier than this, bed is the place of their pre-sleep monologues.[5] Amarjit's song seemed to be providing her with practice in the timing and intonation of a second language. What precisely the child was up to only became clear much later.

What was striking at the time, was her choice of text. Amarjit composed her song out of a portion of the story that deals with the question of possibilities: that a bird might fly, might be made free. These possibilities were narratively and stylistically rooted in the present, in the restrictions that a mother places on a child's desire to act, in the price of the bird. At some level, the text she contemplated in such a sustained way allowed her to think about the difficult linguistic relationship of the present to the conditional — of the relationship between what is, and what might be — not simply as a syntactic matter, but as a social and emotional question too.

Most languages, and the way children are taught to read their written forms, present them with difficulties as regards tense sequence. English tense sequence for example, demands the sophisticated manipulation and re-ordering of function words such as 'will', 'would', 'might', 'did', 'do' and 'used'. At a time when children are still being taught to pay close attention to individual words when reading, the verbal and written responses asked of them demand the ability to manipulate strings of words according to meaning through time. Amarjit was learning to do this in both Punjabi and English. It seemed likely that she used this story — and many others — to help herself with this task, for stories are themselves hypotheses, leading from an easily comprehended present — the interrelation and reaction of people to each other in dialogue — through different states of time. It is the desire of the moment, the yearning expressed in the present ('the bird wants to get out and fly away') that predicates hypothetical and conditional states of affairs, and in this way makes linguistic structures based on 'might' and 'perhaps' comprehensible. That Amarjit read herself in those particular lines, saw her own position between what is and what might be, was obvious; but the transformation of imagery that she achieved, through the reworking of a culture that she found represented in the story-book narrative, only became apparent later on.

A few days after I had recorded her song, I played the tape to the school in morning assembly. There had been a plan to have a friend of Amarjit play the notated tune on her recorder, but it proved too difficult for a beginner to master in so short a time. I explained to the children that I would go back to the story of David and Goliath that another teacher had delivered to them in assembly the week before, and get them to think about how a shepherd who possibly couldn't read and who certainly couldn't read music, learned to play so well that he could please a King. I was going to suggest, I had told Amarjit, that maybe it was because he did something like she did: heard a story that he liked and made a song out of it.

I hated doing assembly. Clause 25 of the 1948 Education Act, which directs that each school day open with a corporate act of worship, places burdens on those of us who know that one tacit reason for our occupying a particular position in the school hierarchy is to relieve colleagues of this awful burden. I had a senior post in that school, and if someone had written my job description, taking assembly would have been listed. It is difficult to explain these matters to outsiders: who among those who read these pages except for teachers will have as atheists to propagate Christianity as part of a job of work, and to engage in matters of conscience that are so dreary, so old-fashioned and so unimportant? If some of us unwillingly take part in a system that disseminates the Judaic-Christian myths, then some of it has to do with an understanding that in many ways, such propagation has absolutely nothing to do with the ideas that are embodied in these re-tellings. I knew as well as everyone else on the staff did that all gatherings of a school together — assemblies, hymn practices, sponsored walks — are for the adults involved like plonking the kids in front of the telly at home, putting your feet up, letting the mind drift: the ease of not being responsible. In 'Shooting an Elephant' George Orwell explains what it felt like to earn a living by acting as the administrative tool of an ideology he despised: as a policeman in Burma in the 1920s, and I found there an expression of my bored oscillation between resentment and obligation when faced with the duty of taking assembly.[6] But this is too grand a comparison for what is, in primary schools, only like doing dinner duty with God thrown in.

And it is harder than that. It would be easier to resist telling children what one doesn't believe if it wasn't also clear that those who do not understand the metaphors of a culture are denied access to power: the pleasure of knowing, structures of thought, interpretive devices. And this giving of access to the symbols of a culture would in its turn have been more gratifying if I hadn't also been taking part in a system of genteel racism that ended every 'multicultural' assembly with a rendering of 'Jesus friend of little children'.

On the day in question, the day I played Amarjit's song in assembly, the recorded song filled the hall, and the children started to laugh. I remember telling myself in a moment of fine, mad, panic that it was all right, that this was just the Fish and Chips for Supper Effect, the laughter of recognition, and release that Leila Berg encountered when she read some of the first Nipper books to London schoolchildren.[7] I smiled fixedly and reassuringly at the assembled, and the laughter died away, ordinary England, obedient to a glance.

But it wasn't release and liberation at all. It was the laughter of confusion and embarrassment — because of the plain, unadorned voice, because Asian children weren't often performers at assembly in that school, for many reasons, which this chapter will attempt to outline. I have returned many times to that cold hall, to that assembly, and indeed, in many narratives I have made out of the incident that I describe here, it has become the focus of my attention, the point of the story. There is still a subterranean account here that goes like this: an account in which I read rejection in the

faces of teachers and children in front of me, believe that some
of my colleagues think that I am comparing a 9-year-old Asian
working-class girl with a reading problem to David the King,
make an unspoken but still quite improper act of identification
with Amarjit, tell the head three days later that I won't do
assemblies any more, that I'll pull my weight some other way,
and everyone in the staffroom thinks that getting out of
obligations is the desired end of making a great deal of fuss
about absloutely nothing at all. But that is the wrong narrative. The point was the song; and the dual concerns — investigation of a language system, and of a social system on Amarjit's
part — that it revealed.

■ Words and Music

The portion of the text that Amarjit was recorded singing is as
follows:

> It was a very beautiful song, but it was a very sad song, too.
> 'Let the bird go!' cried Redigan. 'Do let it go! The song is so
> sad, I can't bear to listen to it. The bird wants to get out and
> fly away.' 'No, no!' said her mother. 'Don't be silly, Redigan.
> That bird cost me a lot of money. You must take it to your
> grandmother. She lives all alone. She likes wild things. She
> can listen to the golden bird singing.' 'But the bird sings so
> sadly,' said Redigan. 'The bird sings beautifully,' said her
> mother. 'You and Colin must set out early in the morning and
> take the bird to your grandmother.' She put the red cloth
> back over the cage, and the bird stopped singing. Colin and
> Redigan got up early next morning and set off to see their
> grandmother. Colin carried the cage with the bird, and
> Redigan carried a basket of cakes. They had a long way to go.
> Their grandmother lived in a little house on the other side of
> the green hills. Grandmother had a bad leg and she couldn't
> walk very far. But she was very happy in her little house.
> There was a big bush of roses in her garden. She had a cow
> and six brown hens. The cow came to the door every day to
> be milked, and the hens lived under an apple tree in the
> garden. Colin and Redigan went to see their grandmother
> every week, and took her a basket of cakes and fresh bread.
> They always wanted to go and see her. She told them stories,

and gave them apples and cakes to eat. She fed the birds
every day. All the birds in the woods came to her garden, and
she was never lonely. She was so happy that she made Colin
and Redigan happy too . . .

On the tape, Amarjit's voice grows tired, and she stops here,
though she may have sung much more alone in her bed at night.
Yet she was quite certain about where she wanted to start, three
pages into the narrative, with the beautiful, sad song. The rest of
The Green Man and the Golden Bird rehearses an old theme, in
which the golden bird, released from its cage by accident,
protects Redigan and her brother from various dangers. The
elegiac simplicity of the opening pages, in which the ideas of
restriction and freedom are presented, does not provide the
overall structure of the story. It seems that Amarjit took from the
text precisely what she wanted, and left the rest.

'Of all the creatures . . . that women writers use to stand in,
metaphorically, for their own sex, it is their birds who have made
the most impression on me,' remarks Ellen Moers in *Literary
Women*. She speculates on reasons for this choice, on the
littleness of birds, the ease with which they can be tortured by
small boys, their half-promise of exotic, sensual delights. But the
two most arresting hypotheses that she puts forward are the self-
containment and self-indulgence of the bird's song, and at the
same time, its representation of confinement, its encapsulation of
the yearning for 'the wings of liberty': 'from Mary Wollstonecraft's *Mary* — to Bronte's *Jane Eyre* — to Ann Frank's *Diary
of a Young Girl* — I find that the caged bird makes a metaphor
that truly deserves the adjective Female . . . a way for the
imprisoned girl-child to become a free adult'.[8]

It is well known among folklorists and anthropologists
(less well known perhaps, among developmental linguists and
educationalists) that the speech play — the catches, jokes,
rhymes, riddles and skipping games — of 7-, 8-, and 9-year-
olds speaking their first language, demonstrates a spontaneous
interest in its sound system. Like all theories of development,
developmental linguistics has been constructed in a highly
specific way. It is, for a start, generally concerned with
young children, children under school age, and it has been re-
luctant to absorb the findings of other disciplines concerning

children's language, such as anthropology — which is, in any case, usually concerened with the language use of older children. What is more, the corpus that informs the theories of language that are transmitted to schools is based on the linguistic development of monolingual children. There is little explanation within the everyday theories thus constructed in schools, of what bilingual children might be up to in performing particular language functions, and there is a tendency to equate the performance of children like Amarjit with that of much younger monolingual children, even to think of them, half-consciously, as babyish or backward.

For instance, most children master the phonological system of their first language by the time they are two, so the eight-year-old repeating and reversing strings of sounds in speech play is not *practising* anything in a way that a baby could be said to be practising when she babbles; the eight-year-old is rather rehearsing a long-possessed skill.[9] At nine, Amarjit was rehearsing Punjabi in this way; but also, at the same time and for slightly different purposes, she explored the phonological possibilities of a second language — the phonological possibilities of English. Her song served her as a quite specific piece of practice in acquiring English; but it also allowed her to explore the poetic function of the language. If children in the process of becoming bilingual set themselves this dual task of rehearsal and delight — and the evidence is that many of them do[10] — then it cannot be equated with an earlier period of *first* language acquisition, but must be seen developmentally in its own right. The elaborate formality of Amarjit's translation from text to song indicates her conscious involvement in this process of language acquisition. What is more (and as is discussed below), the social and psychological *content* of the song was something that she, as a nine-year-old, was deliberately trying to confront and understand.

Amarjit elaborated speech play in a second language by using its musical system. This technique can be seen as her search for a more sophisticated and rigorous means of linguistic exploration than speech play itself provided her with, in that the musical system of a culture can operate as a schematic and abstract representation of its language system. In fact, the comparison of melodic structure and linguistic intonation remains under-investigated,[11] though it is the one that is needed in considering Amarjit's song. It has been argued for example, that the typicality and appeal of certain melodic systems can be accounted for in this way, that

> the peculiar, inimitable evenness of the ska beat may be closely related to the fact that the Jamaican dialect of English is . . . extremely 'syllable timed' — that is, each syllable takes up very much the same amount of time, unlike dialects of southern English, in which stressed syllables are markedly longer than the others . . .[12]

Most of the dialects of English spoken in Britain are in fact stress-timed, as opposed to syllable-timed. This means that 'the main stresses in an utterance will fall at approximately regular intervals, no matter how many "weak" syllables intervene. . . . In individual words too, there is a characteristic main stress'.[13] Learning the characteristic *timing* of a new language is one of the many tasks facing the child becoming bilingual.

Punjabi has a very strong *tendency* towards syllable timing. The poetic system of Punjabi represents in a heightened form the halfway position that it occupies as a language along the continuum of syllable-timed/stress-timed world languages. Punjabi poetry involves the combination and patterning of long and short syllables, and is in this way unlike, for example the poetry of an extremely syllable-timed language like French, where it is the absolute number of syllables that makes a poetic unit. A particular feature of the poetic system of Punjabi is the freedom it gives to the poet to lengthen and shorten syllables for rhetorical effect, so that a superstructure of stress is laid over a basic syllabic system, in a formalised way. The poetry and rhymes that Amarjit knew — the cradle-songs and rhyming games of the Punjab — formalised and elaborated the tendency in everyday prose towards stress-timing.[14]

When Amarjit turned the prose of her reading book into a song, it was possibly her familiarity with Punjabi verse that gave her the extraordinary confidence and facility that she displayed in the contracting and lengthening of phonemes. Her song offers linguistic evidence of the way in which a child employed her knowledge of one language, and the musical system that was based on it, in acquiring another. The song offers the example of a child performing a linguistic device that is known in bilingual children (though rarely witnessed to such a sustained degree): that of mapping the phonological system of a first language on to a second.[15] It shows a child creatively using her knowledge of two language systems, for highly practical purposes, and for the purposes of delight, both at the same time.

■ Song and Socialisation

It is a commonplace within late 20th century theories of childhood education that a child's own experience must be a starting point for learning; and recent elaboration of this notion within the field of multicultural education would emphasise Amarjit's alienation from her reading book, the distance of her own experience from its fairytale Germanic setting, and from the blue-eyed blondes who people its pages.[16] But it seems that what Amarjit did was to occupy, take hold of, and transform the set of symbols that she encountered; for what she found there was most profoundly herself.

Amarjit's poetic and practical interest in the sound system of English that the song embodied is connected to another that children display when manipulating language in verbal play: the formal rehearsal of adult roles, particularly those of sexual and marital relationships. There is evidence from the anthropological study of speech-play in children across many cultures that suggests investigation of the social and sexual world is a primary concern of children from seven to twelve,[17] and Amarjit's song gave her the means to explore the world of adult intention and purpose surrounding her, permitting her to consider an adult sexuality, and what she saw as its implications for her future. Children in the process of becoming bilingual may well combine both concerns in their speech-play, and like Amarjit provide themselves with practice in the phonological and intonational system of English and with an understanding of the process of their own socialisation.

It became clear from conversations with Amarjit's friends over the next year, that the economic basis of their existence was a dominant feature of the girls' understanding of themselves — as indeed it may well be for all girl children, and for working-class girls in particular. However, the part that economic relationships and children's understanding of them play in growth of the sense of self rarely enters into normative accounts of development. The conversation that provided me with the most insight into the metaphoric order that Amarjit transformed when she made her song, was with four ten-year-olds (three girls and a boy) a year later. In what follows, and in considering the children's discussion of weddings, babies, boy-children and implicitly, the dowry system (though it is never directly mentioned) it is important to remember that what the children's words reveal is *their* understanding of a social and sexual future, not my understanding, nor an actual *account* of a social and sexual system.

The children were detailing the celebration and party giving that surrounds the birth of a boy child in the Sikh community: 'when somebody gets a girl,' commented Ravinder Kaur[18] matter-of-factly, 'nearly all the ladies get sad. When they have a little boy, they're happy. . . . They cry when they have a girl'. This account of her own sex was formalised in the telling: she, a dearly loved child, presented a ritual that had a learned explanation. But in their account of parties and celebration, the children struggled to understand something of themselves:

First it's at home, a *gudwara*;[19] then it's a party — two weeks
later it's a party. Then when he has his teeth they give
another party for the teeth. So it's a real good celebration for
the boy. . . . Girls don't usually have parties. . . . They're silly
having parties for girls because boys are — they think boys
are more important than girls.

The children moved between the adult formulation (or rather, what they understood to be the adult formulation) and the economic unit of the known self:

The boy has to have his wedding very specially. He does.
Because the boy is going to get married . . . and the parents
have to give the girls some special things. . . . The other parents
don't have to give the boy anything, so he's very lucky.

The only boy present produced a formulation of the same clarity that Amarjit achieved when she composed her song. Not bearing the same emotional relationship to the economic system that the girls did, Jatinder Singh, after twenty minutes of speculative listening, looked up from his writing and said:

> I know why girls don't have parties. When girls are grown up and they get married, they are going to go away from their home. . . . If they're a boy, they just stay in that place, and the girl's got to come to that place.

Girls were costly items: 'Don't be silly Redigan. That bird cost me a lot of money'.

A year before, and younger than these children, Amarjit had explored the same question. The imagery she took from her book, and her manipulation of it, allowed her to dwell on both economic value and economic restriction. The metaphors she used allowed her not only the idea of 'the wings of liberty', but also, by permitting direct comparison between the expensive bird and herself, allowed a movement beyond the traditional European use of the image that Moers outlined, allowed her to see the flight to freedom overshadowed by restriction.

It seems likely that the *cost* of the bird was the feature of the story that preoccupied Amarjit, for its price expressed the difficulties of the adult role she was trying to confront. By dealing with the bird's price she drew on a set of cultural referents that allowed her to see herself as both valued and resented, the costly item that would inevitably disappear from home, its flight sought out, inevitable, its resting place fragile and secure.

In 'A Daughter: A Thing To Be Given Away', Penelope Brown and her colleagues have described the structural and economic foundation in Punjabi Sikh society for emotional understandings that Amarjit may have been trying to assess. In outlining the external features of a social organisation which puts women 'at the service of men', and in which, having no economic or social alternative, they are inexorably drawn into marriage, they present the dangerous emotional territory that the young Punjabi bride must traverse, the enforced flight from a loving and protective mother to a mother-in-law:

New brides pose a threat of potential breaches of family
solidarity — they have to go through the dangerous process of
aligning their interests with those of strangers and breaking
the ties with their natal families. A mother in her turn must
let go of her daughter. There are many Punjabi proverbs and
sayings about a daughter which illustrate this point:

'She is a bird of passage'
'Another's property'
'A guest in her parents' home'
'A thing to be given away'.[20]

The words of Redigan's mother in the story, where she tells
the child she is foolish for wanting to let the bird go, may
possibly have been interpreted by Amarjit in this way. . . .
The image of the flight to freedom turns in upon itself, the
daughter's leaving seen resentfully, because of the expenditure
involved in rearing a bird of passage. . . .

■ Invisible Children

I am further from Amarjit now. Five years ago I knew her —
complicatedly, but clearly — as a female child, a Punjabi, a
Sikh, a working-class little girl, whose family history lay in the
small farming area between Amritsar and Jallunder. To me,
her individual history represented a new version of the long
practice of change and migration within British society, the
borders of cultures traversed, communities unknown to each
other linked across great distances by a million particular
journeys, the shift from country to city that carried its own
resonance 'between birth and learning', that showed 'history
active and continuous: the relations . . . not only of ideas and
experiences, but of rent and interest, of situation and power; a
wider system'.[21]

To see Amarjit within this trajectory was the only honest
position I could find for the teacher I was, the only possible
figuring of a relationship between a white woman and a black
child, in racist, late-20th-century Britain.[22] Then, five years
ago, I saw Amarjit occupying the more general position of

working-class children in schools: seen as falling short of some measure of 'real' childhood, somehow lacking, inadequate. It was clear to me, as Maureen Stone was to write, that 'black children are a section of the working class in Britain, and whatever is true of the working class generally, it is also true of [them]'. In *The Education of the Black Child in Britain*, she describes how

> the social structure [operates] through schools to reinforce the low status of black pupils. The use of social psychological theories to 'explain' lower class and/or black achievement in schools, I regard as unwillingness to relate social psychological theories to the wider historical, sociological, political and economic factors operating in society, both in terms of working class children generally, and of black children in particular.[23]

I believed then (and it is the argument here) that the theories of linguistic and cultural deprivation that Stone here refers to, and the much deeper set of social beliefs and relationships upon which they are based, were ones that teachers were implicitly expected to work with in primary schools, and that they dictated much of the indifferent response to Amarjit's song.

However, the last five years or so has seen the emergence of a set of ideas within the field of multicultural education that seems to offer an alternative to the hopelessness of deprivation theory . . .[24] But these developments in multiculturalism, and the prescriptions that have been passed on to schools can, in fact, serve to expose a rarely discussed contradiction that operates in the lives of children and teachers. The contradiction concerns the category of 'experience' — children's 'experience' its use in classrooms, and its incorporation into reading, curriculum and learning material. These questions are, in their turn, reflective of a history of relationships within the primary school which, once outlined, can show how the pedagogy designed to encompass Amarjit's experience, actually rejected its creative expression. Amarjit's position within the school system highlights a much wider absence of children's experience from the form and content of their learning.

It is a commonplace within radical critiques of popular

education that 'the history of formal education in this country has not generally reflected the culture of the mass of the people', and that given this, 'it would be quite unrealistic to expect schools to cater to the cultural needs of a black minority of the working class when they have demonstrated their inability or unwillingness to cater to the cultural needs of the majority white culture'.[25] Maureen Stone is writing here of Afro-Caribbean children in British schools, children who, in the 1970s, were often assumed to have 'no culture' at all. Children like Amarjit, on the other hand, can be seen to represent an exotic 'high culture'. The well-worn cultural markers of tourism and cookery books are an entirely unthreatening and permanent form of the cultural exotic: children can paint temples and list the fourteen great gurus, cook samosas in the classroom and demonstrate the tying of a sari, because none of this has anything to do with the processes of history and politics, and completely ignores the processes whereby 'children as they grow create for themselves a living culture out of the elements of the various existing cultures to which they have access'.[26] This is precisely what Amarjit did in making her song; but the educational theory designed to support her actually denied her this act of transformation.

In spite of the strategies designed to support her, children like Amarjit do not exist within the educational system. She exists legally of course, in that she possesses a birth certificate and a passport, and her name is written in many registers of the state. But in school, where pedagogical practice and pedagogical assessment have been constructed on the evidential base of many studies of child development, the experience of minority group children is nowhere entered into the records. For instance, in 1963 the Newsons explained why 'immigrants' were to be excluded from their longitudinal study of child-rearing practices in Nottingham:

> We were primarily interested in normal babies in ordinary family situations. For this reason we deliberately excluded from our sample a number of cases . . . all illegitimate children and all children known to have gross disabilities . . . children whose parents were recent immigrants to the country . . . for the purposes of the study the picture could only be confused by their inclusion.[27]

The Bristol Language Development Study, which was set up in 1972 to study the role of language and parental attitudes in the transition from home to school, and on which an enormous amount of educational assumption and practice is based, specifically excluded 'children with known handicaps, those in full-time day care and those whose parents did not speak English as their native language'.[28]

Amarjit's absence from such studies is a heightened version of the absence of working-class children in general from the psychological, psycho-analytic and linguistic evidence which supports our mid-20th century understanding of what a child *is*. This understanding of childhood has been evolved over the last two hundred years, and is based on the experience of a limited number of middle- and upper-class children. It is this understanding which, in its turn, informs the longitudinal studies from which Amarjit is so conspicuously absent; for though children from socio-economic groupings IV and V are, of course, present in these surveys, the *idea* of the child with which they are observed and questioned makes it possible to define working-class and minority group childhood as an inadequacy, a kind of pathology.[29]

Amarjit, a child who spoke two languages, found herself being schooled within a set of theories that had added her bilingualism to the checklist of disadvantages that marks the deprived child. The history of this attitude towards bilingualism has not yet been written, but it is possible to pinpoint landmarks of dissemination. In 1967 for example, the Plowden Committee recommended that Educational Priority Areas be identified, and that certain factors be taken into account when resources were allocated. Bilingualism was added to a list that included: the presence of mentally and physically handicapped children in an area, the number of parents receiving state benefits, domestic overcrowding, and so on.[30] When Educational Priority Areas were finally set up in 1972, having a first language other than English was rejected as a measure of deprivation;[31] but by then, the Plowden Report had been very widely circulated and discussed among teachers, and there is some evidence that the notion of bilingualism as disadvantage has a currency in schools. When the 'Social Handicap and Cognitive Functioning in Pre-

School Children' Project was set up in 1975, teacher groups working with the Project defined a socially handicapped child as 'one whose home background may be that of a one-parent family . . . of a large low-income family; with the father unemployed; with one member of the family chronically sick; a child left with untrained help before or after school; the only or younger child of elderly parents; or from a home where the language spoken is different from that of school. . . .[32]

There is now, in the 1980s, a considerable body of literature that underlines the cognitive advantages of being bilingual, and this literature shows in general, as Amarjit's song showed in great specificity, that the more a child knows about one language, the more she can transfer that knowledge to acquiring and understanding a new one.[33] Using this structure of knowledge, Amarjit might be seen as a privileged learner, because of her age (and the objective understanding of a language system that age brings) and because, by accident, she found a means of manipulating and transforming the meanings that two linguistic systems presented her with. But the idea that bilingualism confers certain advantages on children has not yet become common currency in schools.

There is as yet no adequate way of talking or writing about the restrictions that are placed upon children by these theories of class and intelligence and language. Brian Jackson, reporting in 1978 from a multiracial reception class in the Midlands, did find a way, but only at the difficult expense of blaming the adults who taught the minority-group and working-class children he spent a year with. He pointed out that in a city where the majority of people are rooted in a working-class culture, a sense of that culture is quite absent from the school:

> Teachers simply do not know about the children's homes, backgrounds, pre-school years . . . [so] the child simply doesn't make sense in school. Many of a teacher's difficulties arise because she is governed by one cultural perspective. . . . [The] universe of early childhood, mixed cultures and the home itself is almost invisible. . . . My reports of a child's domestic life only a few hundred yards away were like the afterwork tales of a traveller from unknown lands. Such images as teachers had of home life . . . were ludicrous folk caricatures which are . . . painful to record.[34]

In this situation there is a whole network of common-sense arguments about deprivation to provide a teacher with comfort: 'she can then either fall back on deficit theories — "What can you expect?" — or simply pass over the matter.'

■ Assembly

The recorded song filled the hall and the children started to laugh. There was no way of figuring, on their part or their teachers', what could have been a good and acceptable piece of work from Amarjit. Transfigured somehow, moved to the other side of town, a child without her history, someone else, perhaps she could have had a school acknowledge her learning as effective, and thus have come to understand the implications of her own insights. The sense of power and the intellectual pleasure of knowing that something has been worked out, were, of course, denied to all the children in that cold hall.

Amarjit's song provided her with practice in the timing and intonation of English, and meditation upon the social circumstances that provide the substructure for the construction of linguistic hypotheses. What Amarjit wanted to think about was change: about now, where a bird is caged, and about a future, in which the bird is free. Her movement towards understanding hypothetical and conditional states of affairs, the connections within time of the present and the future, between what is, and what might be, was based on her identification with the bird's current desire. Amarjit, reading her book, watching herself:

> The song is so sad
> I can't bear
> to listen to it.
> The songbird wants
> to get out and fly away.
> No, no; said her mother.
> Don't be silly, Redigan.
> That bird
> cost me a lot of money . . .

6 True Romances[1]

In the summer of 1983, in the national press first and later in the historical and teaching journals, voices were raised about the teaching of history in the schools. Initially the debate centred on matters of patriotism, of national identity and national pride. The first salvo was — probably quite unwittingly — fired by Lord Thomas who, interviewed in a June number of the *Observer* and asked what were his hopes of the next half-century of Thatcherism, produced six of them, one of which was for 'educational reform which ensures that everyone at school is given a real sense of the history of our nation at least as good as French children learn about their country'.[2]

Response was swift, with Christopher Hill for example, pointing out on more than one occasion that the root difference between the teaching of history in England and France lies in the centrality of the idea of revolution in French culture, and in learning about a past in a social context where 'history is not just kings and battles, [but] is the people on the streets, taking command of their own destiny'.[3]

These violently raised questions about the teaching and learning of history, and the political import of the choice of historical subject matter, are part of a wider set of issues that the educational journals have also been reporting for several years now — issues of curriculum structure and change, of who designs a curriculum, of the relationship of the Department of Education and Science to the local authorities and the

109

schools, of the relationship of schooling to work, and to the existence that recession is mapping out for most school leavers. History, rather than any other subject area, was marked as the scene of conflict within curriculum politics, and historians suddenly found themselves on an educational battlefield. But the early debate placed itself within the secondary school and young children and what they learn in primary school of the past and their relationship to it, remained quite invisible within the argument. This invisibility should not surprise (who among the historians and politicians caught up in the fight paused to be surprised or even noticed their absence?), for young children and the history they learn at school are a case of the unrevealed presence: they are there, but not seen; they spell something out that remains unread.

To bring those invisible children into focus raises questions of politics and the political uses of history that are wider than those revealed when Sir Keith Joseph addresses the Historical Association, or itemises the components of the core curriculum,[4] or even when the History Workshop Centre for Social History is launched, and all our carefully prepared rejoinders are laid on the table. Considering what young children do with history may help us see something of the weight of a common imagination, reveal the uses we make of a common past, show the extreme difficulty that lies in abandoning the territory of our dreams, and the Kings and Queens who walk there. The figurative conditions of the child's existence revealed in this way, we may see something of our own, understand the substructure of desire and intention that underlies our own historical practice.

This chapter contains a series of propositions about what it is that children *do* with history, and the uses they might make of what is conveyed to them about the past. In the least complex of ways, as Christopher Hill's distinction between English and French school history shows, the history presented to children in any society is politically and socially determined. What is presented to pupils under twelve in British classrooms has as much to do with ideas about childhood, theories of child development and learning and educational history as it has with political intention and notions about the nature of the historical enterprise. But what is interesting about classrooms, as is interesting about every other institutional grouping of people for specific purposes, is the disjuncture between what is meant to happen, what those in authority believe is happening, and what actually does happen. In the space between the intentions of educators and what children do with what they are inadvertently given, children in classrooms gain access to a highly conservative historical romance.

Tomorrow afternoon a child somewhere — many children — will sit in a classroom copying the line drawings from a range of reference books for inclusion in her own project folder, 'Life in Elizabethan Times'. It's the afternoon, because the primary school morning is reserved for the hard stuff, maths and English, though they may go under other names. Topic work, what she is doing now, will happen again, sometime later on during the week, when she will get her folder out, try again to put the text of the reference book into her own words, as her teacher said; but she will end up copying it, and go back to tracing the very pleasing intricacy of the court lady's lace collar.

She is sitting with other children around a table, mostly girls. The children have free choice here, and a few feet away, the boys pursue their own interests: the details on a medieval shield, the fixings of a breast-plate, 'Weapons Through the Ages'. The children talk to each other, share the felt tip pens, occasionally point out a picture in one of the books; but they're not really working together (though they know that project work is a time when they 'work together'); they only occasionally discuss the matter in hand, and then as a technical question — the right colour for a petticoat revealed beneath the dress, the sharpness of the lead needed for tracing a farthingale.

The child really wanted to do that topic, chose it, and its title — or as much as anyone in a classroom ever chooses anything. It brings a kind of peace, this making of a product — a folder with a decorated cover — that is done at a slower pace than most things in a primary classroom. The afternoon measures out the pleasurable isolation of a simple task, a space of silence in the surrounding clatter; and it is a lady, perhaps a

Queen, who wears the collar. Part of what is happening is to do with the desire for pretty things: clothes and power.

One way of appropriating this scene is to ask: What happens at this moment? What weight of a common imagination is brought to bear on the tracing of a farthingale? What is rejected or repressed in that moment, what longing embodied in that particular copying of the past? . . . In looking at the little line drawings of poor handloom weavers and Mary Queen of Scots, the Queen is the one likely to win out in the end, because she has prettier clothes to trace around, and the glamour of an army to command. The heroic view of history is not foisted on the unwilling eight-year-old; it presents her with an agenda that the theoretical meeting place between the practice of people's history and the pedagogy of progressivism in the primary classroom simply cannot supply. I think that the child takes the conservative romance and reproduces it in her topic book, in spite of its being racist, and sexist, and relentlessly Anglo-centric, because it serves her purposes, in something of the way Freud discussed in 1908, in 'Family Romances'.

The child, Freud argued, for whom her parents were once the source of all authority and all belief, discovers in the course of development, through the exigencies of family life, and through comparisons made in the social world, that the hero and heroine of her early years are not perfect. In imagination she 'becomes engaged in the task of getting free of the parents of whom [she] now has a low opinion, and of replacing them by others, who, as a rule, are of higher social standing'.⁵ Freud noted the great versatility of this particular fantasy, its 'many-sidedness', that enabled the child to use it to meet every requirement of social life. He noted too, the connection in form between these imaginative constructions and 'historical intrigues' — the dramas of revenge and death and triumph that control the heroic narrative of conservative history. The bravery of Kings, great Queens weeping, the world narrowed to an island, the figures on the stage moved by incomprehensible yet easily labelled motives — greed, wickedness, folly — the heroic history that the child finds between the pages of her textbook and embodied in its illustrations, may perhaps serve her in something of this way, enable her to manipulate her own family drama, and make it work to her greater satisfaction.

The way in which children may use the manipulable figures of romance, in this case, the wicked stepmother, the cruel father, the princess weeping in her high tower — all the fairy tales — has been elaborated by Bruno Bettelheim in *The Uses of Enchantment*. By the use of these figures, and the essential optimism of the fairytale, the child may, he claims, find the courage to acknowledge the conflict that lies at the heart of the family drama, and through such acknowledgement find a usable solution to her own difficulties.[6]

The same gentle optimism pervades both these psychoanalytic accounts of how the child may consciously come to use the symbols of the social world. Freud reminds us that in replacing the real father and mother with a King and Queen, the child is not so much ridding herself of her parents, but is rather exalting them, and attempting to preserve an original affection. He suggested that the project is only 'an expression of the child's longing for the happy vanished days when his father seemed to him the noblest and strongest of men, and his mother the dearest and loveliest of women'. Bettelheim pointed to the essential humanity of the heroes of the fairy tale, to the ordinariness of the problems they confront, to the pleasure and security of the happy ending. The nameless King and Queen of the fairy tale are, in his account, only the King and Queen in all of us.[7]

There is something about this benignity that will not do — or, that will not do if we are to deal with the child's use of the historical romance. It is not part of the psychoanalytic project to reckon with the social and political fact that Oedipus was first a King's son, and then a King himself, but it has to be our project if we are to uncover the possible uses that children make of particular historical narratives. 'Family Romances' describes the process by which children come to use social and class relations to map out their personal drama. In replacing the parents, in fantasy, by those of 'higher social standing', the child will, said Freud

> make use . . . of any opportune coincidences from his actual experience, such as his becoming acquainted with the Lord of

the Manor or some landed proprietor if he lives in the country, or with some member of the aristocracy if he lives in the town. Chance occurences of this kind arouse the child's envy, which finds expression in the phantasy in which both his parents are replaced by others of better birth.[8]

The lived relationships of the social world enter the child's consciousness in this way, and are used for an intimate purpose.

This enterprise may perhaps speak to what some children, in some classroom circumstances, actually do with historical information. Some insight into the possible workings of this process is provided by the distinction that Bettelheim makes between the fairy tale and the myth. The events of the fairy tale are everyday events, ordinary: what could happen to all of us if we went out of the back door tomorrow morning and found ourselves walking towards the Well of the World's End. They are about everybody: the people are 'little old men', 'a girl', 'a seventh sister'. Even when named, the names are not real names, just descriptions — 'Cap O'Rushes', 'Little Red Riding Hood'. The fairy tale offers magic solutions (for that is what we want), but the problems (jealousy, envy, hate, feelings of inadequacy) are quite ordinary ones.

The myth on the other hand, concerns a unique event, with named heroes and heroines; it concerns *something that has happened*. The myth of Oedipus, says Bettelheim by way of example, is not a warning about not getting involved in a triangular family constellation. Rather, it is about *what has happened* to every human being; it is about what *must* happen to you if you are a human being. The myth is terrifying, whilst the fairy tale is benign.[9]

You read the fairy tales to children, and they ritually ask, 'Is it true?', knowing that your answer will be no. But if they asked the same question of the myth, 'no' would be a kind of lie. They do not ask the question at all about the stories in the history books — about the children locked in the tower, the rebellion's failure, the rivalry of two great Queens. They have been told from the very start that all of it is true, that *it really did happen*.

The conservative historical romance that children still

have access to might operate in the way that Bettelheim describes the operation of myths. History does not allow children to leave aside the categories of 'true' and 'not true' in the way that fiction does. Its actors are named; the events took place in time and space; it really did happen. And what really did happen is terrifying. There is nothing within the historical romance to mediate the abandonment of most children who use it. The message that they must read is that they, no more than their parents, are not Kings or Queens or brave knights. They are the poor peasant, the nameless Saxon constructing his rude hut, the serving maid, the rabble, whose rebellion (when it is mentioned, which is not often) is as motiveless as the benignity of Kings. Through using this form of history, and in this particular way, the world and its social relations come to occupy the child in a problematic fashion; that is, the relations that are symbolised and used for the purposes of romance and fantasy, represent a difficulty that they did not represent for the children who were the subject of Freud's observation (even though those children may not themselves have been the sons and daughters of Lord Mayors, or members of aristocratic families).

The very stuff of dreams measures out the centrality of some people's relationship to the world, the marginality of others. It is not in the dream, nor in the fantasy itself, that the problem lies, but in its interpretation: given what we know of the world, there are only a limited number of ways of understanding the castle on the hill, the feast laid out for the battle's victors . . . . 'As a child', a crippled birdseller told Henry Mayhew in 1850, after he had recounted a recurring dream, 'I was in great distress . . . I've sometimes sat down and cried . . . I hardly know why I cried. I suppose because I was miserable. It's nothing to do with me who's king or queen. It can never have anything to do with me.'[10] But it did have something to do with him; for the only way he could speak of his exclusion from the earth was to use the figures that stood in the way of his appropriating it.

The Written Self

7 Kathleen Woodward's *Jipping Street*[1]

Jipping Street is a psychological account of growing up female and working class. It is about a mother who is not the martyred saint of traditional male working-class autobiography, whose child, Kathleen Woodward, is bound to her not by love, nor gratitude, but by a fierce sense of resentment and debt. On a first reading, the insistent repetition of the narrative seems to speak out of historical darkness. But, in fact, what Kathleen Woodward has to say here about the relationship of mothers and daughters in working-class households is written in many places, it is just that we have few ways of reading about the tension and despair of our first affective relationship. 'I hate my mother', said Maggie Fuller in *Dutiful Daughters*, and we are not really in a position to understand what she meant.[2]

First published in 1928, *Jipping Street* offers an account of the author's childhood and adolescence in Bermondsey, some time before the First World War. It confirms other accounts of working-class childhood at the turn of the century, particularly of children's usefulness in 'the helping years' before starting school and going out to work.[3] The account Kathleen Woodward presents of her childhood introduction to socialism, her search for self-education through membership of socialist, suffrage and free-thought groups, throws light on other autobiographical descriptions of similar political educations of the 1890s and 1900s.[4] The diffuse religiosity that came to permeate London socialist groups in the years before the

First World War is outlined here in the chapter 'Sons and Daughters of Revolt',[5] and her plain and pecuniary account of women and trade union organisation is a piece of counter evidence to more conventional records of the relationship between work and politics in this period.

So if Kathleen Woodward's book is to be read as history, then it confirms to some extent other reports of working-class life and working-class politics in Edwardian London. But readers mining the book for historical evidence should be warned: *Jipping Street* is not what it seems, and it needs to be read as case-history rather than history. Details of time, place and politics are used by Kathleen Woodward to construct a psychological narrative rather than a historical one, and because of this, the *meaning* of events described is of a different order from that of the very same events when written about elsewhere.

Kathleen Doris Woodward was born in September 1896, in Peckham — south of the Old Kent Road, in fact, a geographical boundary that she gives to the Bermondsey she describes in *Jipping Street*. She was one of five children, and her father was a lithographic printer, a skilled man, though at the time of Kathleen's birth working as a casual labourer in the printing trade. It is not clear if the family later moved north, towards the river, into Bermondsey proper; but as Kathleen Woodward implicitly recognised when she set her childhood there, to be born in the ordinary poverty of South London's endless streets is not enough, not bad enough. The writer must move north, or east, closer to the river, to Mile End or Whitechapel, in order to place a childhood in a real slum, and make it worthy of attention.

By setting her childhood in pre-First World War Bermondsey, Kathleen Woodward recognised an almost virgin literary territory. When a philanthropic settlement was established there in the 1890s, its founder noted that it was

> at that time the most neglected neighbourhood of poorer London . . . the south side was practically off the map, derelict. It had neither the advantages nor the disadvantages of the appalling East End. It had not been written up like the Mile End Road or the Ratcliffe Highway . . .[6]

By 1911 however, Bermondsey had been written up, by Alexander Paterson, in *Across the Bridges*.[7] His description is echoed in Kathleen Woodward's; but Jipping Street never actually existed, though it was placed by its author with great topographical detail upon the Bermondsey map. The closest geographical match to it is Weston Street, which at the end of the century ran from Guy's Hospital, south to the Old Kent Road. But houses described in the book were not a feature of Weston Street, and no canal ever ran parallel to it. The wharf on the canal where rubbish is shot into waiting barges and the suicides hover in *Jipping Street* has a clear model in St. Saviour's Wharf, on the Thames itself; but it is a fair walk from the Jipping Street Woodward portrays. Jipping Street was not real, and it is likely that its creator wanted us to recognise it as a state of mind, a slough of despond. Writing thirty years before Kathleen Woodward did, Arthur Morrison described the emotional topography of any poor London street. 'Where in the East End lies this street?' he asks;

> Everywhere. The hundred and fifty yards is only a link in a long and mightily tangled chain — is only a turn in the tortuous maze. The street . . . is hundreds of miles long . . . there is no other way in the world that can more properly be called a single street, because of its dismal lack of accent, its sordid uniformity, its utter remoteness from delight . . .[8]

At the age of twelve, Kathleen Woodward by her own account, found factory work on the north side of the river, and then, perhaps a couple of years later, returned to Bermondsey to work as a machinist in a clothing factory. This must have been about 1910 (*Jipping Street* is as vague about time as it is precise in its misleading topography), and the first external corroboration of Woodward's account concerns the years in the collar factory just before the War, described in the book in 'Escape'. When Kathleen Woodward published her first book *Queen Mary* in 1927,[9] several newspapers took up her story at precisely the place where *Jipping Street* ends, recounting how 'a worker in a South London collar factory was rescued by the late Mary Macarthur, the trade union organiser and friend of the Queen.'[10]

Mary Macarthur, Secretary of the National Federation of Women Workers, was active in Bermondsey twice during the period when Kathleen Woodward was an adolescent worker there, first during the Bermondsey Uprising of 1911 when, inspired by the all-London walk-out by dockers, 'without any organisation, without any lead, thousands of [Bermondsey] workers, men, women and girls, came out on strike';[11] and again in 1913, when she worked to extend the provisions of the National Insurance Act (1912) to the shirtmaking, food preserving and sugar confectionary industries — all Bermondsey trades that employed large numbers of women and girls.[12] It is likely that Mary Macarthur and Kathleen Woodward met during 1911 (the character of Miss Doremus in *Jipping Street* may well be a portrait of Mary Macarthur); but the precise nature of the 'rescue' performed by her is not yet clear. At the outbreak of war, Mary Macarthur was co-opted onto the Central Committee on Women's Employment, which was presided over by Queen Mary — sewing and knitting by ladies for the war effort was undercutting wages of women in the clothing industry. Mary Macarthur acted as the Committee's Honorary Secretary, and there developed between her and the Queen what Kathleen Woodward refers to as 'an extraordinarily romantic if unknown story called by certain women in the Labour Party "the case of Mary Ann and Mary R" [Regina].' Mary Macarthur died in 1921, but whatever the quality of her friendship with the author of *Jipping Street*, it is certain that the range of acquaintances she developed during the War years helped Kathleen Woodward obtain the interviews that made her first book such a success.

The closing date of *Jipping Street* is probably 1915, and the War provided its author with the means to get up and out. By 1925 she was living in a flat in Middle Temple, sharing with a female friend, an American student. In the years after leaving Bermondsey she worked her passage across the Atlantic as a stewardess, worked as a receptionist at a London club, wrote children's stories, worked as a freelance journalist, and on the staff of the *Daily Express*.[13] She also spent some time after 1928 on the *New York Times*. Kathleen Woodward converted to Roman Catholicism in the 1930s, and went on writing until her death in 1961. Her last book, *The Lady of*

Marlborough House (a more elaborate version of *Queen Mary*) appeared in 1938.

When *Jipping Street*, her second book, appeared in 1928, reviewers used it to outline the early chapters of a romantic life. The publication of *Queen Mary* the year before had shown its author to be one who had already made the traditional journey of the fairy-tale, across the river, to the other side. She was 'the daughter of a washer-woman who grew up to be the biographer of a Queen', 'a London factory hand who wrote the Queen's life.'[14] Amidst the rave reviews, both here and abroad,[15] some critics noted *Jipping Street*'s oddness as autobiography, and placed it on the literary borderlands of the novel. They were then able to read it in the tradition of the novel of 'low-life', or the semi-sociological revelations of books like Arthur Morrison's *Child of the Jago*,[16] and to see its pages peopled by lovable or horrifying Dickensian characters.

Yet at each point of such characterisation, Kathleen Woodward takes her readers to the point of ironic conceit: the gentle Marxist basket maker — who slits a child's throat on Clapham Common; fast Lil, who gets her deserts and whose dead child is laid out in a *cake* box. It is as if the author taunts us with the possibility that it really could have been as bad as that, as if the goose girl in the fairy-tale were to casually pen in the chilling details of her life after the transformation had already taken place, and she had already come to inhabit the royal palace. In fact, it becomes clear that, consciously or not, Kathleen Woodward wanted her readers to understand the tricks she played with autobiography and narrative, her reversals of topography, and her ironies of characterisation and literary allusion.

It was words that paid for Kathleen Woodward's tranformation across the river, and *Jipping Street* is a book about words, particularly words as escape routes. Like many of the men who later remembered their education through the socialist and free-thought groups of Edwardian London, she took to journalism. But she never came, as some of those men did, to condemn the lure of 'the beautiful words', nor to reject the blandishments of the 18th and 19th century classics by which they educated themselves. Teenagers of the 1900s, drunk on their own oratory, the rolling glory of their quotations, eschewed the sense and satisfied their souls with the sounds, seized wooden boxes and stood on them in the snow outside public houses, and uttered the beautiful, moving, sensuous words. Kathleen Woodward's story is one of seduction and betrayal by the beautiful words. The sonorous repetitions of *Jipping Street* give the violent events she describes the ambiguous qualities of a dream, and the reader asks, against her will, was a grandmother *really* swung round the room by her hair? Did her mother *really* split the mad grandfather's back open with an axe?

Yet there is no ambiguity about the major relationships of this book. Kathleen Woodward's mother is the central character of *Jipping Street*, and the enabling and gentle figures of Jessica Mourn and Marian Evelyn throw into relief her daughter's stark portraiture. There is no mistaking what is meant in this account: Kathleen Woodward will allow no one to fall back on the myth of working-class motherhood.

Recent reinterpretations of psychoanalytic theory have provided striking accounts of the way in which the mothering of daughters produces in little girls the need and desire to mother in their turn. Accounts like that of Nancy Chodorow in *Mothering*[17] may come to be modified and extended by the case-history that is *Jipping Street*, for what results from the relationship between mother and daughter described here seems not to have been the need to mother, but the impossibility of Kathleen Woodward's reproducing herself. On the evidence of *Jipping Street*, she knew as a child that she was a burden to her mother, that she need never have been born, that mothers could indeed kill their children. The child shrank from sexual knowledge, from an understanding of a process that had brought her into being, and that gave women 'so little pleasure, so little joy'.

The contradiction of knowing as a child that whilst one exists, one also need never have been, is a great impetus to thought, a fine honing for a child's intelligence; but it implies as well, a death of sensuality. What has been indicated in books like *Maternity: Letters from Working Women*[18] is here made a little plainer. We need to know more, perhaps by a different reading of the few texts of working-class women that we already possess, of what the implications for sexuality are of this particular psychological history.

Jipping Street indicates what this psychological history might be, and its value as evidence may well lie in places where it breaks the rules of autobiography. In autobiographical narration, what matters is the order and veracity of the events described. To reverse the order is to falsify the account; to omit something is to alter it.[19] The autobiographical narrator presents herself as a witness to real events. It is therefore possible to tell lies in autobiography, to bear false historical witness, in a way that it is not possible to tell lies in the writing of a fiction. However, in the construction of psychological narrative — in the making of case-history — truth and order do not matter in the same way. If the events described are falsified, the reader still ends up with the same story in the end: the individual's account of how she got to be the way she is.[20] The events described carry their own meaning. A happening or a relationship may be removed from its 'real' context, and described in another setting; but any falsification this may involve does not alter the status of events and relationships as psychological evidence, though questions must certainly be raised about them as historical truth.[21] Ideas and feelings have, after all, to be embodied in some way: the particularity of *Jipping Street* is that its author uses working-class life and socialist politics to embody hers, rather than the cultural referents that we are accustomed to from traditional case-history.

If *Jipping Street* is to be read in this way, then it deserves the status of underground literature, for it tells a story that neither the confines of descriptive sociology nor the strictures of a new feminism can allow. It is about the ambivalence and restriction of the relationship between mother and daughter, about a mother no longer split into good and bad, as in the fairy-tales and psychoanalytic theory, but powerfully integrated, terribly confining. It is a corrective, written fifty years ago, to all those recent accounts that seek to define the mother/daughter relationship as one of nourishment and support; and it is a salutary reminder that class circumstances alter psychological cases.

Ellen Woodward displayed the stoicism and endurance

that has been described as the rationalisation of oppression.[22] Often, her façade of endurance cracked, and she expressed herself in extreme violence towards her children. The child Kathleen accepted the physical violence calmly, but she violently rejected the dreary stoicism of her mother's vision: 'shut your mouth and go on.' This a book about being the daughter of such a mother. It is about all those mothers who tell you, impossibly, that it is unbearable, but it has to be borne. 'If only there were not Jipping Street, and the factory, and mother . . . '; intolerable burden, impossible legacy.

8 Written Children:
Margaret McMillan, Marigold and Mignon[1]

I shall begin in the confessional mode, by telling you about my problem. It is that — as you will see — I have trouble moving between the boundaries of two disciplines, in this case, those of history and literary studies; what happens — as you will see — is that I move between saying that something *was* the case, and that something was a representation, used for ideological purposes. What I want to talk about is the way in which a historical and cultural development in the period 1880–1930 expressed itself in certain literary changes, which I understand to be expressive of material and political change: new versions of the meaning of childhood, at many levels, in one society, at one point in time. But it seems singularly difficult to deal with the 'what happened', in relationship to a trope, an image, a figure. The problem is of course, an imperfectly understood (inadequately theorised) movement from textuality and representation, to something that 'happened'. There are solutions to this problem of course, but I think they are not for me. There is the solution, which is to behave as if it all 'happened' historically, to say that *Sesame and Lilies* is as much a historical event as the industrial capitalism it criticises. But that does not really help with the placing of event, relationship and chronology in historical time: which I feel obliged to do. There is the solution that suggests that nothing 'happened' at all, that it is — was — all text. But I simply cannot seek a solution in that direction.

Anyway, I hope we will be able to discuss my problem afterwards, when you see more clearly exactly what it is.

I've just finished a book, and given the manuscript to the publisher. In its 650 pages, I think there is just one good idea, and it is that one good idea that I am going to talk about. The book started out being a biography of Margaret McMillan (1860–1931), influential early member of the Independent Labour Party (ILP), socialist journalist and propagandist; but has ended up as something that has the title *Childhood, Culture and Class in Britain, Margaret McMillan, 1860–1931.* It is though, still very much tied to the figure of Margaret McMillan, and my suggestions, about the way in which childhood became an emblem, or representation of human *insideness*, or *interiority* in this period, have emerged from ten years' close acquaintance with McMillan's writing and political work. But I think that is all you need to know about her — so that I may begin — is the content of my assertion in the book, the argument of the 650 pages: that in the forty or so years after 1890, McMillan *rewrote* working-class childhood in this culture.[2]

To suggest this is not to employ some metaphor, vaguely invoking a discourse of the social subject (in this case, that of 'the working-class child'); it is rather to consider seriously the huge output of her writing, the lectures she gave, and the books she published on this topic. The figures of working-class childhood that McMillan presented to the readership of the *Clarion* and the *Labour Leader* and in the fiction she produced for these and other journals in the 1890s needs an analysis that can deal with the subjects of her writing as both invented and real — as literary figures, and as representatives of actual children living in particular social circumstances, in Bradford in the 1890s, and in Deptford after 1910.

What I've done in the book, is trace McMillan's rewriting within British socialism, and show that it was used to help form ILP and Labour Party policy on childhood. What helped shape this policy was not just sets of statistics concerning child ill-health and hunger, not just the sociological shape of deformed and defrauded childhood, but also, and at the same time, the moving, sentimentalised and 'sacralised' child-figures who dwelt in McMillan's prose and her platform oratory.[3]

I have to sketch out one whole area of my argument now, so that I can get on to the second, which forms my topic today. The sketch goes like this: developments in scientific thought in the 19th century showed that childhood was both a stage of growth and development common to all of us, abandoned and left behind, but at the same time, a core of the individual's psychic life, always immanent, waiting there to be drawn on in various ways. A good deal of work still remains to be done on shifts within physiology and later, psychology, that established this particular perception, of human beings located within time by their own history of personal growth; but certainly, in the *literary* representation of children this implicit understanding of human subjectivity, showed in the way the child-figure came to be used as an extension of this self, a resource for returning to one's own childhood, and as an image of ones extension in time.

Not only was childhood represented in these new ways from the 1860s onwards, but histories were written of it. McMillan herself wrote fragments of this kind of history, using the markers of literature and art to measure out a 19th century 'invention' of childhood.[4] John Ruskin's art-history of working-class childhood was published in 1884, and it seems likely that McMillan's account was derived from his. In 'Fairyland', Ruskin noted the beauty with which children were depicted in the work of Rubens, Rembrandt and Vandyke, and then went on to describe how 'the merciless manufacturing fury, which today grinds children to dust between millstones and tears them to pieces on engine wheels', had compelled British painters to represent working children in 'wickedness and misery'. Using the same literary landmarks as McMillan was to employ, he suggested that 'in literature we may take the "Cottar's Saturday Night" and the "toddlin' wee things" as the real beginning of child benediction'.[5] McMillan's depiction of working-class childhood, the precise evocation of beauty in sordid surroundings, the *meaning* of the child thus depicted as an already-thwarted possibility, lay within this tradition of literary, aesthetic and cultural criticism.

This child, noticed by many 'in pale and corrupt misery',[6] was the means by which the city might be held up for condemnation. Ruskin noted in 1884, a number of artists who had 'protested, with consistent feeling, against the misery entailed on the poor children of our great cities — by painting the real inheritance of childhood in meadows and fresh air'.[7] McMillan's camp school in Deptford was an intensely practical manifestation of this romantic critique of capitalism: children's adenoids were operated on, remedial gym straightened backs, bodies were washed and made beautiful; children put on weight rapidly. But *written* about, within this aesthetic and cultural tradition, the children who were healed and schooled there became figures that represented the multilayered meanings of 'natural' childhood. 'The love of spring may have been chilled for the moment by the cold wind of our industrial system', wrote McMillan in 1906, evoking the possibility of lowering national rates of infant mortality. 'But it is bound to revive. And it is love that will save the myriads who embark on the rough seas of life from going down so soon into the dark waters'.[8]

The child as potential rescuer, or reclaimer, of corrupt adulthood, was, as we all conventionally know, a feature of the Romantic, post-Wordsworthian depiction of childhood, and as a literary territory, this 19th century component of this understanding has been very well mapped out, particularly in the work of Peter Coveney.[9] One of McMillan's literary achievements may come to be seen in the way she wedded this particular legacy of Romanticism within British culture to socialist thought, in a new version of an established literary figure, 'the child'. . . .[10] The process is made clearer if we recognise that this child was always much more than a literary trope, was available as well as one of the means by which scientific and social thought mapped out the psychology of childhood, and the stages of child language development, throughout the century.[11] It was an idea that also provided a context of understanding for the anthropological study of childhood, that established the norms of development with which we operate in modern times.[12]

McMillan seems to have turned her written attention — her literary and journalistic attention — to childhood for the

first time in December 1895, when she published the story
'Gutterella' in the *Weekly Times and Echo*.[13] Here, the
childhood of the working-class heroine, and the child Gutterella's passionate love for her father, are used only to prefigure
her doom, Gutterella's inevitable course through the match
factory, phossy jaw, casual sexual relationships, and death. For
the next twenty years of fiction and non-fiction writing,
McMillan was to use accounts of the corruption of childhood
under industrial capitalism in this way, in order to make a
more general point about working-class life, presented as it
was in 'Gutterella', as 'a solitary groping from cradle to
grave'.[14] At the beginning of 1897, McMillan published the
two-part 'Lola'. Repeating the structure of 'Gutterella', 'Lola'
is a moving account of a workhouse child's growth into
womanhood, and ensuing deterioration into death.[15] At first
sight, the use of the figure of the workhouse child is an odd
device for McMillan to have chosen, for she was never
involved in workhouse education. Although McMillan showed
a taste for exotic children (gypsy maids, Highland crofters'
daughters and the like) Lola, in spite of her dark and brooding
beauty does not really fit into this category either. Rather, she
is a workhouse child because then she can be utterly hopeless
and abandoned, as is demanded in a certain type of romantic
fiction of childhood. She is a girl, because within the literary
culture attendant on this romance, it is easier to look at girls
and women, easier to probe their psychology, than it is to look
at little boys. The fictional 'Lola', a girl and a workhouse child,
allows McMillan to explore two central themes of the story:
the influence of childhood experience on psycho-sexual
development, and the notion of the unconscious mind.
Unloved as a child, Lola cannot love in adulthood, is unable
even to make friends with her fellow servants when she takes a
job as a housemaid:

> The cook and the table maid . . . pitied Lola. They would
> have been kind to her, but she had such a strange way with
> her. She was not quarrelsome nor ill-tempered. . . . But there
> was something about her that repelled. Her eyes never
> softened, her eyes never lightened even when she laughed,
> and she would have said good-bye forever in the same tone in

which she said 'good-morning'. . . . Something was wrong
with her. She was like a plant without roots, that grows fast
but falls at night. 'Unhappy the heart', says a great poet,
'which has not loved in youth'. . . .[16]

Lola marries, but leaves her husband within six months: she
was, says McMillan, 'a wayfarer in life. Every house she
alighted in . . . was an inn. And her husband was a chance
traveller like the rest . . . it is certain that poor-law children,
when they grow up, can be married like cuckoos . . . . ' The
only figure to promote love in Lola is a visiting educationalist,
a woman who runs a model school in the country. Lola is
haunted by the memory of her after their brief meeting, stands
on street corners scanning the crowds and looking for her.
Everyone else was 'part of the blank wall of the past, but she
was like a dream-face, flitting forever between her and the cold
stone'. Lola thinks of the child-rescuer on her deathbed.

In one extraordinary scene of Lola's young adolescence,
she dreams (an event not usually allowed to fictional working-
class children in this period — nor any other, come to that),
and through the dream she is allowed by McMillan to express
envy:

> Sometimes she dreamed that the big sea came and lifted her
> away. Far away she knew, there was life — stirring deep and
> glorious; new and strange things slumbered and played in it
> — things of which she had no hint, no clue. She dreamed
> not as happier maidens dream, but in a wilder element, with
> no point of return, no ark of peace, no glad sweet wakening
> — for she had no reminiscences, no friendships, no regrets.
> The past was blank to Lola as a prison wall. She took the
> material for her dreams from the sights and sounds of
> yesterday. Always sights at which she gazed as an outsider.
> Always sounds whose inner meaning escaped her. One
> evening she had found herself in the grounds of a rich man.
> There was a great tent on the lawn, and within the tent a
> number of ladies and men were dining. Lanterns hung from
> the roof, and there were flowers and music. The ladies had
> jewels on their necks, and the crystal and silver on the table
> shone under a soft but brilliant light! Lola looked, and her
> brow darkened. Next day she heard the children in the Park
> prattling to their mothers and nurses, and the soft low tones

with which the women answered them annoyed her. She went home quickly, carrying the loving words with her, like burrs on her dress.

By 1897, when this story was published in the *Clarion*, McMillan had already visited Charcot's clinic in Paris, and reported on it for *Clarion* readers.[17] At one level, this piece is a useful reminder of the existence of the idea of the unconscious before Freud, its origins to be traced through the Romantic movement, and in developments in neurological science in the second half of the 19th century.[18] But more particularly, what the fictional Lola — her dreams, her repressed desire — allowed McMillan to do was explore the psychological effect of deprivation in childhood in fictional form. At the same time as this was written, she pursued these questions in her physiological and educational pieces in the *Bradford Labour Echo*.[19]

'There is', wrote McMillan in 1899, 'a strange lack of life and spontaneity' in such children. 'They are depressed, and their depression is obvious even in their noisiest moments. They do not complain. They never complain. . . .'[20] Both the fictional 'Lola' and the real Bradford children that she described in her journalism had been thwarted in development. More fortunate children, operating through play, gathered material 'for the higher mental life which is to follow, just as in the sub-conscious life of infancy, they once gathered materials for the conscious life today.' The way in which she depicted working-class child life operated then as a warning to her socialist readership: 'the mental life flows from the sympathetic and sub-conscious, and from these alone it is nourished. Woe then to those whose life-river is troubled near its source'.

In the book, I have traced the way in which a particular theory of physiological development allowed McMillan to believe that working-class children could be rescued from deprived circumstances, made whole, well and strong, and educated to become agents of a new social future. The particular purchase of the physiological paradigm for McMillan seems to me to lie in what has been described as a major shift of the 19th century, from idealism to materialism, and the widespread adoption of the new holistic physiological model in many areas of scientific and social thinking, in which it was the *interaction* between the parts of an entity that described the whole. In McMillan's fictional and factual description of children, it was the interrelationship between body and mind, blood and brain, hand and eye, that made up the child.

There was as well, another set of ideas, popular in the 1890s, that allowed working-class children to be seen as possible agents of the new life by McMillan. In McMillan's writing and propaganda work a certain notion occurs again and again: a telling phrase — 'little children have brought us all up from barbarism' — echoes.[21] It was only much later that its source was revealed, in a now-forgotten but contemporaneously immensely influential book, Henry Drummond's publication of the Lowell Lectures in the *Ascent of Man*, in 1894.[22]

Drummond's book was an exegesis on what the author called 'the evolution of love'. Darwinism, he argued, had been misunderstood, in that the struggle for existence had been confused with evolution itself. In fact, in this account, there are two struggles to be seen taking place in the history of the human race, one being for life, and the second for the love of others: 'from selfdom to otherdom', said Drummond, 'is the supreme transition of history'. *The Ascent of Man* set out to reveal 'the stupendous superstructure of Altruism.'[23]

Drummond argued that in human history, it was 'in the care and nurture of the young, in the provision everywhere throughout nature for the seed and the egg, in the infinite self-sacrifices of Maternity' that altruism had found its main expression.[24] Within this account, human children had a particular significance, because the human mother was able to recognise her children as being like herself, and thereby able to move evolution on from a mere 'solicitude for the egg', to a full-blown maternity:

> if a butterfly could live until its egg was hatched . . . it would see no butterfly come out of its egg, no airy likeness of itself, but an earth bound caterpillar. If it recognised the creature as its child, it could never play mother to it.[25]

With the creation of human children then, 'Altruism found an area for its own expression as had never before existed in the world'.[26]

Drummond's work, and her use of it, allowed McMillan to establish working-class childhood as both an arena for political action *and* as a figurative device. I shall return to this last point of Drummond — the visual connection between human child and parent — towards the end of this paper.

McMillan achieved her literary effect through a kind of rhetoric of sentimentality, and her childhood fiction still has the power to move the reader to tears. Moving the reader to tears is the topic I now wish to consider. In 'Kindergarten', Franco Moretti tries to explain what the means are by which certain narratives make the reader cry.[27] He argues that moving moments in such stories are established when the point of view, or perception, of one of the characters, coincides with the perception of the reader, who has just made his or her way through the narrative. Effects of pathos — being moved to tears — have also to do with the timing of this coincidence of points of view. The coincidence is particularly moving when, in Moretti's words 'it comes too late' — the most obvious expression of this too-lateness, or tardiness, being the death of one of the characters. We cry then, because we understand that the course of events is irreversible; our tears are the expression of our powerlessness to alter the course of events. As Moretti says, 'This is what makes one cry. Tears are always the product of powerlessness. They presuppose two mutually opposed facts: that it is clear how the present state of things should be changed — and that this change is impossible'.[28] McMillan's fictional depiction of working-class childhood, from the mid-1890s onwards, moved between the idea of possibility — that things might be made better, that a regenerated child might regenerate a class, regenerate a nation; and her presentation of the process by which *this did not happen*. Her melodramatic child-deaths, or the beautiful, ravaged dying of the child-woman 'Lola', stretched out on her workhouse bed, show what could have been, and what did not come to pass, both at the same time. This was the way in which McMillan wrote about working-class childhood as part of working-class life, establishing its bleak trajectory as a

figurative device; and so the notion of regenerated childhood
as social salvation carried within it the sign that these things
should *not* come to pass.

The fictional 'Lola', who died in the pages of the *Clarion*
in 1896, was brought to life again in a series of pieces that
McMillan wrote for the *Highway*, the journal of the Workers'
Educational Association, between 1911 and 1912. With the
overall title of 'In Our Garden', the third and most reprinted
piece was an account of the night when the first Deptford
child slept out in the garden of the Clinic.[29] In describing the
progress of Marigold's arrival, disrobing, washing, and set-
tling down to sleep under the stars, McMillan made great
literary claims for this Deptford seven-year-old, a cos-
termonger's child, calling her, in her title to the piece, 'the
English Mignon', and using as an epigraph the opening line
from the infinitely sad song of yearning that Goethe's Mignon
sings, and that was later set to music by Schubert: 'Kennst dü
das Land . . .':

> Know you the land where lemons are in flower,
> Where the golden oranges glow in the dusky bower,
> A gentle wind descends from the azure sky,
> The myrtle is still and the laurel stretches high,
> Is it known to you?. . . .[30]

Wilhelm Meister, Goethe's *Bildungsroman* of 1795–6, was
much in the news in 1910–1911, for an earlier version of the
novel, entitled *Wilhelm Meister's Theatrical Mission*, written
between 1777–85, had just been discovered. A part-transcrip-
tion of the manuscript reported in the British press
highlighted the earlier version of Mignon's song.[31] In evoking
Mignon, the strange, androgynous, autistic girl-child of the
two versions of *Wilhelm Meister*, McMillan attached a
particular weight of meaning to her own Marigold. To the
reader, the connections between the two child-figures are
manifold. Goethe's Mignon is an abducted Italian child
working as an acrobat with a troup of travelling players when
Wilhelm Meister first encounters her. She promotes in him
'intense pity', and an overwhelming sympathy and fascina-
tion.[32] The bodily postures of the child acrobats, of whom

Mignon is only one, are seen as 'strange dislocations', and Mignon herself, though very beautiful, suggests a similar deformity, for 'her limbs promised stronger growth, or else announced a development that was retarded. . . .'[33] Meister buys the child from her exploitative employer, and she becomes his servant, though Mignon herself takes the young man as her father.

Mignon's ambiguous gender (she is at first 'he' then 'she' and sometimes 'it') her silences, her hysteria are part of what make her attractive to Meister, and what promote in him a great tenderness. Careless of her feelings though, he does not see what Mignon herself cannot articulate, which is the young girl's developing sexual love for him. Mignon, who throughout the novel appears at the moments of Meister's romantic and sexual attention to other women, actually witnesses a sexual encounter between him and an actress, in the bedroom where she has hidden herself to wait for him.[34] It is this scene that begins Mignon's descent into death: 'she suffered unbearable torment, all the vigorous emotions of passionate jealousy were combined with the unrecognised demands of an obscure demand'.[35] As child-figure, and as a girl-child she has to die, and indeed does, welcoming the release from life, in front of Meister's very eyes, in the famous lines: 'Look how your heart is beating' — 'Let it break. . . . It's been beating too long anyway'.[36]

The import of Mignon for McMillan seems apparent enough, both in the child's strangeness and deformity, and in her potential as reclaimer of sensibility in the adults around her. She is at once a representation of Meister's own inner conflict, his inability to grow and develop, and of natural growth in general, inhibited by social forces.[37] The child Mignon is also preternaturally clean, and spends much time washing her clothes and herself.[38] Her music is the sum of her oddness and her beauty of soul; and McMillan described the 'English Mignon' singing her prayers to herself she lay on her camp-bed in the Deptford garden, in a passage that begins: 'In houses,' whispers the little one, 'where it is dark and ugly, and people in the room, I will say them; but here I sing instead. . . .'[39]

Marigold's ardour and impulsiveness of affection and

embrace echo that of Mignon too: like Goethe's child, Marigold remains elusive, as when 'suddenly [she] flings her arms round her friend's neck, and, always holding aloof, looks at her with eyes full of love. She looks at Nurse, and keeps aloof even when holding her fast'.[40] What is more, the child-figure of the 1790s was the fruit of a double and shocking incestuous relationship, and it is possible that McMillan sought to indicate the horrors of her own child's home circumstances by evoking her.

It is probable that McMillan did intend the reader to make all these connections between Mignon and Marigold, and to bestow on the working-class seven-year-old of 1911 the same depth of interiority, dignity and meaning that Goethe gave to his child-figure. However, the only direct reference that McMillan made to *Wilhelm Meister* was when she presented the child's facial beauty. 'She wears', wrote McMillan:

> the poor raiment of the slum child — a thin, soiled pinafore, long skirts and clumsy shoes; but on her head, over a triangle of short, thick golden hair, is a blue knitted cap, which blot of vivid colour draws the eyes away from the poor raiment. Then one notes the beauty of the face, the broad, low brow, the exquisite lines of lip and chin, the nose, which like Goethe's Mignon, is extremely lovely, and above all the ethereal blue eyes, set rather far apart under wide, dark eyebrows. . . .

In *Wilhelm Meister*, Mignon marks the hero's particular failure of sensibility, and when she dies, Meister understands, too late, the aetiology of that failure. Death elevates Mignon in social status too, but that elevation also comes behind its own time. Franco Moretti has called the death of Mignon the exemplar of Goethe's philistinism.[41] But the reader reserves outrage for Geothe's vulgarity in the reading of Mignon's funeral obsequies, where the embalmed child, endowed with the flush of life by the cosmetics that she had so painfully rubbed from her cheeks at the end of her career as an acrobat, lies in her open casket, whilst angelic crowds of little boys debate in chorus her various symbolic meanings.[42]

There has been some debate of late, about whether what actually makes the reader cry is, as Moretti has claimed, that *it is too late*, or whether the convulsion of pity and tenderness is dependent not on the death, or annihilation of promise, but rather on the audience's sense that *if only* things had arranged themselves differently, opportunity for fulfillment would not have been lost.[43] *If only*, it is said, as a response made through the tears, confirms both that there has been loss, or death, but also, at the same time, affirms that *it could have been*. So, it is argued by Steve Neale in 'Melodrama and Tears', that at the moment of powerlessness to change things, which is what tears express, there is in operation a fantasy that things might be quite different from the way they are. Another way of putting this might be to say that when tears come to the eyes, two levels of time are in operation — now, where things as they are say *it did not happen, it is too late*; and the conditional past, where *they might have been*.

This rewriting of Moretti's thesis has considerable purchase, except that Mignon's death says only: it is too late — and says precisely that *because* in 'Kindergarten' Moretti constructed the argument around different *child*-figures, not around adults, as in the revision of his argument. The horribly rouged dead-yet-living child lying in her open coffin may well suggest what could have been, for it is by lying there that her aristocratic heritage is revealed. But the embalmed child does not move us to tears, as does the living and dying Mignon. Indeed, as new and different meanings were accreted to the idea of childhood from the late-18th century onwards, we could say that children themselves became the central repository for the sense of loss and yearning that the words 'too late' embody. Robert Pattison, in *The Child Figure in English Literature* has noted that in post-Wordsworthian sensibility, childhood is understood as 'a condition which for the vast majority of men is irretrievably lost as soon as completed'. He further describes it as 'a lost realm, somewhere in the past of our lives and the past of our culture. . . .'[44] This idea can be approached in a different though complementary way, as I have suggested, by pointing to the massive development in understanding of human growth that the century we are discussing witnessed. The building up of scientific evidence about physical growth in childhood, the marking out of stages of development and the processes of language acquisition, all describe an actual progress in individual lives, which increased in symbolic importance during the 19th century, whereby that which is traversed is, in the end, left behind and abandoned, as the child grows up and goes away. In this way, childhood as it has been culturally described is always about that which is temporary and impermament, always describes a loss in adult life, a state that is recognised too late. What is more, the idea of things being *too late*, as exemplified in McMillan's rewriting of Mignon, express a conflict and ambiguity that must always attach to this kind of use of children in literary and symbolic terms. The manipulation of two levels of time (the here-and-now; the might-have-been) that the *if only* represents, cannot really come into play with the child-figure, for children are quite precisely a physiological chronology, a *history*, as they make their way through the stages of growth. The solution of the writer trying to use the social fact of childhood in a symbolic way, and as representative of an adult state of mind, is usually to kill the child-figure. In *Wilhelm Meister*, Mignon dies at the realistic level because she has suffered too much, and because the narrative of her own life brings her to this point. At the symbolic level she expires because Meister has achieved adulthood, maturity and an inner integrity, and Mignon is no longer useful as representative of his former disharmony.[45]

We must suppose that by so deliberately operating this set of references, by making Marigold a version of Mignon, McMillan was both making a political statement, telling her readers at a practical level, that help needed to be given to inner-city children at the optimum time for human development, and also, at the same time, manipulating much that was unspoken. Marigold was not doomed, as Mignon is, and she does not die; but whilst McMillan's child expresses hope, she also means: *it is too late*, a fact of which her author was quite aware. McMillan writes tenderly of her, asleep in the garden; and then asks

> Will she go back to the dark ugly house? Yes. As the nights grow long and chill, she must go back. She will sleep again in a foetid room, and for this poor resting place the coster must pay such a heavy rent that there is little left over to spend in food and other things for Marigold.

Marigold, it seems, could only achieve the beautiful land of Mignon's song for a very short time; she was a moment of hope, before she had to leave the garden.

Much later, in 1917, McMillan completed the story of Marigold for her readers, in her book *The Camp School*:

> 'Was she saved by the Camp?' some gentle voice may ask.
> No, she was not. Some were saved . . . [but] Marigold was not among them. She tasted the joy of one new summer.
> Then her father, the hawker, was killed. Her mother 'moved'.
> We saw her long after. Her lovely face had coarsened so as to be almost unrecognisable . . . . Why dwell on one tragedy among so many thousands?.[46]

My concern is with the social implications of symbolising childhood, and the kind of symbolisation that McMillan tried to put on a political agenda. There is much historical work to be done here, though I am now most interested in the sketch-maps stored towards an answer, that have been drawn up by literary theorists whose work I have briefly used. I think as well, that it will be useful to pursue Mignon though the pages of Carlyle, her sexualisation as a child-woman by both Scott and Dickens, and their attendant refusal of Mignon's essential characteristic: which is her madness. It seems to me that this is how I have to start a historical quest, in literary and representational terms, by recognising that children are the first metaphor for all people (as Drummond so clearly told his readers of the 1890s), whether they have children or not, whether they are literate and in the business of constructing metaphors or not: a mapping of analogy and meaning for the self, always in shape and form *like us*, the visual connection plain to see. As they are produced materially out of women's bodies, and as in all known societies women, whether actual mothers or not, have played the greater role in their care, we should expect variation in the uses of childhood made by men and women; but not that much variation, as it is in the power of children to represent the loss of the self and the extension of the self into the future that the theoretical purchase lies.

9 The Radical Policeman's Tale:
working-class men and writing in the 19th century[1]

My book *The Radical Soldier's Tale* was published recently, and it is John Pearman and his writing, the subjects of that book, that I am going to talk about. Originally, I called my manuscript 'The Radical Policeman's Tale'; but there was some strange idea that the title *Radical Soldier* would make for better sales in the US. The restoration of my original title here should help me explain to you why, after spending twenty-five years as a policeman, John Pearman did not have a story to tell about being one; wrote rather, a military story, about the eight or so years he spent in India.

Despite the military emphasis of my account, and the title he gave to his own manuscript (he called it 'Memoirs of late Sergeant John Pearman'), John Pearman was a radical, republican, freethinking policeman who worked for the Buckinghamshire Constabulary from 1857 until 1881. He was stationed at Eton, in the environs of Windsor Castle, from February 1864, until he retired. In the eighteen months — or maybe two years — after being granted a pension at Michaelmas Quarter Sessions in 1881, he wrote his Memoirs, presenting in the 278 page notebook that I am going to talk about, his life as both a policeman and a soldier, and an analysis of the ideologies that divided people from each other, in the societies he had known, and those he had read about.

John Pearman's 'Memoirs' are worth dealing with in some detail, I think, both because they make up a working-class autobiography that throws light on popular political thought

in the mid-Victorian years, and because they show very clearly
a man using writing to further his political understanding, and
his understanding of himself as someone shaped by the social
and political world he was describing.

John Pearman has actually been published before. In
1967, the Marquess of Anglesey (who is the authority on the
history of the British cavalry), advertised in the national press
for private diaries and memoirs of 19th century cavalry life,
and he was contacted by a George Pearman, who had in his
possession his grandfather's notebook, which contained a
lengthy description of his service in the King's Own Light
Dragoons between 1843 and 1856. The Marquess was interested. He considered that 'from the point of view of military
history [the memoir] has some importance. While not adding
greatly to our knowledge of the campaigns [against the Sikhs],
it does supply a number of new details.'[2] Responding to the
description it offered, of the British army in India before the
end of East India Company rule, and Pearman's description of
the wars in the Punjab between 1845–1849, which preceded
Britain's annexation of those territories, he published a part
transcription of the 'Memoir', and a commentary on it, in
1968, under the title of *Sergeant Pearman's Memoirs*.

The author of the 'Memoirs' was much misrepresented in
this publication. What Anglesey did in fact, was to transcribe
the first 152 pages of the notebook, which deal with Pearman's
Indian years and the Sikh Wars, and briefly summarise the
hundred or so remaining pages, including some long autobiographical extracts dealing with Pearman's police career. He
did this for reasons that he thought would be obvious to his
audience: 'Here,' he remarks, 'Pearman indulges in page after
page of philosophical and social reflection, few of which are
original or of particular interest.'[3] His editing of the manuscript also involved his correcting Pearman's spelling, tidying
up his grammar, and often, altering his sentence structure. By
cutting the narrative of the Indian years off from the political
ideas that Pearman used to give meaning to this narrative,
Anglesey was able to see Pearman as an a-typical soldier of the
1840s, an odd-ball, whose condemnations of army life had
some connection with the fact that he was 'considerably above
the ordinary run of men in the army in the mid-19th century,'

and whose 'resentment of the gap between officer and men' was an aspect of personality, rather than of political analysis.[4] What he really objected to in the last 120 pages of the 'Memoir' was that, as he put it 'in old age Pearman became excessively class conscious'. What his editorship did in fact, was to prevent any presentation of the process by which John Pearman used a political consciousness to recast the story of his own life.

In my introduction to *The Radical Soldier's Tale*, what I have tried to do (and what I am attempting to indicate here) is to find the groundwork of John Pearman's radicalism; to see the consciousness of his sixties forged not only out of ideas fairly newly received from secularism and freethought, nor just from the discussion of various socialisms that emerged in the land reform movement of the late 1870s; but also out of his active reworking of his own experience, especially the experience of the Indian years. Here, I think I must tell you (for this paper does not demonstrate this point) that he seems to me to have made an intellectual leap that there was no exact model for in the radical and secularist press that he had access to: for he saw British imperialism of the mid-19th century as being directly connected to questions of land ownership in Britain, as part of the same system whereby some men took land from others, and cut them off from its enjoyment. Indeed, he had literally *seen* the appropriation of the earth by kingly power, had been one of its hired bravos, in India, in the 1840s.

John Pearman's struggle to understand, to achieve a written and radical social analysis, derived, I believe, from three main sources: from his experience as a member of the uniformed working class (as a railway worker, a soldier, and a policeman); from talking and reading about a wide range of ideas through a long working life; and finally (and most clearly evidenced in the 'Memoir') from the act of writing. Imperial events of the late 1870s, and of 1881–1882 — British annexation of the Transvaal, and the defeat of the Zulu nation at Ulundi in July 1879, the first Boer War of 1880–1881, and British occupation of Egypt in the summer and autumn of 1882 — all, I think, gave contemporary shape to John Pearman's past, to his memories of serving John Company in India, of a time when, as he put it 'if they were Thieves and

Stole the Country I must say they gave some of it to the Blood
hounds (I.E Soldiers) who hunted down the rightful owners
. . . .'

Writing, considered as a psychological and linguistic
process, can act as a powerful synthesiser of ideas and reality,
of belief and experience. But (and I will give you my
conclusion now) that synthesis did not occur in John
Pearman's case. We can see the manuscript as a testing of the
wisdom of popular freethought against a man's life story; and
we can see that the two did not fit; the one only partly
illuminated the other; something was not achieved. I think
that we can see John Pearman's own recognition of this
dislocation taking place at several levels throughout the text,
and that a recognition of it, of some sort, can be argued for in
the following ways: in the narrative break that occurs just over
halfway through the 'Memoir'; in its author's discordant and
contradictory attitudes towards discipline that can be read in
the manuscript; and in the syntactic structure he used when
dealing with this contradiction. I shall mention these points
briefly now, by way of introduction; but will return to the
question of discipline in particular, later in this talk.

The most obvious point of dislocation is the place where
the narrative shifts dramatically, around pages 153–156. Up to
this point, Pearman has written a military memoir, an account
of enlistment, journeying, travail, and battle. There are
similarities in form between his account, and other narratives
of the Sikh Wars; these in their turn, link with working-class
memoirs of the Peninsular and Crimean Wars. There is no
way of telling if John Pearman had read these published
accounts before he set out to write his much later one;
however, he used a narrative form in the first part of his
'Memoir' that was quite conventionalised in the writings of
the rank and file.

Half way through the notebook, this conventionalised
narrative breaks down, and Pearman's account becomes a
written political argument into which he inserts autobiographical detail at various points, for the purposes of illustration.
One of the autobiographical traditions to which Pearman may
have had access was that of the 17th century: the Puritan
spiritual autobiography was an interpretative form, dealing

with the understanding of events rather than the narrating of them. Linda Peterson has argued most persuasively that this hermeneutic form was used in 19th-century writing about the self.[5] Certainly, if it were a legacy for 19th century writers, it may explain why 19th century autobiography includes much material that seems 'unautobiographical' to the 20th century eye: commentary, extemporisation, essays on various topics. As we do not know what John Pearman read by way of autobiography in his lifetime, and therefore do not know whether his models were working-class military autobiographies (possibly within the hermeneutic tradition), or modern middle-class autobiographies (nor indeed, whether he read anything like this at all), we have to look at what it is within the text that seems to cause the striking break between the military memoir and the play of ideas that makes up the second half of the document.

What moved John Pearman away from narrative and towards interpretation was the end of his career as a soldier. He tried to revive this structure by going on to write about his career as a policeman (so that he might take a life spent in uniform as a framework), but that attempt does not last long. It was soldiering that brought forth a story, and the rest of his life that produced explication. It seems then, that there was something about being a soldier that allowed him to tell a tale.

This narrative fracture is connected, I think, to the tension that John Pearman came to see lying between experience and explication. He will write of the ordered beauty of a great army ready for battle; and later, he will show how clearly he sees the connection between military panoply and kingcraft, land ownership and imperialism. He will write of his connection with 'the poor brotherhood', the outcasts of the earth, and he will trenchantly analyse a system that makes criminals of working people; and then he will say: 'but still I like Law and have always tried as a Soldier and a policeman to maintain it and to keep up Discipline'.

The two do not fit; these things cannot be put together; and this realisation is expressed in the particular syntactic structure that he uses at moments of maximum contradiction. He links the contradictions together in a paratactic chain: he cannot make the connections between them, only present them, one after the other, with that unsatisfying, unsynthesising 'but':

> one man as much right to the earth as another. but I know we must have rulers. but not as they now live in Luxury and riot. God made animated nature all ruled by a certain Law of its own But man as Prostituted that Law and made artificialial Laws to suit his own purpose. . . . Look at the pride of the Church the Bishops must have his Coach to go to church on Sundays. . . . But we must highly respect the founders of many religions . . .

One of the things I want to do through John Pearman's writing, is to take on the historians, take on their — our — general refusal to consider writing as anything but a transparent container for what is being sought: the facts, the events, the content. I want to suggest that an understanding of writing as a linguistic and psychological process is in its own way a possible means of historical analysis, able to reveal that which cannot be revealed in any other way.

There is another purpose, or point of reference, here as well, that I ought to mention at this moment. I think that over all of this, there broods a historical enterprise undertaken on behalf of another working man, who lived three hundred years before John Pearman, and far away and in another country: I mean Carlo Ginzburg's Menocchio, the miller investigated by the Inquisition, whose cosmology Ginzburg tries to reconstruct in *The Cheese and the Worms.*[6] I take issue with the analysis that Ginzburg makes, but I have learned a great deal from the way in which he presents Menocchio as a liminal figure, a man on the edge of things (though it is Ginzburg's critics who have noticed this rather than Ginzburg himself). In 16th century Europe, mills were situated on the outskirts of settlements; millers had commerce with economic worlds that were wider than the village, with urban centres and new ideas. In my book *Policing the Victorian Community*, I described the way in which, by enforcing a particular kind of work discipline, 19th century police authorities put their working-class recruits into a position that could be described as liminal: constables were cut off from the communities of their birth, stationed at a geographical distance; they were dressed in a uniform, and expected to live by the rules of sobriety and self-discipline; and possessed of these attributes, were sent out to watch a society from which they had but recently been removed. In Parliamentary Commissions of Inquiry and in Chief Constables' reports of the 1860s and 1870s, I kept coming across a particular image: constables on night duty are ordered to watch the beer-houses; they are to watch through the windows, or at the open door, but to keep their distance from that light and conviviality. They are not to speak to the drinkers, not to step over the threshold or through the door that distances and makes theatrical what was, until yesterday, a familiar life. Being in an awkward position between two ways of life, two systems of belief — liminality — has its effect on those who stand in this position. Nineteenth century policemen in English provinces lived on the edges of communities (like 16th century Italian millers, indeed), lived there both topographically and emotionally; they were in a particularly good position to obtain reading material, hear arguments, think through what had been presented to them, by way of official and unofficial information.[7] This indeed is the place where I would take issue with Ginzburg, or rather find his model inappropriate for my purposes. For *The Cheese and the Worms* operated by opposing the world of books and ideas to a 'real' and oral and peasant culture. In John Pearman's case though, we are dealing with a working man who lived in a literate society, in which, on the evidence of his text, published and official ideas continually interacted with ideas that he had obtained from other sources, other people, during the course of a life.

A careful reading of John Pearman's last 150 pages shows him reading widely in the radical and secularist press of 1880–1882 particularly in the pages of Charles Bradlaugh's *National Reformer* and George Standring's *Republican*. In many cases, it has been possible to trace the articles he read, not because he copied them out in the notebook, but because he employed ideas from them to add to his own analysis. It is also quite clear that he was reading Henry George's *Progress and Poverty*, was watching the national press for news of Britain's imperial exploits in Egypt and South Africa; and also reading a great deal else that I shall never be able to trace.

What I believe happened to John Pearman is this: he retired from the police and moved from his police cottage at Eton, where he had been stationed since 1864, to Windsor. He was then in a position to get hold of and read a wide range of journalism and other political commentary. He also had time, and a blank police notebook. He started to write a soldier's story: a tale of marching, fighting and enduring. I would suggest that it was writing the soldier's tale itself that brought him, at a precise historical moment to the analysis that he achieved. For the main part, the first part of the manuscript is quite innocent of the scathing condemnation of British imperialism that is the feature of the second part — except at one point. Remembering the Battle of Chilianwala of January 13 1849, the penultimate battle of the Sikh Wars and disastrous for the British, with a very high casualty rate, he wrote:

> The Battle lasted until Dark at night when both armys Stayed on the ground and the killed and wounded Lay were they Fell our small army lost about 2 Thousand and the Enemy it was said Lost near 5 Thousand so what with men and horses the place was covered with dead and dying that night I prayed to god that I mite never see that sight again . . . night closed the sad sight and the rain came down as if to Cleans us from our past sin. for I verily believe man was not made to kill his fellow man. It has become the order of man since by our Artificial Life and keep the rank of nations . . .

By my reckoning, it is now early 1882 — say Spring or very early Summer — the papers are full of South Africa, and the aftermath of the Convention signed between the British and the Boers in 1881. Soon, Britain will despatch another army to Egypt. I think that John Pearman wanted to get to the end of his soldier's tale, so that he could deal with the historical import of the telling of his own life story:

> when we find a part of the world that would be of use and a profit to us we at once covit the same. but then it is peopled by a dark skinned race Gods people but what of that God as not made their views to meet ours in this . . . so we wish to make Christians IE Covit their country it will bring a good return for the outlay — our first step send out 6 or 8

missionary men with many faces but one head and such as
will in a short time bring about what is wanted. . . . Well to
bring about our next step send a few soldiers they will soon
show the way to become Christians. The next step is you
must pay for the Loss you have put us to by being so
stubborn as not to accept our views of religion. So you must
pay the cost. now comes the grand step Annexation of their
country and in a short time a few years we send them a
Bishop and all his host and you must pay for that likewise . . .

I think that with a text like this, particularly as it is a text in
which there are formal errors, it is possible to argue for a
particular effect of composition in writing: writing made the
meaning of John Pearman's past plain to him, and in conjunction with what he was reading in those eighteen months
enabled him to make analysis out of experience. Also, and
more prosaically, as a policeman he had spent a quarter of a
century writing. It was through the written word, through the
daily filling-in of journals and entry books, that 19th century
police hierarchies managed their personnel. John Pearman was
a man to whom writing was an everyday event. What he set
out to do in the autumn of 1881 was not for him an unusual
activity.

This is to take part in the claim for a wide psychological
effect of writing on individual consciousness. I want to make
claims for much smaller ones; to argue that spelling errors for
instance, allow the historian to make some kind of resurrection
of the way in which people spoke in the past, and also allow a
reconstruction of the process by which they were taught to
read. More importantly, I want to argue that in John
Pearman's text we can see him constantly shifting between a
model of writing that understands written language as speech-
written-down, speech-transcribed; and a model that understands writing as a linguistic system in its own right: writing as
discourse. I shall not claim that these are very large or very
important means of historical reconstruction. Unless you are
rivetted, as I am, by the way in which all emergent writers of
English over-extend the '-ed' rule for regular verb endings to
irregular verbs, then I think that this low level of linguistic
analysis is tedious to listen to (much easier to read), and I
don't intend to bore you with it now. But I do want to mention

it, especially that distinction between writing as speech-written-down and writing as discourse.

First, I want to make it plain what kind of model of language I am working with: that is, that my understanding of writing is cognitive and developmental. It is taken from a view of language learning and language development, in which literacy is understood to have particular psychological effects, which I think is a model that has some usefulness for the historian. I also want to make it clear that I believe that I am dealing with observable psychological processes undergone in real historical circumstances.

I think that John Pearman's document, considered as the result of the psychological process of writing, does allow us some limited access to a state of mind, a way of thinking, from a century ago. It is for this reason that my transcription of the 'Memoir' is a literal one, that is, that it reproduces John Pearman's spelling errors, his syntactic structure, and is faithful to his line endings. These features have to be used as part of the process of historical interpretation; in an edited transcription, these features are lost.

I'd like to pursue this question of the psychological effects of writing, by looking at John Pearman's 'Memoir' as a working-class autobiography. By seeing how his writing matches what we know of other working-class writing in this period, I hope to be able to say something clearer about the particularity of John Pearman's achievement. In general, 19th century working class autobiography was the survey of a life from a fixed viewpoint, an attempt to make sense of a life and to order events and the experience of relationships into a coherent narrative sequence. Usually, as was the case with John Pearman, the autobiography was undertaken at the end of a working life, in conditions of greater leisure than had been experienced during it. But John Pearman's 'Memoir' does not fit into this pattern. As I have already emphasised, the second half is only occasionally written as a life story. Here, Pearman produced a kind of dialogue of ideas, into which he inserted autobiographical items at different points. A typical shift of topic in this way is to be found on pages 188–189 of the 'Memoir', where reflection on the way in which the rich can evade the consequences of breaking the law, leads to a reflection on the life of the poor: 'we cannot find much to live for ours is a life of heavy toil to get a bare liveing and amas money and whealth for the great men of the day.'

Generalised reflection then leads Pearman to his own story: 'But I must be very thankful that I have never been out of employment or without a Shilling Since I first took to keep myself at the Age of 13 years . . .' The 'Memoir' here is a collection of jagged observations, difficult shifts of topic, incomplete self-portraits. He did not smooth himself into the rounded character who makes a journey through life, but rather presented the unfinished items of a psychology. The 'Memoir' is an account of thinking as much as it is of living; and it is with this idea in mind that I want to turn to a consideration of John Pearman's understanding of himself; for self-understanding attained through writing is a claim made for it by historians of working-class writing. I want to look at soldiers' stories, for that is what John Pearman began by writing.

To go for a soldier was an uncommon experience for 19th century working-class men: in the 1840s and 1850s only about 1 per cent of the male population was under arms. It was an uncommon experience in statistical terms, but at the same time, it was the most common metaphorical expression of a man's life. There are more autobiographies written by working-class men become soldiers than by those become miners, or agricultural workers, or weavers, though all of these were much more common 19th century experiences, and John Pearman's soldier's story is often strikingly similar to other published ones that also deal with Britain's colonial campaigns in India. There is the sea journey and its entertainments, the sharks caught and shot, the same shock of surprise on landing, the same magical journey up the Ganges. James Gilling, publican's son and hairdresser from Worksop bound for the Punjab with the 9th Royal Lancers in 1845, sailed past Benares and was reminded of the chapbook fiction of his youth.[8] Much writing like his made explicit reference to chapbook fiction, sometimes directly presenting itself as part of the genre, as did William Hall's published *Diary* of 1848, which on its title page mentioned not only the battles that the pages held, but also 'numerous shooting excursions in India after

Game of all descriptions including the lion and other wild beasts of the jungle.'[9]

In the folk fairy tale of chap-book fiction, hundreds of Jacks are sent out into the world, to kill giants or behead dragons. In a 19th century development of this old tale, the soldier-hero abstracts himself from the reality of comradeship and the communality of campaigning, and presents himself as the lone and intrepid traveller and fighter, as William Hall did. I think that it's important to note that in published accounts of 19th century soldiering written by working men, it is rare for the communality of war to be presented, as John Pearman presents it.

The folk-fairy tale has served certain functions in Western society that I think it is important to discuss at this juncture. There is a substantial body of literature concerned with the uses that young children make of the fairy-tale, in circumnavigating the crises of development. Within this psychoanalytic framework, Bruno Bettelheim has shown us too, that fairy-tales can suggest to young children that the weak and powerless (children, Jack the Giant Killer, Tom Thumb) may defy the great, and not be annihilated. We do know in fact, from both psychological and historical sources, that the folk-fairy tale has been used by and been useful to a great many people growing up and surviving in this culture, over the last four hundred years.[10]

So the working-class soldier's presentation of his story, in a manner that echoes the adventuring of Tom Thumb, Jack the Giant Killer and Thomas Hickathrift, may suggest something of the same usage. What we should be alerted to above all, in pursuing this line of thought, is that the structure of the folk-fairy tale allows the expression of feelings about the self. It allows those feelings to be expressed in a highly conventionalised and formulaic way to be sure; but the soldier-hero, like Jack, can move through the emotions of fear, anger, desperation, loneliness and extreme aggression. What makes the universe in which he journeys and battles is beyond his ken: he moves in a mysterious world, where things just happen; he is powerless to understand it, like a child. What John Pearman achieved within the form of 19th century military autobiography (and I think this was only one of his achievements in writing) derives from his knowledge (which was not these other men's knowledge) that it was not his war, that it was rather a war of capital, of the landed interest, of the rich and powerful, and of official Christianity. Knowing this, he was able to present his time in India as a time of conviviality and comradeship, an experience that was not bound by the expectations and ideology of his leaders, and in which there was space to live and to tell his own story. The denial of communality, the self-presenation of lone heroism, of self-as-Jack-the-Giant-Killer that is a feature of other working-class military autobiography in this period, was perhaps an oblique recognition on the part of the writers, of something that these men knew, but could not acknowledge as John Pearman did: that the ideological setting to their adventures made them strangers in the world.

The soldier could tell a story. For a very long time, I would suggest, it was the only story a common man could tell, as far as audience approval across class barriers went. What is more, the affective depth of the soldier's tale permitted the man writing an exploration of the self that in general, we reckon was allowed women, but not men, writing in the 18th and early 19th century. It was a manipulable framework; and it allowed exploration of a range of emotions. It served John Pearman well, I think, and led him on the path of interpretation. But John Pearman could not tell a story about being a policeman. Why not? I only have partial answers to this question. First, he possessed an analysis of law and society that saw policing as part and parcel of the political and economic order. Having described (and condemned) that, he had implicitly discussed (and condemned) policing. Second, policing was dull, in a way soldiering was not. He could not make the elegant and intellectually demanding analysis of the rural Buckinghamshire that he policed in the way that India had allowed him to make analysis. This point connects with a third, which is that *there are no stories about being a policeman* (though of course, the 1880s do witness the emergence of a sub-genre of low comedy, to do with burly frames, stupidity of mind, big feet, and funny hats). Fourth — and perhaps we can talk about this — the very liminality of the policeman's position prevents the telling of a tale. I am not sure of the mechanism of that prevention, but I am sure it is of ironic proportions, and about the differing commentaries on class position, being on the inside and on the outside, that are embodied in the difference between the possible narrative of the soldier, and the policeman's failure as story teller.

Writing History

10 Forms of History, Histories of Form[1]

In modern literary studies, biography and autobiography are not usually considered together. But that is what I intend to do in this paper — make some observations about the history of these forms, and some suggestions about how a consideration of women's written life-stories might serve to shift the demarcation line between the two. I shall raise these questions by discussing the biography that I have been writing over the last year (and working on for much longer than that); that of Margaret McMillan, who was born in New York State in 1860 of Scottish emigré parents, grew up in Inverness, and who died in 1931, an earlier career in socialist and Independent Labour Party (ILP) politics forgotten in the a-political celebration of her as a saviour of little children.

This paper then, involves a discussion of literary form, of what literary forms permit and what they prevent in particular historical contexts. This means that I shall be discussing the constraints that the form of biography presents me with, writing of a historical figure, now, in the mid-1980s; the constraints that the form of autobiography offered to Margaret McMillan, writing her own, very odd, life-story in 1927. In her *Life of Rachel McMillan*, she purported to write the biography of her sister Rachel, and in fact, wrote her own.[2] Particularly, she effected this disguise of herself (if that is what it was: perhaps it was a display, or an interpretation of herself) by appropriating her sister's childhood. Later, I want to return to the figure of the child, and its use in women's life-stories.

'That', as Margaret Mcmillan once said to a student taking down a lecture from her dictation, 'that will do for the exordium, now for the peroration.' I shall now turn to the problems of writing a biography of Margaret McMillan, problems that are, I think, to do with a) the current state of feminist biography, and the history of biographical form that it carries about with it; b) the legacy of a certain kind of women's history; and c) the subject herself.

If Margaret McMillan is known at all today, it is through a body of educational writing that celebrates her work in early childhood education during and after the the First World War. Several hagiographies, which call her variously prophet of childhood, pioneer of nursery education, and a modern Santa Barbara were published between 1930 and 1960, and they serve to neatly sever off her first fifty years, when she was a member of the Independent Labour Party and socialist journalist and propagandist, from the last twenty (her time as prophetess, seer and saint) after she established an open-air treatment centre and school in the slums of Deptford, in 1910.[3] No one who is familiar with popular history of childhood, in which, as kind people rescue children from factory, mine and physical deterioration and things march to an enlightened present throughout the 19th century, or who is aware of the history of education, which has usually eschewed politics as one of its central organising devices, should be surprised at the effective disappearance of McMillan's first fifty years, within this biographical corpus.

The way seems clear for the historical biographer. A historical biography, one that elevates the political and social setting to the life above its narration, must restore a background to McMillan that deals in terms of culture and class. It must, for instance, make something of her having been born in Westchester County, in New York State, of her father's death in 1865, of the return of a mother and two small daughters to Inverness, to a house of cold, Presbyterian restriction, an expulsion from a garden of paradise and a garden of childhood, and a prefiguring of the garden in the slum that was the Deptford Centre, half a century later. It must make something of a history of the Highland Clearances, their reverberation and consolidation in both myth and political organisation in the Highland capital during the 1860s and 1870s. A historical biography must place the working life of two lower-middle-class young women, of Margaret and her sister Rachel, in some perspective, must acknowledge that McMillan was unusually well educated for a girl from her background, being sent to Germany and Switzerland to train as a finishing governess. It must speculate reasonably on the years she spent governessing in the English shires, speculation that will involve arguing that the fiction she produced for the labour press in the 1890s constitutes some evidence of this period, which is otherwise quite lost to historical view. It must place McMillan's 'conversion' to socialism in the context of the great Dock Strike of 1889, and within the trajectory of British ethical socialism. It must say what being recruited to the ILP in 1893, moving to Bradford to teach a course of adult education in the Labour Institute there, and being elected to three school boards in the city suggest about the possibilities for women's economic and political activity in the 1890s. It must say something important (or at least interesting) about the possible relationships of women to political structures at the end of the last century, exampled in McMillan's involvement in municipal affairs, and about the disenfranchisement of women at this level, in an enactment of 1902. It can present her move back to London, in 1903, as a removal from such political structure and political support, and can discuss her courses of adult education, lecturing and writing as an early example of the modern intellectual woman's hustling of a part-time living. This historical biography can get its fun by delineating a new myth, a myth of Corinne (though in fact, Ellen Moers got there first, as she so often did) in which the female figure on the socialist platform, the woman speaking there, possesses a charisma and calls forth an adulation that even Keir Hardie could not command.[4] What it certainly has to do is discuss her role as intellectual of the ILP, as translator of a range of physiological and psychological ideas into a coherent theory of childhood and socialism, with redeemed and regenerated working-class childhood the path to revolutionary change. It can show how, through all her fiction, all her journalism, she rewrote and reconstructed her own childhood, and found new places for it within her autobiography, so we might see that significant legacy of British romanticism, the Wordsworthian child, the marriage between immanence and mortality, a child-figure that measures out a particular aetiology of the self, being used by one woman, in one particular historical context — and for a political purpose, to boot. For of course, what is particularly interesting and important about McMillan's quest for her own lost childhood (a quest that can be seen as the organising principle of the life-story as told in Europe since the early 19th century), is that she reorganised and reasserted her own past not just in the words she put on the page, but in the lives of others: the others being poor children, working-class children, the 'children of the dark area'. As theoretical rabbit, this particular biography can pull out of its hat the observation that McMillan's theory of childhood was taken over lock-stock-and-barrel by the ILP, but that neither the executive nor the membership knew, nor cared to know, the roots or the implication of their party policy on childhood, and it can ask: what is an idea or a theory when those who hold it do not know its provenance?

Raymond Williams argued that in spite of its seeming simplicity, biography, along with memoir and history, is a difficult and perplexing form, partly because in so rigorously asserting its generic factuality, as opposed to the fictionality of myth, or epic, or drama, the writer can disguise his or her use of epic, drama and romance in the narrative.[5] On this point I shall be quite upfront, and show that I know what I am about. I shall describe McMillan's apostasy of 1929, when this veteran socialist spoke on a conservative platform for Nancy Astor's nursery school campaign; and I shall write that apostasy as tragedy, if I can. Finally, as its engine of internal deconstruction and as major rhetorical device, the biography has to foreground its major source, which is McMillan's own *Life of Rachel McMillan*, autobiography written in the the guise of biography, and show how the living Margaret canonises her dead sister Rachel, so that this doppelganger bears the whole narrative of McMillan's life. In the end, I want my biography to serve as an exploration of the Romantic variant of the form, in which the biographer seeks a shade of herself in the subject she delineates, in the pages of her book.

A historical biography can do all of this, and might even be able, neatly, to raise the question of how literary form influences overt and implied representations of the self. And so what, then, is the problem? Biography is a truly popular form, as a glance at any best-seller list will show; and the biography of women, that has been produced out of publishers' women's studies lists in the last five years or so, has shared this general popularity. Current women's biography owes much of its success, I would speculate, to what makes the form generally popular, and that is first, the confirmation that biography offers, that life-stories *can* be told, that the inchoate experience of living and feeling can be marshalled into a chronology, and that central and unified subjects reach the conclusion of a life, and come into possession of their own story; and second, the way in which biography partakes of the historical romance. By historical romance (which I suppose should more properly be called a romance of history) I mean the hope that that which is gone, that which is irretrievably lost, which is past time, can be brought back, and conjured before the eyes 'as it really was'; and that it can be possessed. Biography takes us closer to its subject matter than does other historical writing, and within the romance of getting closer, women figure with more depth and delight. It is by the satisfactory *detail* — which can be sartorial, emotional, domestic — that women are the visible heroines of the historical romance. This delightful weight of detail, littleness, and interiority, is recognised in most literary histories, for whilst it is evident that this culture has bestowed interiority on women at many points and in different ways over the last 300 years, and that the emerging biographical novel has not been the sole vehicle (we would have, for example to look at forms as diverse as the *vita*, the written psychoanalytic case-study, the great-heroines-series of Fifties comics and reading primers) it is nevertheless valuable to see Samuel Richardson's *Pamela* of 1740, as some kind of Ur-text in this regard. All accounts of the development of the novel as a form point to the great divide between Henry Fielding — all surface for his characters, all motivation from without, all classical trope and allusion — and Samuel Richardson, whose fifteen-year-old Pamela is all selfhood, all inside, and whose depth as a point of reference for female interiority has been immense.

It could reasonably be observed at this point, that whichever way I tell it, I am on to some kind of winner in writing the biography of a woman. What *are* the problems? Partly, they come from knowledge about existing forms. Put at its simplest, McMillan was a public woman who lived in a public space, and the modern categories of women's history and women's biography make that remarkably difficult to deal with, unless I proceed by revealing the detail that lies underneath the public figure — a path not open to me, as I shall explain.

I shall comment on women's history first of all, for one popular legacy of the work that has been done in this field over the last fifteen years, is an altered sense of the historical meaning and importance of female *insignificance*. The absence of women from conventional historical accounts, discussion of this absence (and discussion of the real archival difficulties that lie in the way of presenting their lives in a historical context) are, at the same time, a massive assertion of what lies hidden. A sense of that which is lost, never to be recovered completely, has been one of the most powerful rhetorical devices of modern women's history. This sadness of effect is also to be found in much working-class history, where indeed, a greater number of lives lie lost. But a comparison between the two shows I think, that in women's history, loss and absence remain exactly that — loss, absence, insignificance — in a way that is not the case in the writing of people's history. The organising principles of people's history — the annals of labour, class struggle, the battles of trade union history that might foreshadow a greater and final revolutionary struggle — all allow the lack of detail a greater *prefigurative* force than women's history can allow the women whose absence it notes from the recorded past. Oppression and repression and silence have a *meaning* within the narrative structure of labour history that is not the case in women's history. This seems to me to be a real narrative constraint in writing the biography of a woman who lived and had her being in a public world; for biography has to partake of general and current historical understandings of women's lives, which has given absence a meaning, but a domestic and a highly detailed one, in a minor key.

I think that this 'meaninglessness' needs to be distinguished from the literary delineation of 'uneventfulness', which has also structured much biography of women — and for a longer time than the insights of women's history have. Lives of famous women have been presented initially through a domestic detail that asserts how little really happened to them; then a heroine is delineated by her eruption from uneventfulness, into public life. In this way, the 19th century heroine of biography in particular remains an exceptional figure, one whose life-story explains only itself. Partly, this has been to do with the absence of analyses of women's structural relationship to the societies in which they became actors; but the exceptional female figure, or heroine, has also been produced out of the biographer's use of a personal, or individual, frame of time. Early uneventfulness, in which nothing much happens to the heroine, is seen to produce and shape what happens later, within a public space. In this way, the public life is presented as a reverse image of the old, uneventful life, rather than as a set of interactions between the subject and the political and social circumstances she finds herself in. So, as in the tradition of the exemplary religious biography from an earlier period, that which is created in adversity, in isolation, in a life where 'nothing happened', is understood to produce later conduct.

These old assumptions about an individuality formed in struggle and isolation have been reinforced to some extent, by a modern psycholgy of women, the use of which permits a universalisation of domestic conflict. A struggle with a father then might foreshadow a social struggle, against the assumptions of a patriarchal society. Dependency, and the frequent failure of women to make a break from it is then seen as a transhistorical factor, and allows a life-story to be considered in terms of relationships with others and their vicissitudes.

You will see that, as far as Margaret McMillan goes, these conventions place me in real difficulty, for this public woman left no collection of letters, no journal with which to peel away the layers of public form, in order to reveal the true woman. I can do something with the huge output of her journalism, particularly with the fiction that uses the figure of the child, and I can certainly historicise the setting to her life. But the life story I shall tell will not yield any more than have the earlier ones, nor than she did, in her *Life of Rachel McMillan* in 1927. Above all, I cannot attempt to unveil her, for the delectation of an audience: I have no secrets to tell about her. Within the form, such secrets are usually sexual, and McMillan appears not to have had a sexual relationship with anyone, ever. She prevents delineation of an interiority: she demands a public life I think, that might perform the trick — not of dissolving the opposition between between inside and outside, for that is not possible — but of letting us see, briefly, momentarily, how we might find new means of interpreting lives that have been lived. It has to take as its central image that arresting rhetorical moment of the woman on the public platform, or even more appropriately — and we have a witness to this moment — of the woman in the public square, in the market square, Nottingham, the miners' strike, 1893, and Percy Redfern, the drapers' assistant uplifted by her words, 'touched by something vaguely, unattainably fine. . .', remembering them more than half a century later, in his book of 1946.[6]

It was Mikhail Bakhtin who, in discussing Greek rhetorical autobiography and biography, took us to the public square, the place and form of the ancient state, the civic funeral and memorial speeches there delivered, in which biographies 'there was not, nor could there be, anything intimate or private, secret or personal . . . (where) the individual is open on all sides, he is all surface . . .'[7] To have found McMillan in a public square is one of the moments that gladdens the heart of the historian, and the writer of the biography can use the analogy to draw the reader's attention to the dead weight of interiority that hangs about the neck of women's biography (that hangs about the neck of women). But in fact, that prehistory of the form, in which there is no inside, only surface, and where both biography and autobiography serve the same political and civic function, does not serve to explain either the difficulties that lie in the way of writing McMillan's life, nor the trouble she had in telling her own.

English biography is generally seen as emerging as a literary form in the 17th century, as part of a larger body of writings that dealt with spiritual journeys undertaken in individual lives. The Puritan autobiography is the best known — and most investigated — component of this genre, and was designed to situate a life within the context of God's purpose, and, at the same time, to give an account of its *meaning*, through that very placement within the time and space of a particular spirituality. The important point here is that time and space were specified, in that religious and social milieux came to be described in some detail, and from this mass of secular detail within a religious form there developed a specifically historical consciousness, that is, an understanding of the self as formed by a historicised world, by a setting that exists and changes separately from the human actors who find themselves within it.

When spiritual autobiographies of the seventeenth century, and later developments in the form, are labelled interpretative, it means that for their authors, and for a community of readers, the purpose of the lifestory lay not so much in its narration, but rather in the meanings it was possible to make out of it. In the same way, the spiritual biography was exemplary in form, its purpose being not just to give an account of a life, but also to make a demonstration of the possible purposes, meanings and uses that might be made of that life-story by others. In her book *Victorian Autobiography*, Linda Peterson describes an almost total alienation of women from the form.[8] She implicates in particular conduct book writers like Hannah Moore, who expended many words in the early 19th century telling women that the female mind was incapable of making connections between ideas and entities, incapable of drawing out meaning and purpose from the events of a life, incapable of hermeneutic activity (a point that Mary Wollstonecraft had also made, in the *Vindication of the Rights of Woman*, but with less self-congratulation and more regret than Hannah Moore). Peterson describes Harriet Martineau as a rare 19th century female autobiographer, able to perform the interpretative task because she was able to substitute the doctines of Positivism for Biblical Christianity, as a hermeneutics.

So, the biographical and autobiographical terrain was a male one, and as late as 1938, Virginia Woolf still understood biography to be the form that served above all others to express and affirm a particular kind of masculinity.[9] Nevertheless, the 1920s (the time when McMillan wrote her own *Life of Rachel McMillan*) saw an important appropriation of these forms by women. The following argument is based on the work of Kathryn Dodd, who has discussed this rapid growth of women's life stories after the First World War by considering Ray Strachey's *The Cause*, that classic text of the struggle for women's suffrage.[10]

This was published in 1928, and delineates a history of British feminism and the suffrage movement through a celebration of the achievements of exceptional middle-class women. Dodd sees in *The Cause* a woman writing a history of women constructed out of numerous biographies and within the framework of Baldwinite constitutionalism. She sees Strachey ignoring actual histories of militancy in favour of a depiction of women succouring and uplifting the needy, notably working women and helpless children. (It was indeed Baldwin's Conservative government that granted the universal franchise that gave women the vote in 1928, not as a capitulation to feminist demands, but as a matter of constitutional inevitability.) Only very broad and general histories of literary form could see the startling appropriation of a hermeneutic form by women in the 1920s as directly connected with the bestowal on them of political meaning and status, though I do think that uses of literary forms in particular periods must always to be partly explained by the political and structural relationship of people to the society in which they write.

To some extent then, that kind of political context may explain McMillan's writing of *Life of Rachel McMillan* in 1927; and indeed, in this odd book, something of the same reworking of the past that Kathryn Dodd has noted in *The Cause* is at work, for in *Life of Rachel McMillan* the care and succour of little children, which had in fact been carried out as a matter of political conviction and political policy, becomes the regenerative motor of the world and the history McMillan tells — a progressive cause that lies beyond 'politics'.

However, what is more interesting for current purposes is McMillan's writing of a life-story in the guise of her sister's. For about Rachel, there is nothing to tell: she really did possess secrets, but McMillan was not going to reveal them. In keeping them she tells her own story, but minute by minute returns to the fiction that it is Rachel's life she is imparting. I still do not know how I am to read this trope (nor how I am to give it meaning when I write). There were other autobiographical moments in Margaret McMillan's life, for as a leading member of the ILP she was frequently interviewed and asked to contribute articles to the labour press with titles like 'How I Became a Socialist'. Through all of them, it is possible to see her working towards the point where Rachel's suffering as a little girl can be offered as the device on which all the political work, all the rescue of other children, in Deptford, in Bradford, rests.

I have already mentioned the particular legacy of Romanticism within western society that has been the establishment of childhood as an emblem of the self lying deep within each individual. I would suggest that in looking at the history of biographical and autobiographical accounts of women's lives we look particularly at the use of their own childhood, as a means women found to make interiority, smallness and insignificance work as a mode of interpretation. But I am stuck here, between an interpretation that will allow us to see McMillan's use of the notion of childhood as a hermeneutics, as a complex way of revealing and giving meaning to the self, with a use of time that is backward-looking, that looks back to what is already given in the figure of the child — stuck between that, and an interpretation that would see her actual writing of other childhoods, working-class childhoods, as an evasion of the interiority, privacy and littleness that forms of femininity, current at the turn of the century, current now, would have her use to explain herself.

I have told the story so far, of the writing of two biographies, their intersection with autobiography and history, and the questions they have raised. I have moved about in the chronology, though I could well have begun with the public man in the public square, and ended with the interior depth of the subject of modern women's biography.

But this seemed the best way of drawing attention to the intersection of literary forms with each other, and the political settings that have and do govern depictions of women's lives — and in order to suggest that I want to make the implied meaning of McMillan's own life and writing some kind of denial of interiority — which denial may be a pretence, or a fiction, but one which might do some political or public good, by suggesting that the boundaries of these forms, which are more than literary boundaries, might be traversed.

11 Horsemen[1]

■ **George Ewart Evans, *Spoken History*, Faber, 1987**

There is the idea of the story-taker, the necessary collaborator in the act of telling, the one who listens, shapes the narrative by assuming that there is something there to be told; who takes the story, not as appropriation, but as part of a deal, so that the outcome — an entity, a story — might be placed there, in the space between the listener and the teller. The presence of the story-taker wards off the question 'So what?'. According to William Labov, a story-taker from a tradition quite different from the one George Ewart Evans represents, a sociolinguist rather than a folklorist, that is the response that every good narrator is continually evading: 'when the narrative is over, it should be unthinkable for a bystander to say "So what?".'

The story-taker was first identified by the branch of folklore studies that has recorded and transcribed children's narratives over the last forty years, though he appears as timeless as the huckster or the trickster, a man without place or history himself. In fact, he began to assume professional status at the end of the last century, when folklorists started to collect and analyse the stories of country people in a systematic way. Later, in this century, sociolinguists like Labov, pursuing linguistic complexity in the face of theories of linguistic inadequacy and linguistic deprivation, recorded the verbal

171

accounts of adolescents, complex New York street-fighting stories of the 1960s, which when transcribed and analysed, asserted a grammar of Black American English. Some accounts that appropriate the clinical practice of psychoanalysis to narratology, suggest that since the 1890s, the storytaker's purpose in the consulting room has been to give back to the analysand the story of his or her own life, welded into chronological sequence and narrative coherence, so that at the end of it all, the coming to psychic health might be seen as the reappropriation of ones own life-story. The most familiar modern professional story-taker is probably the oral historian, with tape recorder placed discreetly to one side, prescribed smiles and nods of encouragement: 'Can you tell me a bit more about that?' Such professionals really do tape and take away the stories they hear, though it is the social anthropologist rather than the historian who experiences the dilemas of possession in the starkest of ways. In publishing *Nisaí The Life and Words of a Kung Woman* in 1981, Marjorie Shostak had to reflect on the propriety of making a book out of the words of a woman whose world did not encompass literacy, nor an understanding of the production and consumption of texts.[2]

These have not been George Ewart Evans's problems over the past thirty years, in which he has published ten accounts of rural life and folklore, told largely in the transcribed words of the many men and women he has spoken to, particularly in East Anglia and in the Glamorganshire valley in which he was born, in 1909. For most of these accounts, as he reminds his readers in *Spoken History*, he sought out people born in the 1880s and 1890s, and they certainly knew what he was doing among them, taking notes at first, later with a tape recorder. As the first generation of consistently schooled rural poor, they possessed a sophisticated understanding of the meaning of books and the purpose of making them (though the literary furnishings of their imagination are not really discussed by Evans, anywhere in his corpus).

Spoken History is an account of the evolution of this particular story-taker's craft, and the influences on him. It is a meditation on all the material he has published since the mid-1950s, gathered around the themes of place and work: the material that came out of Wales and Ireland, farms and fishing, men's work with horses. Like Robert Roberts, another recorder of the lives of the poor born at the end of the last century, Evans grew up in a grocer's shop, not in the classic slum of Salford, but in the mining valley of Abercynon.[3] The children of shopkeepers in poor working-class communities were apparently able to learn the useful strategies of liminality, of being both part of the culture that surrounded them by class allegiance and sympathy (as in the case of the Roberts and Evans families) but also in contact with wider worlds of commerce and ideas. Their families were possessors of secrets: they grew up in households where the financial interstices of the surrounding streets were bread and butter matters, but about which a proper discretion was maintained. Evans has retained an honourable reticence through his long life as a folklorist, or oral historian, and there is a good deal of charm to it. What must captivate, as the narratives are handed over, is Evan's recognition of the charm of other men, who tell good stories in public bars, grip with their detailed accounts of something done, a process of labour completed, the account of it precisely offered. What is unsaid, what the formality of the exchange does not permit, is eloquent in its silence. That the men he has talked to have rarely offered personal stories, never talked of love, nor sex, nor what they watch on television, is much to do with Evans's conviction that 'in tackling the main work of a community we identify the main historical topic. His work is the centre of a man's life: all, or most, of his physical and mental energy goes into it . . . .'

It is this conviction on Evans's part that has, on the one hand, allowed him to present the farm labourer as bearing the huge symbolic weight that this culture has bestowed on him, since Richard Jefferies allowed Hodge to lumber into view, in the 1880s: a huge, romantic figure, of elemental simplicity of mind. Indeed, Evans's earliest work can be clearly placed within the artistic neo-Romaticism of the Second World War and the early Fifties, and its celebration of rurality as patriotism in English life. But at the same time (and this is Evan's contributuon to the tradition he has worked within) his taking of narratives within the contained area of work and labour has allowed him to reveal great complexity of mind, to bear witness to the intelligence with which work is accomplished, processes of labour are refined, and working lives are led.

The discretion and formality, the recognition of privacy and dignity that evidently characterised Evans's interviews, are to be seen in his autobiography, where the account of an obviously troubled adolescence and family life is told with such reticent warmth, that to think of asking for more seems an impropriety. This autobiography was told in *The Strength of the Hills* (1983), where he described his Board of Education scholarship to University College, Cardiff to read classics; being bound to teaching when he finished, yet loathing it; his attempts to write fiction; his discovery of a life's work in East Anglia, where, freelancing in the Fifties, he brought up the children whilst his wife worked as village school teacher. He has never been far away from the people he has written about: he calls most of the East Anglian farm-workers he has recorded, his friends. By sympathy, and by the social positioning his wife's job brought him, he has belonged to the complex rural communities in which he found himself.

Spoken History pinpoints the crucial experiences and encounters that helped Evans evolve his craft (his discovery of the work of Lewis Henry Morgan through Engels, his meeting with Seamus Delargy, Director of the Irish Folklore Commission, his work for Charles Parker in sound radio, in the 1960s). In this way, *Spoken History* is a companion volume to *Strength of the Hills*. He reflects on his craft, by exploring the differences between social anthropology, 'folklore', 'history' and 'oral history'. The book reproduces a good deal of the material that is to be found in the sequence that started with *Ask the Fellows Who Cut the Hay* (1956), and presents some hitherto unpublished material, collected in Blaxhall village in the 1950s. Evans would rather have called himself a social anthropologist than a historian, but the accidents of life, and the relative nearness of the Thompsons' Centre for the Study of Oral History at Essex University led him to oral history, though he criticises the genre for 'an over-emphasis on the *oral* component . . . and a comparative neglect of the *history*.' This must be a reference to the formal origins of oral history in the US, where the lifestories of significant citizens were collected in a Columbia University project from the 1940s onwards. For Evans, these public figures did not embody 'the mythical and non-rational elements' that he has so consistently encountered in his own work, especially when talking to old men about their work with the horses. Literally, these old men *were* history, exemplars of 'historical depth'; and should the horseman's belief in magical rites, in for instance, the efficacy of the frog's bone in jading horses, be doubted, then what they had to say might be verified by turning to 'their particular document . . . the whole world as . . . anthropologists have demonstrated during the last hundred or so years, by their researches among primitive peoples.' *Spoken History* is a powerful retelling of the myth of a single origin, and Evans argues that students of oral history should not find it strange that distant people from cultures remote in time and space might offer evidence of a universal communality, for 'under their surface differences [they] belong to the same human ground-plan . . . are moved by the same human laws.'

Evans's first books were prompted by the urgent need to capture the past of a rural society before it disappeared, for mechanisation, particularly in arable country like East Anglia was bringing about a greater change in farming practice than the society had ever before witnessed. He wanted to record the men and women who were, in the 1950s and 1960s, 'survivors from another era', particularly the men who in his description, found themselves with no one to tell their story: 'the work had changed so very much after the horses had gone . . . so that the young men and the retired workers had very little in common . . . the old were glad of someone to talk to'.

The books of the 1960s and 1970s elaborated the pattern laid out in the first, as did his short stories in *Acky* (1973), and his fiction for children. For Evans, all the accounts he has taken and reproduced offer extraordinary confirmation of the belief that that there is 'no backward limit in time to which it is not possible for oral tradition to refer'. Particularly, here in *Spoken History* he reflects on the material he collected for *Horse Power and Magic* (1979) and *The Horse in the Furrow* (1960) and argues that the lineage of horsemen's beliefs give access to 'the prehistory of our islands. Up to the present only the findings of the anthropologist have been accepted . . . .'

Once, reading *The Pattern Under the Plough* (1966), Raymond
Williams looked up from the formula on the page, that 'a way
of life that has come down to us from the days of Virgil has
suddenly ended', reflected on the ever-receding lost rural past
of English literary culture, the immutability of the terms
'country' and 'city', our profound desire for lost ruralities, and
wrote then, in response to this (and many other works as well)
The Country and the City. Whatever it is we want from the
countryman's voice, talking out of an eternal past, Evans's
work has to be seen as a directive force among those memoirs,
observations and histories of rural life that, in Williams's
estimation, actually cancel lived and experienced histories, of
land tenure and land ownership, histories of labour, of class
relations, in the English countryside. In *Spoken History*, we
can literally see the cancellation take place before our eyes.
Towards the end of the book, Evans reflects briefly on the
bitterness about the old days evinced by so many men, when
they were treated like 'medieval serfs'. He refers his readers to
an appropriate piece of evidence in *Horse Power and Magic*,
and goes on in the same breath to say that it was contained in
'one of those long accounts, full of contributory details that are
nevertheless worth recording'. The point of the account
becomes a blacksmith's rasp, and the uncommon item of
information that rasps were sometimes turned into gardening
implements.

The historical romance that Evans delineates, the desire
for the past to be there, within reach, is matched by a linguistic
romance, in which the accounts of farm practice, themselves
embodiments of an unbroken tradition stretching back to the
beginnings of recorded history, are told in an *appropriate*
language, 'that is fitting to the material information conveyed',
helping to give it 'a proper and more durable clothing'.
Remembering the men and women born at the end of the last
century, and recorded by him thirty years ago, Evans recalls
their using a language that was 'steeped in centuries of
continuous usage, describing processes and situations and
customs that had gone on uninterruptedly since farming
began. It was as if their work, the work of their hands, had
fashioned their tongue, and moulded their speech to economi-
cal and often memorable utterance.' So as the men sit and tell

their stories, the words themselves are items of evidence: each utterance contains and holds the past. Horace White dies, and Evans records that 'he was not a man you could easily forget. As well as being a very companionable exponent of oral history, he was the sort of man you were always glad to meet'. The young cannot be this kind of companion — except significantly, Mervyn Carter, born in 1936, dyslexic and unschooled. His range of knowledge about the horse and his willingness to impart it are implicitly linked to his illiteracy, for in this romance of language, writing is separated completely from speech, and the oral culture is described as the primary and the first. And yet: the old men whose words provided Evans's life work grew to maturity in a literate culture, where the written constantly interacted with the spoken, were schooled as children in a form of language that taught them something of the ways of rhetoric that would not have been available to the children of the rural poor living only a century before, never mind in the time of Virgil — through the syllabification demanded by hymn-singing, the shape of the words on the page of the reading primer, the pauses and stresses of long pieces of recitation, committed to heart. And by separating speech so definitely from writing, Evans is unable to reflect on the central contradiction of all studies of spoken language, which is that they have to be made a text before they can be looked at, used, heard: before they can be taken. The process of his own extraordinarily elegant transcriptions, in which the stress and cadence of speech is indicated by a particular use of punctuation marks and the careful placing now and then, of a dialect word in modified orthography, is presented as quite transparent throughout all his books.

What lies behind Evans's craft as transcriber is respect for those whose stories he writes down, and the conscious desire to render them with dignity. Anyone familiar with the tradition of countryside literature from the late 19th century, and Sturt's and Jefferies's transliterations of Hodge's words, knows how easy it is to use dialect to make a man look a fool, so that we might smile, and raise an eyebrow at the quaintness of vocabulary, the plodding of a mind. Evans's style of transcription and his beliefs about language have asserted themselves against this tradition of condescension. When a history of popular theories of language in this society comes to be written, Evans's books will have to be seen in connection with a radical assertion in the schools, made since the 1960s, of the validity and worth of working-class children's speech against various theories of deprivation, and beliefs about a poverty of thought connected with particular patterns of language. Once written, that history would show the difficulties of the radical position, and the way in which it has led to a denial that people may actually be deprived of modes of language, in the same way as they are denied access to other aspects of the material world. Outside the school, but motivated by the same radicalism, Evans has asserted a compelling dignity and primacy of language among the rural working class, a true, original language of men, that is as engrossing a political idea as it was when William Blake learned of the real, original language of nature from the Swedenborgians. Given that we do not yet possess a social theory of language that can acknowledge deprivation without attributing stupidity to the disinherited, we can say that though his work represents a linguistic romance, it represents a necessary political position as well.

George Ewart Evans's earlier books were decorated with Bewick wood-cuts; the later ones, like *Spoken History*, owe much to David Gentleman's line drawings. Usually placed at the head of a chapter, they can be surrounded in the mind's eye in the same way as Bewick's can, by the enclosing circle, so that we might reach out and grasp that little world, take hold of the lost green place, that the words caught here speak to.

12 'The Mother Made Conscious':
the historical development of a primary school pedagogy[1]

The dictum — that the ideal teacher of young children is like 'a mother made conscious' — is Friederich Froebel's (1782–1852), the educational philosopher and founder of the kindergarten movement, and it belongs to the 1840s. But as a piece of educational prescription it has much more recent echoes, particularly in educational advice offered to teachers since the last war, by Donald Winnicott and other members of the British psychoanalytic movement. This article sets out to deal with the development within primary schooling, of certain sets of ideas that have linked the teaching of young children with an understanding of mothering, and the contradictions that this largely inexplicit and unexamined notion spells out for women and children in classrooms, particularly working-class children and their teachers.

The arena for this development has obviously been the school; but the primary school, and its history, can be used to explain more than itself. All those who have anything to do with children have low status in our culture. Mothers and teachers are obvious occupants of this position, but so are people who work on childhood within the fields of sociology, psychology and history. The indifference of historians towards the questions raised by a study of childhood can perhaps be attributed to a more general reluctance within the discipline to engage with the idea of the life-cycle, of development and change within individual experiences and their intersection with historical time.[2] Childhood *is* about change, and development: it is an essentially transitory state. What this reluctance means, in effect, is that there are as yet few ways of using childhood as an interpretive device, as something that might tell of historical and political developments. But in fact, it is possible to enter the classroom and see there at work a process by which, over the last century and a half, the relationship between women and children has been established as a cultural and social one, understood to exist above and apart from the relationship of biology. It is possible to use childhood as it is lived out in classrooms and as experienced by the women caught there as teachers, as a device of historical interpretation.

The notion of teaching as a kind of mothering and the belief in the benefits to children of maternal attitudes, seems to derive from two sources: from the educative sphere of the middle-class mother in the domestic schoolroom of the 19th century; and from a translation, for the educational market, of the natural, unforced education that 19th century observers saw being imparted by poor (preferably peasant) mothers to their children.

The educative role of the middle-class woman in the home is well documented, though much evidence is still scattered widely through unpublished autobiographies and developmental diaries.[3] Developmental diaries, which seem to have been quite widely kept by middle-class mothers, detailed their children's acquisition of language, their education in morality, and the methods by which they were made literate, as part of the naturalistic observation of 'child life'. Occasionally, children's own diaries, like those of Marjory Fleming and the Coleridge sisters, reveal the process of this domestic education.[4]

Middle-class women like these were the directors of their children's education, and they approached their task with a high degree of self-consciousness and intellectual awareness. Quoting the late 18th century philosopher Thomas Reid, Catherine Stanley of Alderley, Cheshire, who kept a developmental diary of four of her children between 1812 and 1820, thought that:

If we could obtain a distinct and full history of all that hath

passed in the mind of a child from the beginning of life till
it grows up . . . this would be a treasure of natural history
which would probably give more light into the human
faculties than all the systems of philosophy about them
from the beginning of the world . . .[5]

For Elizabeth Cleghorn Gaskell, mothering was a moral as
well as an intellectual responsibility, the diary she kept of her
first child's development a reflection of her belief that 'all a
woman's life ought to have reference to the period when she
will be fulfilling one of her greatest and highest duties, those of
a mother'.[6]

Journals like these, which have provided the
unacknowledged bedrock of modern developmental psycholgy, indicate a duality of responsibility within domestic
child-care: mothers like Anna Alcott in the USA and
Elizabeth Gaskell in the UK were both the nurturers and
educators of their children. Concerned with them as emotional
and psychological beings, a mother's task was also to provide
for their intellectual advancement. The conflation of mothering small children with educating them has left a significant
legacy for child-care in Britain. 'The increasing pressure on
teachers in day care centres, preschools and primary classes, to
respond to the apparent needs of children assumed to be
unmet by their busy . . . mothers', that Lilian Katz noted in
the US in 1982, along with 'a growing enthusiasm for parent
training and parental involvement in schooling',[7] is *not* a
recent development in this country, where the role of mother
was aligned with that of educator by the very women who in
their journals and day-books provided the 19th century bank
of data by which modern children's assumed needs have been
assessed.

Later in the 19th century, the child-study movement and
the emerging disciplines of child psychology and developmental linguistics spoke specifically to fathers, and men's
accounts of their children's development were increasingly
published.[8] Many of these case-studies concentrated on
specific aspects of development, as did Darwin's brief account
of the growth of the sense of self in his little boy, and Ronjat's
description of his child's bilingualism.[9] The feature of the

informal, unpublished mother's journal on the other hand, was her acknowledgement of intense involvement in the moral and intellectual development of her children, and her identification with their needs and desires. Felt identification and involvement, coupled with the scientific detachment demanded of the mother as observer, produced many documents of extreme tension.[10]

What these middle-class mothers were doing was using intellectual curiosity and exercising educational attainment within an approved domestic sphere. As the arena of public education widened in mid-19th century Britain, many attempts were made to extend the educative role of the middle-class woman from the domestic schoolroom to the public classroom.[11] When Martha Maria von Marenholtz-Buelow publicised Froebel's German kindergarten system for a British audience in 1855, she spoke of a woman's educational mission that combined the educative with the moral, arguing that a woman

> should be enabled to take upon herself those responsibilities which men cannot always undertake with actual propriety, and look after those interests which nature expressly intended to be committed to her charge. The position of woman, as mother, nurse and instructress of childhood, embraces the lofty idea of the female sex having being appointed by Providence to be the legitimate support of helpless humanity . . . [12]

In publicising Froebel's educational philosophy, Marenholtz-Buelow hoped to draw on a practice that was long established in middle-class families. But the notion of teacher-as-mother that she presented to the public, derived in fact, from a very different source.

The good mother did naturally, observed Friedrich Froebel in the 1840s, what the good teacher must extrapolate from her practice, must make overt, and use. The good teacher must

> waken and develop in the Human Being every power, every disposition . . . Without any Teaching, Reminding or

Learning, the true mother does this of herself. But this is not enough: in Addition is needed that being Conscious, and acting upon a Creature that is growing Conscious, she do her part Consciously and Consistently, as in Duty bound to guide the Human Being in its regular development.[13]

Froebel's mother-made-conscious had a precedent. Johann Pestalozzi, the Swiss philosopher and pioneer of education for the poor, published *Lienhard and Gertrude* in 1780, and the fictional Gertrude's upbringing of her children was used to outline a pedagogy.[14] Both Pestalozzi and Froebel used naturalistic observation of mothers interacting with their children to delineate maternal practice as the foundation for a new educational order. Froebel knew Pestalozzi's work, had spent time at his experimental school at Yverdun, and used the older man's insight that 'mothers are educators of their children, and [that] we can learn from their methods'.[15] Observation like this, by male educational theorists, of the behaviour of mothers with their children (particularly, in Froebel's case, 'in the cottages of the lower classes') established 'the tendencies of the maternal and infantile instincts' as the basis of a pedagogy.[16]

This pedagogy, appropriated from the behaviour of the peasant mothers that Pestalozzi and Froebel observed, centred on the qualities of instinct, feeling and 'naturalness'. It presents a striking contrast to the *intellectual* involvement in child development expressed in the case-studies from the middle-class nursery mentioned above. 'It was not Froebel's idea', commented one of his late-19th century supporters,

> to substitute philosophy for maternal instincts, but to show that in the treatment of their children by successful mothers, a principle was involved which might be understood and applied to all who have to train young children, whether nurses or teachers . . . [17]

The principle involved was the idea of growth as a natural unfolding, a kind of emotional logic of development; and what was asked from the mother, the nurse and the teacher, was an empathy, an identification with the child. The cult of the

Romantic child in literature, as well as in the publicity machine of the Froebelian movement, all ensured a substantial middle-class audience for Froebel's philosophy of education.[18] At this level of the transmission of ideas — family magazines, books of advice to mothers, late 19th-century translations of Froebel for the educational market — Froebel did not suffer the neglect that Pestalozzi is reported suffering at the hands of philosophers of education,[19] and his ideas were immensely influential in establishing a British school of child-centred education. The 'social and literary romanticism' which one commentator sees as the dominant set of values and aspirations in teacher education this century, has been nourished by these Froebelian roots.[20]

But Froebel's educational philosophy was also applied to working-class children. Private, charitable kindergartens, established in poor districts of industrial cities in the 1860s and 1870s did work that was established as Board of Education policy from the 1890s onwards.[21] The naturalness that Froebelianism emphasised, the child's need to touch, handle, and construct, to be in touch with nature in 'airy, bright schoolrooms', provided a consistent point of contrast with the actual lives of small children in inner cities at the turn of the century. The contrast between the artificiality and corruption of the city, and the natural environment that the countryside offers, has been a consistent theme of English progressive education, reflecting the persistence of a much wider cultural ideal, the rural as representative of 'a natural way of life: of peace, innocence and simple virtue'; the proper place for a child to flower.[22] Drawing on this contrastive imagery, and describing the differences between school and home life, it was impossible to avoid condemnation of the latter. In 1919, Margaret McMillan wrote about 'Dennis', who lived

> in a worse street than Jerry's. It is a huddle of houses with dark greasy lobbies and hideous black stairs leading down into cellars. Dennis's mother lives in one of the cellars. It is so dark that when one goes in one sees nothing for a few moments. Then a broken wall, and a few sticks of furniture appear, and a dark young woman with touzled hair and glittering eyes looks down at us. Dennis is a great pet in the Nursery. On his firm little feet he runs all round the big

shelter and garden exploring and enjoying everything . . . he
breaks into a kind of singing on bright June mornings, the
wind blowing . . . his eyes alight with joy. In the evening his
older sister comes and carries him back to the cellar . . .[23]

It was for Dennis, for 'the child of the mean streets and of the
slum that [Froebel] dreamed his dream of child gardens',
wrote McMillan in 1926.[24] The camp schools that she
established with her sister Rachel in South East London in the
years before the First World War stood as a twenty-year
reference point for the difference between what was, and what
might be.

In staffing their schools, the McMillans looked to the
same source for teachers of poor children as had Madam
Marenholtz-Buelow half a century before, arguing that in the
slum nursery the middle-class girl's desire to serve, to learn, to
find herself, could be fulfilled.[25] However, any woman,
whether she were of the middle class or not, who was asked to
perform the prescribed act of identification with poor children, to provide them with conscious mothering, was placed in
a position of deep conflict and ambivalence. This ambivalence
towards children of the working class within primary education is one of the most significant legacies of the historical
development of Romantic child-centredness.

The dissemination of Froebel's ideas, from the early
publicity of the 1850s, to his establishment in many modern
text-books of educational thought as a key figure in the
development of child-centred education, demonstrates one
way in which the feminine — particularly the delineation of
teaching as a conscious and articulated version of mothering
— has been established within educational thought. Few
British primary school teachers will complete a period of
training without hearing of Froebel and gaining some access to
the idea that developed out of his Romantic pantheism.[26] But
the idea of teaching as a version of mothering has more
complex social and political roots than this account of the
transmission and adoption of ideas implies. The conflation of
the two roles draws on generalised social perceptions of what is
fit work for women, and there is a modern literature of
educational prescription that asks women to call upon the

principles of good housekeeping in the arrangement of the classroom domestic day. 'No reasonably intelligent woman', wrote Lesley Webb in 1976:

> finds it impossible to make a home within even the most unlikely four walls. For teachers, the task of making a classroom into a temporary home and workroom . . . is . . . rarely one that is beyond their home-making skills.[27]

It remains to be discovered how much this practical aspect of mothering is a function of classrooms that are set up to promote children's self-directed activity through the school day. Did the Standard II classroom of 1910, fixed desks in rows, instruction from the front and the blackboard, need this kind of good housekeeping? Perhaps the organisation of material and equipment elaborates the practical role of the mother/teacher in the classroom. Froebel's didactic apparatus took a lot of organising, and 19th and early 20th century accounts of kindergartens devote a large amount of space to the practicalities of keeping house in the schoolroom.[28]

Ideas about teachers as mothers-made-conscious began to enter the state educational system in the years before the First World War — 'Treat each child as if he were your own' — exhorted the McMillan sisters of teachers on many occasions between 1890 and 1914;[29] and in the 1960s and 1970s D.W. Winnicott's influential works told teachers of young children to model themselves on good — or 'good enough' — mothers.[30] The young teacher needs to learn about mothering through 'conversation with and observation of the mothers and children in her care'. Having no biological orientation towards the children she teaches — except indirectly through identification with a mother figure' — she must be brought gradually to see that there exists 'a complex psychology of infant growth and adaption'.[31] Made conscious then, she can start to construct the delicate equilibrium between the desire to teach, to influence, to fill children with knowledge; and the recognition that she must draw back at each moment of desire: wean, and let the child go free. 'If teachers and pupils are living healthily', said Winnicott, 'they are engaged in a mutual sacrifice of spontaneity and independence'.[32]

The metaphorical groundwork of this relationship, this

tension between the desire to influence, and the acknowledgement that the responsible mother must withold influence in
order to provide for the child's growth, is located in the
earliest processes of human life, in feeding, ingestion, reten-
tion and elimination. It is the emptiness within that produces
in both teacher and child the need to influence and to be
influenced.[33] But Winnicott dealt in more than metaphorical
relationships. The psychological process he describes, and the
prescribed educational practice that arises out of it, are both
rooted in social understanding. Just as the family has,
throughout our recent history, been associated with the
'natural processes of eating, sleeping, sexuality and cleaning
oneself', and women, through their role in caring for children
within it, have been most intimately connected with these
processes, so any teacher in her pinny clearing up after a
painting session in an infants' classroom might agree that her
low status is located in her connection with these 'most
primary and compelling material processes'.[34] Primary school
teaching allows women, as it has done for a century past, to
elaborate this function within a system of wage labour. The
development of compulsory mass education allowed a large
number of women who were not actually mothers, to take the
attributes and skills of that state into the market place.

A great deal of recent work on the position of women and
girls in education has dealt in terms of their invisibility. The
amount of teacher time devoted to interaction with boys rather
than girls, and the small and declining number of women who
reach the top in school or teaching union hierarchy, have
received wide attention.[35] Recently, a content analysis of basic
texts in the philosophy of education has been grounded in the
argument that in educational philosophy as in political theory
'women, children and the family dwell in the "ontological
basement", outside and underneath the political structure'.
Jane Roland Martin calls here for the educational realm to be
'reconstituted', and for modern analytic philosophy of education to investigate questions about 'childrearing and the
transmission of values . . . [to] explore the forms of thinking,
feeling and acting associated with child-rearing, marriage and
the family', in this way making 'concepts such as mothering
and nurturance . . . subjects for philosophical analysis . . .'[36]

Yet far from dwelling in the basement of British educational thought, the mother-made-conscious is central to its ideology, and different voices, speaking at different moments over the last century and a half, have urged teachers to take upon themselves the structures of maternal thought. Indeed, given the consistency of this advice to teachers, it may be fruitful to see educational history itself as one of society's ontological cellars, the place where secrets may be found, the workings of the household above made plainer.

Donald Winnicott's advice to teachers was delivered in radio broadcasts and books in the post-Second World War context of theories of maternal deprivation.[37] It drew then, on quite different social roots from the earlier advice to teachers, exemplified in the Froebelian school and outlined above. Yet across the centuries, the methodology that lay behind the pedagogical prescriptions remains strikingly similar. It is clear from the recently published account of Winnicott's work in *Boundary and Space* that his delineation of 'the ordinary devoted mother' was based on his work with patients and their mothers at Paddington Green Children's Hospital between 1923 and the early Sixties.[38] The majority of these mothers were working class. Like Froebel, Winnicott found a model for good mothering in the natural behaviour of the poor, though its context had shifted from the country to the city.

It is unlikely that Winnicott knew of a history of advice to teachers into which his prescription fitted. Froebel was among the first to establish a theory of individual child psychology and to describe childhood in terms of developmental stages,[39] and child analysis inherited this psychology, not so much as psychology in itself, but rather as a generalised cultural perception of childhood.

The social context for the dissemination of the idea of teaching as a version of mothering, was the feminisation of a trade. In the early part of the 19th century the majority of teachers of young children were men.[40] Samuel Wilderspin for example, recommended their employment on the grounds that their position at the head of a family would have acquainted them with the intelligent exercise of judicious tenderness.[41] Robert Owen's infant school at New Lanark was run by men teachers, one of whom, Robert Dunn, Owen considered to be 'the best instructor of infants I have seen in any part of the world'.[42] Women — wives, daughters, sisters — assisted these male pedagogues, but not until the last quarter of the century did women constitute a majority of elementary school teachers.[43]

In theory, school teaching could be seen as practice for women's real role — as a mother — and attempts were made at various points during the 19th century to attract entrants from the middle class.[44] But the education of the poor remained an unpopular field for the philanthropic efforts of the wealthy, and the majority of female recruits were drawn, as were their male colleagues, from the skilled and semi-skilled working class.[45] In the late 1880s, attested one teacher, 'the elementary schools of the land . . . were staffed with teachers drawn almost entirely from the same ranks as the children'.[46]

The tension between the origins of those women 'going up into the next class' in this way, and the insecurities of their social position in the late 19th and early 20th century have been frequently described. It is possible that working-class recruits brought with them attitudes towards children and ideas about childrearing that provided them with strong resistance to the official ideology of child-centredness. For what has been dealt with here *is* an official ideology, transmitted in text-books, in initial and inservice training, and through the activities of a local and central inspectorate.[47] The place where this ideology meets other, half-articulated, 'commonsense' theories about childhood, is a shadowy one. It is only possible here to speculate about what those other theories might be, but it is important to do this, for they have some bearing on the elaboration of ideas around the central image of teacher as mother. In fact there are hints in the literature that two views of mothering are in inarticulate conflict in many schools. The official texts speak of a contained liberality, the freedom for children to move and discover as they might in a good bourgeois home. But many teachers, like many working-class parents, know that it is much better if they are all sitting down, getting on with something.[48]

Disseminators of the official ideology seem nearly always to have been aware that the reality could never hope to match the image, and the ideal primary school teacher has hovered for a century now, in the timeless present tense:

> They have the charm of great actresses. They move
> with wonderful grace. Their voices are low, penetrating,
> musical . . . Their dress is beautiful and simple, and nothing
> is so remarkable as their power — except their gentleness.[49]

Margaret McMillan called this piece of 1908 'Schools of Tomorrow'; but even the descriptive sociology of the time put teachers in the same ethereal place. Describing Bermondsey infants and elementary teachers of 1911, Alexander Paterson noted that their faces reflected

> no discontent, no weariness of spirit or monotony of work.
> They seem born to the task . . . Their mothering instinct
> endows their teaching with personal force . . . The relation of
> teacher and child is happy and natural because the teacher is
> absorbed in the human interest of her work . . . Teaching is
> so much more natural to the woman's nature . . .[50]

The reality cannot match the prescription because it is impossible for the mother-made-conscious to mother working-class children. The prescribed act of identification with the child implies a further and harder one, with the children's mother, that 'dark young woman with touzled hair and glittering eyes', playing out a travesty of motherhood in her cellar dwelling.

The official ideology outlined above was developed within a set of social theories that already, at the end of the 19th century, saw schools as places where working-class children might be compensated for belonging to working-class families. The force of innovation in nursery schooling in the early and middle years of this century centred on the belief that a working-class child could be physically and emotionally compensated for her disability, while the earlier years of state education had seen the role of the school as compensating for the absence of morality and discipline in working-class homes.[51] The British nursery/infants school saw compensation in terms of cleanliness and love, whilst more recent developments in compensatory education have dealt in terms of cognitive and linguistic deficits. By filling working-class children with rich experiences, schools may hope to fill the emptiness, make up for the 'noise, crowding and physical discomfort' of the child's home, in which 'the usual (i.e middle-class) parental role of tutor and guide is largely lacking'.[52] This last part of the story is well known.

It is possible then that this understanding of working-class childhood as an inadequacy, a fall-short of some measure of real and normal childhood, has provided a specific vehicle of resistance for teachers implicitly asked to become mothers to working-class children, for the real mothers of the children they taught were not able to provide models for their practice. The history of pedagogy in a class society, in which the mothers of the children found in classrooms cannot provide a model for educational practice, and where it is equally difficult to make an act of identification with their children, may go some way towards explaining the position of working-class children in school, and the theories that have evolved to explain their inadequacies.

In British child-centred pedagogy, women have not been excluded from the educational realm, 'concepts such as mothering and nurturance' have been established as official prescription, and the feminine has been recommended as an educational device. As historians and teachers — and especially as women — we should look very carefully at exactly what it is that has been established, for it will have escaped few readers' notice that the precise virtue of the mother-made-conscious is that she does not have to be very clever. In one of the few accounts of primary schooling that acknowledges the reification of the feminine within pedagogy (Elena Giannini Belotti's account of Italian nursery schooling) the feminine is characterised by the enforced and socially approved female virtues of triviality, timidity, conservatism, and anti-intellectualism.[53] We have yet to work out what the implications are for children schooled within the framework of these virtues.

The replacing of women in the history of education and educational thought is hampered, not only by this first difficulty — the elaboration and formalisation of the feminine

within the theory and practice of primary schooling — but also
by a second difficulty: the possibility that such a resurrection
and re-writing may actually serve to disguise a historical and
cultural reality. The feminine nurturance of the primary years,
and the child's eventual emergence into secondary schooling,
could be seen as an educational analogy of the kind of history
that 'records man's escape from and triumph over the
submerging claims of domesticity and nature (closely
identified with the engulfing feminine) . . .': another version
of the flight from nature to culture.[54] As long as traditional
feminine virtues are confirmed within the practice of primary
schooling, then care and nurturance of children must be
constituted in opposition to their intellectal growth, and
academic attainment must be presented to them as something
for which they may strive, but which very few of them can
actually hope to achieve.

Finding women excluded from official descriptions of
social practices such as education, there is a strong temptation
'to reject all official experience as relevant to female experience'.[55] But within the prescriptive literature of primary
schooling in Britain, the feminine *has* been made official. To
deny this presence, to see female experience only as rejected
experience, lying outside the public realm, is to fail to take
hold of the analytic devices which may help us recover the
historical experience of real women and real children in
classrooms of the recent past. In other words, women are
already in that place: within the educational realm. There is
little point in trying to regain territory that is already occupied
in so many problematic and convoluted ways.

13 The Watercress Seller[1]

This is about the encounter of one middle-class man with one working-class eight-year-old girl, on the streets of London, sometime in the winter of 1849-1850. Through this encounter, I want to look at others that have taken place between various adults and various children, within the recent history of this culture. Not all of them have been the product of real meetings on wintry pavements, as the one I am going to descibe was. Some have been fictional, or meetings made within other kinds of texts, made across time and through the written word, or through a camera lens, or through the glass of social investigation. All of them, I shall argue, have been meetings that have served a particular cultural purpose, and they raise more general questions: of history, of the uses of the past in human culture, of sexuality, of representation. The problems of those meetings were to do with the disjuncture that the participants represented, and became aware of in the course of their dialogue; but there are also for us, problems of evidence involved in those encounters. Evidence from children, and about children in the past, throws into relief general problems of historical interpretation. History, as a methodology, is concerned with the reconstruction, interpretation, and use of the past, so it may be as well that it has something to say about that past that occupies all of us, whether we are historians or not — the personal past of each individual childhood.

My interest in these questions came about in two ways. I am a historian who, through the accidents of life, came to spend several years working with children. I taught them, and later I wrote about them. The question I am working on at the moment is historical: the use of the figure of the child, particularly the working-class child, within British socialist theory and the labour movement, at the end of the last century. My experience, of actually working with children, has made me aware of the split that exists between children and 'the child'. Both history and many psychologies tell us, in very different ways, that 'the child' is a construct: that beyond a bit of anatomy and physiology, and perhaps the order of language acquisition, there is not much there that isn't a matter of adult construction, adult projection. There is no 'real', or 'natural' or transcendental child. At the same time, children are *there*, in life as we know it, in social and historical time. They are lived with, worked with; they are there, in networks of social and political relationships. And so we will continue to act as if there is a real and natural and transcendental child. We may know enough about English Romanticism to see what it is we're up to as we search the past for real children. But we will go on doing precisely that: constructing hope, and belief and desire and political futures, using the figure of 'the child'. So there is a tension between what the historian has led me to in the following argument, and what actual relationships with children have led me to. And of course, my hope is that this argument will make a useful connection between the two.

This argument is about an obsession. First of all, it is my obsession, read out of the obsession of a mid-Victorian, middle-class social investigator; and then it is part of a more general cultural obsession. Henry Mayhew, the journalist and social investigator, originally published much of the material that makes up the four volumes of *London Labour and the London Poor* in a series of articles in the *Morning Chronicle* newspaper, that ran from December 1849 to February 1850. *London Labour and the London Poor* is usually seen as the first sociological investigation into the life of working-class London. In histories of the development of social investigation, it is typically linked with Charles Booth's mammoth survey of the late 1880s, *Life and Labour of the People of London*. What is particularly valuable for the historian, is that in his much earlier survey, Henry Mayhew recorded his conversations with a very wide range of poor Londoners, and reproduced them in transcript.

During his first period of investigation, sometime in the winter of 1850, he interviewed an eight-year-old seller of watercresses — a street trader — probably somewhere in the Farringdon area, for that was where the child lived, and where she worked. Mayhew interviewed many little girls that winter, and later on, in the 1850s, as he prepared material for the enlarged edition of *London Labour* of 1861. It is important to note here that he interviewed many more female children than male (indeed, he does not seem to have interviewed any boy under eleven). This interest in little girls was certainly to do with his self-confessed concerns about their moral welfare. I think that we should see it as well, as part of a history of sexuality in the 19th century. In her discussion of the debate that surrounded the age of consent campaigns of the 1880s, Deborah Gorham has drawn our attention to the ways in which the sexual life of girls and women was seen as more significant than that of boys and men, their very being more sexually symbolic.[2] In the same way, as more and more work is done on 19th century constructions of femininity, the ideal-type of Victorian woman emerges as a kind of child, sharing frailty of body and innocence of mind with contemporary understandings of girl children. In these ways, it is not surprising that Mayhew was more interested in little girls than he was in little boys.

He spoke then, that winter, to many little girls; but the street seller of watercresses was the one who affected him the most. I have tried to deal with his puzzled and complicated approach to this child in both *The Tidy House* and in *Landscape for a Good Woman*. He did not know what to make of her: she puzzled him: she repelled him: he felt attraction towards her. For him she was a child, and not-a-child; and something else. He possessed though, an available repertoire of affect with which to write about her: conventional horror and pity, which was the rhetorical mode of the vast majority of 19th century investigators of working-class life. 'There was', he wrote

something cruelly pathetic in hearing this infant, so young

that her features had scarcely formed themselves, talking of
the bitterest struggles of life, with the calm earnestness of one
who has endured them all. I did not know how to talk to her.
At first, I treated her as a child, speaking on childish subjects;
so that I might, by being familiar with her, remove all
shyness, and get her to relate her life freely . . . but the look
of amazement that answered me soon put an end to any
attempt of fun on my part.

The child confounded him: he could not explain her: the
theories of childhood and working-class life he possessed
failed him. Indeed, the child went on to talk about play, about
games, about family affection, and revealed (more apparently
to the historian of the 19th century than to Mayhew himself,
though it was he who recorded the evidence) a highly
organised family life and household economy. 'I always gives
mother my money,' said the child, explaining that

> she's so very good to me . . . She's very poor and goes out
> cleaning rooms sometimes, now she don't work at the fur
> [trade]. I ain't got no father, he's a father-in-law. No; mother
> ain't married again — he's a father-in-law. No; I don't mean
> by that that he says kind things to me, for he never hardly
> speaks. When I gets home after selling cresses, I stops at
> home. I puts the room to rights; mother doesn't make me do
> it, I does it myself. I cleans the chairs, though there's only
> two to clean. I takes a tub and scrubbing brush and flannel,
> and scrubs the floor — that's what I do three or four times a
> week . . . I never had no doll; but I misses little sister —
> she's only two years old. We don't sleep in the same room; for
> father and mother sleeps with little sister in one pair, and me
> and brother and other sister sleeps in the top room. I always
> goes to bed at seven, 'cos I has to be up so early . . .

What makes this evidence so powerful and so revelatory is, I
think, the deep interest in his own reactions to this little girl,
and to other little girls, that Mayhew felt. Along with the
Commissioners of Inquiry into Children's Employment of
1862, and those who worked for the Commission of Inquiry
into the Employment of Children in Agriculture of 1867, both
of which offer extensive documentary evidence of upper-

middle-class men talking to working-class children,[3] Mayhew watched and recorded his own reactions to the smiles that enlivened passive faces, was gratified when a pretty glance or the rounded cheek of babyhood showed through the dirt. 'She smiled', he wrote of one pleasingly clean little crossing-sweeper, 'like a baby in its sleep when thinking of the answer'. These children were true mirrors for these men, mirrors of their own cultivation of the idea of childhood.

Six years later, in 1856, John Ruskin walked through St. Giles on the way from his house to the British Museum, and took part in that same reaction of exquisite sadness felt at the contemplation of warped lives, cramped hopes, opportunity lost. He looked at the children's faces, as they played in the street, and recorded that 'through all of their pale and corrupt misery,' they recalled 'the old Non Angii, and recall it not by their beauty but by their sweetness of expression, even though signed already with trace and cloud of coming life'.[4]

This sense of exquisite sadness served these men in some way (exactly how, I shall suggest in a moment); and the feeling was also part of an enduring and romantic vision of working-class life. Part of what I mean is to be found for instance, in those passages of *Mary Barton*, where Elizabeth Gaskell describes the cosy littleness of the Barton parlour, simple and heart-wrenching detail upon domestic detail called up to make us understand a simplicity and sadness in this form of life.[5] Or to take a more recent example, another passage which celebrates the same domestic simplicity in almost the same terms: Richard Hoggart's *Uses of Literary* of 1957, where a rag rug comes to symbolise a great and enduring simplicity of working-class life.[6] I would suggest that it was a need that propelled this sentimentality, the same need that propelled the watching of poor London children in the 1850s. This need is part of a romance, a longing, that in Mayhew's and Ruskin's prose, is for something gone, and lost beyond all retrieval. I hope to be able to make this particular point clearer in a moment.

In quite fundamental ways, Henry Mayhew could not *see* the Little Watercress Girl. He was, for instance, quite uncertain about her status on a modern developmental map. His inability to see her as an eight-year-old, in the way that we might see her, has been given theoretical foundation by Steven

Marcus, in his discussion of Sigmund Freud's similar difficulties in this regard, when he contemplated the adolescent Dora.[7] Deborah Gorham, in discussing Victorian child-prostitution (or rather, the moral panic that surrounded the idea of child prostitution in the 1880s) reminds us that working-class women, girls, and girl-children, were human beings of lesser social worth than themselves, in the eyes of the middle- and upper-class men who bought their sexual services.[8] There was that too, in Mayhew's encounter with the Little Watercress Girl: a far more common purpose for stopping girls and young women in the street than investigation into their trade and economic circumstances. That was not Henry Mayhew's purpose, but that purpose hovers there, throughout the whole interview. He himself expressed concern about the sexual danger that little girls ran, stopping strange men in the streets to try to sell them bootlaces and matches.

Mayhew could not see this child; but I have spent ten years wanting to. In writing *The Tidy House*, I discovered that one of the things I was up to was equating one of the writers of the story, one of these modern children, a child called Carla, with the little watercress girl . . .[9] That equation, of the modern child with the Victorian child, got me a long way; it was a device that allowed me to explore a history of working-class childhood in the book. But after writing the book, and to deflect my attention from seeing what it was that I had wanted and needed from Carla and from that other, long-dead eight-year-old, I set out instead on the path of trying to discover what it was that Mayhew might have seen and understood as he stood there talking to that child, wintertime, Farringdon, 1850 . . .

I started looking for Mayhew with Doré's image of the 1870s, of children playing in a rookery, and assumed that something of his representation of street life would have dictated Mayhew's vision, as much as it did my historical one.[10] I then moved to (roughly) contemporaneous photographs, at first, ones taken by John Thomson of 1876, that display the same sense of an alien culture displaying its rituals to the observer, and to his other images of working-class childhood, notably his 'Beggar Child' of 1876.[11] Why do the details of that particular photograph mean so much to me? Why do I dwell on the necklace as much as on the sores on the dancing girl's face? I want to read these photographs: to be allowed in — quite as much as did this horde of male photographers who wandered the highways and by-ways of poor London in the 1860s, 1870s and 1880s, snapping poor children. (Or more often, taking them to a studio and snapping them there.)

I felt closer to Mayhew's vision with John Allison Spence's 'Slum Child' of 1851, seeing how powerful would seem the smile of childhood to the middle-class observer, were it to surface through the grime recorded here; and seeing how the impassive stare of Robert Crawshaw's 'Two Beggar Girls' might have disturbed Mayhew very much indeed.[12]

In this pursuit of Mayhew's perception, I found my little watercress girl, in John Allison Spence's 'Rag Picker's Daughter' of 1849. Still, in my imagination, when that child of Mayhew's does not wear Carla's face of 1976, she is here. I wanted her like this of course, wanted her not to be looking at the camera, not to be fixed by Mayhew's enquiry; but herself, looking elsewhere.

There were two things that I was not aware of, or was unwilling to admit, as I collected slides of these photographs. The first repression has become clearer, as historical scholarship has got to work on the photographic image. I am thinking here of work on the unstable nature of the pornographic image in the mid/late 19th century — a question that has been particularly scrutinised through the photographs that Munby took of Hannah Cullwick, where certain poses he placed her in, which are irreducibly pornographic to the modern eye, were obviously not intended to be so by him. (Others were, and we can read them as such.) Certainly, and for a very long time, I passed over the pages in my major source book for these photographs, which show little girls in explicitly erotic poses. I divided the portraits of street life in Ovenden and Melville's *Victorian Children* from these. I was, I think, evading the connection of images, a connection which lies irreducibly in the figure of the little girl herself (all the photographs in a book called *Victorian Children* are of little girls). Perhaps, in this way, I was ignoring an important source of Mayhew's vision (and indeed, of my own). When I discovered, rather late in the day, that my source book for these searches and imaginings was indeed, a text book of kiddy porn, my suspicions about the febrility of my search were confirmed;[13] and so was the understanding that the lost object cannot, indeed, be found.

For even at the time of my pursuit of someone else's vision, I did know that the Little Watercress Girl was indeed Henry Mayhew's child, a figure wrought out of his perception and his transcription of her words. She is not to be found looking away from his gaze, as the rag-picker's daughter looks away. This is particularly hard for me. All disciplines possess their romance, and of course, there is a romance of historical practice. Beyond all the hard and practical work in the archives, the patient compilation of an argument from fragmentary sources, there is a wish, or a desire: *that it might be found*; that the past may be delivered up whole. My own romance is still that I may find this child, that there is enough evidence in her narrative, enough detail of her life and the life of her household, to trace her, perhaps through census material, or through an as-yet-unfound survey of street-trading in Clerkenwell.

This romance, this particular romance, is my own desire for this child, read in the light of Mayhew's desire for her (which was indeed, different from mine; and the same, in many ways). In one way, I have found the child, for I see her now as the shade of *Landscape for a Good Woman*, the means by which I allowed myself to recall my own childhood, and write another account of working-class childhood. She was important because of a series of particular meanings that are attached to watercress, to coldness — being cold — to confrontations with male authority, to my father, to being eight-years-old; and to a fairy-tale, Andersen's 'The Snow Queen', which is itself about a great many of these things. More generally than all of this: the Little Watercress Girl is what I want: the past, which is lost and which I cannot have: my own childhood. She is my fantasy child; and in a different way, she was Mayhew's fantasy child too.

You will see then, I hope, that historical inquiry into childhood must lead us to these real theoretical and practical difficulties. From my perspective, it is clear that we need to do several things. We need to make plainer to ourselves the arena of Romanticism and post-Romanticism within which we describe and theorise childhood. This will involve recognising how little distinction we actually make between real children and our fantasies of children. Then perhaps, seeing the usefulness of this confusion (the usefulness of recognising the confusion) we may be able to use it for research purposes. We need to understand the place of our own childhood in our intellectual as much as our psychic life, and to see that the historical framework within which we work can make paedophiles of us all, at some moment or another: that as we watch, talk to, teach and write about children, we desire them, want something from them, which is our own lost childhood.

Childhood is a particular problem for the historian: we are up to something when we work on the history of childhood that we are not up to when we work on other categories of people in the past. The problem is to do with the place that childhood occupies in our culture: the way in which our dealings with children are seen as an objective measure of our civilisation and our humanity. It is for this reason that the kind of history that records a steady march to an enlightened present, lingers persistently in the history of childhood. It is for instance, the history that we all learn at school: that once there were poor little climbing boys, and that then kind people rescued them by putting them in school: and that things are better now. Both the Romantic movement and psycho-analysis have taught us that in cultural terms, and over the last two hundred years, that childhood is that which lies eternally within us, and the thing we can never have: which is our own particular piece of lost time. I would argue, with Dominick LaCapra in *History and Criticism*, that the historian has a massive transferential relationship to the past.[14] I would say that this transference becomes particularly acute and particularly interesting when children are the subjects of historical research, because of the place that children occupy in human culture and human imagination. The history of childhood, and its historiography are important, because they will tell us something particular about what we are up to in 'doing history'.

I can't go beyond this. What I have done is tell you about my own transferential relationship to the past — and I hope, something about Henry Mayhew and an eight-year-old girl. What we can talk about, and what I hope you will be interested in discussing, is class and gender in the study of childhood, and the way in which, over the last two hundred years of cultural life, the little girl has become 'the child'.

Notes

The place of publication is London, unless otherwise indicated.

■ Introduction

1. See for example, Morris Golden, 'Public Context and Imagining Self in *Pamela* and *Shamela*', *English Literary History*, 53:2 (Summer 1986), pp. 311–29.
2. Nancy Armstrong, *Desire and Domestic Fiction*, Oxford University Press, New York, 1989.
3. ibid.,
4. Samuel Richardson, *Pamela, or Virtue Rewarded* (1740), Penguin, Harmondsworth, 1980. Introduction by Margaret A. Doody, p. 20.
5. Jocelyn Harris, *Samuel Richardson*, Cambridge University Press, Cambridge, 1987, pp. 15–32.
6. Margaret Anne Doody, *A Natural Passion: A Study of the Novels of Samuel Richardson*, Clarendon Press, Oxford, 1974, pp. 35–70.
7. Terry Eagleton, *The Rape of Clarissa*, Blackwell, Oxford, 1982, p. 5.
8. ibid., p. 17.
9. Florian Stuber, 'Teaching *Pamela*', *in* Margaret Anne Doody and Peter Sabor (eds), *Samuel Richardson: Tercentenary Essays*, Cambridge University Press, Cambridge, 1989, pp. 8–22.
10. Richard Hoggart does discuss these feelings (though not the chorus) in *The Uses of Literacy* (1957), Penguin, Harmondsworth, 1958, pp. 241–52.
11. John Locke, *Some Thoughts Concerning Education* (1693), John W. and Jean S. Yolton (eds), Clarendon Press, Oxford, 1989, p. 265.
12. ibid., pp. 199–200.
13. Samuel Richardson, *Pamela, or Virtue Rewarded* (1801), Vols 3 and 4, Garland, New York, 1974, Vol.4, p. 308.

14. W. H. Auden, 'Homage to Clio', *Collected Shorter Poems, 1927-1957*, Faber, 1966, p. 307.

15. Paul A. Roth, 'Narrative Explanations: The Case of History', *History and Theory*, 27:1 (1988), pp. 1-13.

16. Raymond Williams, *Keywords: A Vocabulary of Culture and Society*, Fontana, 1984, pp. 87-93.

17. Raymond Williams, *Marxism and Literature*, Oxford University Press, Oxford, 1977, pp. 14-18.

18. Pamela the 'vulgar, practical little soul' is described in Clara Thompson, *Samuel Richardson: A Biographical and Critical Study* (1900), Norwood Edns, Darby, PA, 1978, p. 156; quoted in Eagleton, op. cit., p. 32.

19. Richardson (1801), op. cit., p. 398.

20. John Carroll (ed.), *Selected Letters of Samuel Richardson*, Clarendon Press, Oxford, 1964, p. 184.

21. Franco Moretti, 'Kindergarten', in *Signs Taken for Wonders*, Verso, 1985, pp. 157-81.

■ Landscape for a Good Woman

1. Originally published in Liz Heron (ed.), *Truth, Dare or Promise: Girls Growing Up in the 1950s*, Virago, 1985, pp. 103-26.

2. George Herriman's Krazy Kat cartoons, syndicated throughout the US from 1913 onwards, are reproduced in *Krazy Kat Komix*, vols 1-4, Real Free Press, Amsterdam, 1974-5.

3. Tamara Hareven, *Family Time and Industrial Time: The Relationship Between the Family and Work in a New England Industrial Community*, Cambridge University Press, New York, 1982, p. 355.

4. That is, never applied to the Guardians of the parish for financial help under the Poor Law.

5. Jill Liddington and Jill Norris, *One Hand Tied Behind Us: The Rise of the Women's Suffrage Movement*, Virago, 1978, pp. 93-5.

6. Kathleen Woodward, *Jipping Street* (1928), Virago, London, 1983. My Introduction to this book is reprinted below, pp. 118-25.

7. V. S. Naipaul, *A House for Mr Biswas*, André Deutsch, 1961. Naipaul has written about composing the book in Streatham Hill, in the *New York Review of Books*, 24 November, 1983.

8. Gareth Stedman Jones, *Languages of Class: Studies in English Working Class History, 1832-1982*, Cambridge University Press, Cambridge, 1983, p. 246.

9. Jeremy Seabrook, *Working Class Childhood*, Gollancz, 1982, p. 147.

10. ibid., p. 202.

11. ibid., pp. 21-36.

12. John Berger, *About Looking*, Writers and Readers, 1980, pp. 90-1.

13. ibid., p. 94.

History and Autobiography

1. This paper was originally presented to the Ruskin Centre for Social History Conference on Autobiography, in May 1986. I gave an earlier version to a seminar at the Birmingham University Centre for Contemporary Cultural Studies in March 1986.
2. My Introduction to *Jipping Street* is reproduced below, pp. 119–26.
3. See above, pp. 21–40.
4. See for example Karl J. Weintraub, 'Autobiography and Historical Consciousness', *Critical Inquiry*, 1 (1975), pp. 821–48.
5. Sigmund Freud, 'Family Romances' (1908), *Standard Edition of the Complete Works*, IX, Hogarth Press, 1959, pp. 234–41.
6. Lewis O. Mink, 'Everyman His or Her Own Annalist', *Critical Inquiry*, 4 (1981), pp. 777–83.

Prisonhouses

1. This is an abridged version of the article published as 'Prisonhouses', in *Feminist Review* (Summer, 1985), pp. 7–21, and reprinted in Martin Lawn and Gerald Grace (eds), *Teachers: The Politics and Culture of Work*, Falmer Press, Lewes, 1987, pp. 117–29. The historical arguments that were its springboard will be found below, in 'The Mother Made Conscious', pp. 179–92.
2. Ruth Adam, *I'm Not Complaining* (1938), Virago, 1983.
3. Jeanetta Bowie, *Penny Buff: Memories of a Clydeside School in the Thirties*, Arrow, 1978.
4. Sylvia Ashton Warner, *Teacher* (1963), Virago, 1980.
5. Charlotte Bronte, *Villette* (1853), Penguin, Harmondsworth, 1979, p. 348.
6. Alice Schwartzer, *Simone de Beauvoir Today*, Chatto/Hogarth, 1983, pp. 734, p. 76, pp. 114–15.
7. Stephen Humphries, *Hooligans or Rebels? An Oral History of Working Class Childhood and Youth, 1889–1939*, Blackwell, Oxford, 1981.
8. Elena Giannini Belotti, *Little Girls*, Writers and Readers, 1973, p. 124.
9. Timothy Ashplant, 'The New Function of Cinema', *Journal of the British Film Institute*, 79/80 (April, 1981), pp. 107–9. See also Tim Mason, 'The Writing of History as Literary and Moral Art', *The Times Higher Educational Supplement*, 1 December, 1978, pp. 14–15.
10. Harold Silver, *Education as History*, Methuen, 1983, pp. 17–24.
11. William Taylor, *Society and the Education of Teachers*, Faber and Faber, 1969, p. 12.
12. Karen Clarke, 'Public and Private Children: infant education in the 1820s and 1830s', *in* Carolyn Steedman, Cathy Urwin and Valerie Walkerdine, *Language, Gender and Childhood*, Routledge and Kegan Paul, 1985, pp. 74–87. See also David Vincent, *Bread, Knowledge and*

Freedom: a study of nineteenth century working-class autobiography, Methuen, 1981, pp. 62–75.

13. Philip McCann and Frances A. Young, *Samuel Wilderspin and the Infant School Movement*, Croom Helm, 1982, p. 175.

14. Nancy Chodorow, *The Reproduction of Mothering*, University of California Press, Berkeley, 1978, pp. 199–201.

15. Sara Ruddick, 'Maternal Thinking', *Feminist Studies*, 6:2 (1980), pp. 341–67. Adrienne Rich, *Of Woman Born*, Virago Press, 1979.

16. Marilyn Helterline, 'The Emergence of Modern Motherhood: Motherhood in England, 1899–1959', *International Journal of Women's Studies*, 3:6 (1980), pp. 590–615.

17. ibid, pp. 611–12.

18. Ann Oakley, *The Sociology of Housework*, Martin Robinson, Oxford, 1974, p. 177.

19. Madeleine Davis and David Wallbridge, *Boundary and Space: An Introduction to the Work of D. W. Winnicott*, Penguin, Harmondsworth, 1983, pp. 96–142. D. W. Winnicott, *The Child, the Family and the Outside World*, Penguin, Harmondwsworth, 1964, pp. 179–239.

20. Charlotte Bronte's 'Roe Head Journal' (entry for 11 August, 1836) quoted in Winifred Gerin, *Charlotte Bronte*, Clarendon Press, Oxford, 1967.

21. I was asked by the editors of *Feminist Review* to insert the explanatory paragraphs between pages 54 and 55. I have retained them here, though I still think that the reader is quite capable of seeing what is going on, without the disruption of this explanation.

■ The Tidy House

1. Originally published in *Feminist Review*, 6 (1980), pp. 1–24. This is an expanded version of that article, incorporating some material from 'Schools of Writing', *Screen Education* 38 (Spring 1981), pp. 5–13.

2. This was written in the summer of 1980.

3. The interrelation of names in 'The Tidy House' may make this as difficult to read as it was for me to transcribe. Apart from fashion, which dictated the naming of the characters (1976 was the first summer of Jamie Summers, the Bionic Woman) it is important that Carl is the masculine of Carla, and that Jeannie is at once the name of a longed-for girl child, Carla's own younger sister, and the independent woman of 'Jack Got the Sack'.

4. Opal Whiteley, *The Fairyland Around Us*, privately printed, Los Angeles, 1918. Opal Whiteley, *The Journal of an Understanding Heart*, The Atlantic Monthly Press, Boston, 1920. Ellery Bede, *Fabulous Opal Whiteley*, Binfords and Mort, Portland, Oregan, 1954. Elizabeth Bradburne, *Opal Whiteley, the Unsolved Mystery*, Putnam, 1962.

5. Jane Boulton, 'Stories for Free Children', *MS* (55), 1976. Jane Boulton, *Opal*, Macmillan, 1976.

6. Ruth Manning-Sanders, *Tripple-Trapple*, BBC Publications, 1973.
7. John Berger, *Permanent Red: Essays in Seeing*, Writers and Readers, 1979.
8. In 1980, I knew of Frank Sidgwick, *The Complete Marjory Fleming*, Sidgwick and Jackson, 1934, and Ellen R. C. Creighton, *Ellen Buxton's Journal*, Geoffrey Bles, 1967.
9. In the *Screen Education* article, I used the Diary of Florence Lind Coleridge, Coleridge Collection, Humanities Research Centre, University of Texas at Austin. See also Ednah D. Cheney, *Louisa May Alcott*, Roberts, Boston, 1889; Margaret Emily Shore, *Journal of Emily Shore*, Kegan Paul, 1891.
10. William Labov, *Language in the Inner City*, University of Pennsylvania Press, Philadelphia, 1972, pp. 354–396.
11. For the full passages of writing, see above, p. 67, and p. 72.
12. Henry Mayhew, *London Labour and the London Poor* (1851), Vol. 1, Cass, 1967, p. 477.
13. Henry Mayhew, *London Labour and the London Poor* (1861–62), Vol.2, Cass, 1967, p. 506.
14. Graham Ovenden and Robert Melville, *Victorian Children*, Academy, 1972.
15. Mayhew (1851), op. cit., p. 151.
16. Ellen Moers, *Literary Women*, The Women's Press, 1978, p. 197.
17. Mayhew (1851), op. cit., p. 480, p. 481, p. 487.

■ Amarjit's Song

1. This is an altered and shortened version of the chapter originally published in Carolyn Steedman, Cathy Urwin and Valerie Walkerdine, *Language Gender and Childhood*, Routledge and Kegan Paul, 1985.
2. Sixth Report of the Children's Employment Commission (1862), PP 1867, xvi, p. 132. David Vincent, *Bread, Knowledge and Freedom: A Study of Nineteenth Century Working Class Autobiography*, Methuen, 1982, pp. 89–92, p. 107. L. S. Vygotsky, *Mind in Society*, Harvard University Press, Cambridge, Mass., 1978, pp. 97–9.
3. Jean Piaget, *Dreams and Imitations*, Routledge and Kegan Paul, 1954, pp. 89–104.
4. Sheila McCullagh, *The Green Man and the Golden Bird*, Hart-Davis, St Albans, 1976.
5. Vera Southgate et al., *Extending Beginning Reading*, Heinemann, 1981, pp. 188–9. Ruth Weir, *Language in the Crib*, Mouton, The Hague, 1970.
6. George Orwell, 'Shooting an Elephant' (1936), in *Collected Essays, Letters and Journalism of George Orwell: An Age Like This*, Penguin, Harmondsworth, 1970, pp. 265–72.
7. Leila Berg, *Reading and Loving*, Routledge and Kegan Paul, 1977, pp. 87–8; *Fish and Chips for Supper*, Macmillan, 1963.
8. Ellen Moers, *Literary Women*, The Women's Press, 1978, pp. 245–51.

9. Mary Sanches and Barbara Kirshenblatt Gimblett, 'Children's Traditional Speech Play and Child Language', in Barbara Kirshenblatt Gimblett (ed.), *Speech Play*, University of Pennsylvania Press, Philadelphia, 1976, pp. 165–210.

10. Sabrina Peck, 'Child-child Discourse in Second Language Acquisition', in Evelyn Hatch (ed.), *Second Language Acquisition*, Newbury House, Rowley, Mass., 1978, pp. 383–400. John H. McDowell, 'Sociolinguistic Contours in the Verbal Art of Chicano Children', *International Journal of Chicano Studies Research*, 13: 1–2 (1982), pp. 165–93.

11. See John Lyon's discussion of this point in *Introduction to Theoretical Linguistics*, Cambridge University Press, Cambridge, 1968, pp. 19–20.

12. Johnny Copasetic, 'Rude Boys Don't Argue', *Melody Maker*, 19 May, 1979, p. 41.

13. Roger H. Flavell, *Language Users and Their Errors*, Macmillan, 1983, p. 55, p. 17.

14. My thanks to Dr Christopher Shackle of the School of Oriental and African Studies, University of London, for the information he gave me about the poetic system of Punjabi and the artistic and domestic culture that supports it. For a description of the the wider poetic system into which that of the Punjab fits, see S. H. Kellogg, *A Grammar of the Hindi Language*, Kegan Paul, 1938, pp. 546–84.

15. Susan Ervin Tripp, 'Is Second Language Learning Like the First?', *TESOL Quarterly*, 8:2 (June 1974), p. 124. Jules Ronjat, *Le Developpement du langage observé chez un enfant bilingue*, Champion, Paris, 1913, pp. 17–35.

16. See Hazel Carby, 'Multi-culture', *Screen Education*, 34 (Spring 1980), pp. 62–70, for a discussion of popular multicultural education. See also Barry Troyna, 'The Ideological and Policy Response to Black Pupils in British Schools', in Anthony Hartnett (ed.), *The Social Sciences in Educational Studies*, Heinemann, 1982, pp. 127–43 for the legislative base for multicultural education. See Bob Dixon, *Catching Them Young* (2 vols), *Volume 1: Sex, Race and Class in Children's Books*, Pluto Press, 1977 for an assessment of children's reading material within the thoery; and for the role of 'experience' within 'multiculturalism' see R. Jeffcoate, 'A Multicultural Curriculum: Beyond the Orthodoxy', *Trends in Education*, 4 (1979), pp. 8–12.

17. Karen Ann Watson Gegeo, 'From Verbal Play to Talk Story: the Role of Routines in Speech Events among Hawaiian Children', in Susan Ervin Tripp and Claudia Mitchell Kernan (eds), *Child Discourse*, Academic Press, New York, 1977, pp. 67–90. Kirshenblatt-Gimblett (1976), op. cit., pp. 65–110. Brian Sutton Smith, *The Folkgames of Children*, University of Texas Press for the American Folklore Society, Austin, 1972, pp. 485–90.

18. For the Sikh naming system, see A. G. James, *Sikh Children in Britain*, Oxford University Press, 1974, p. 24. W. Owen Cole and Piara Singh Sambi, *The Sikhs: Their Religious Beliefs and Practices*, Routledge and Kegan Paul, 1978, pp. 113–14.

19. The children used the word for the place where the Sikh scriptures are

kept, that is, the temple, or a room set aside in a private house for worship, to describe the ceremony itself. James, op.cit., pp. 30–52. Owen Cole and Singh Sambi, op. cit., pp. 112–13.

20. Penelope Brown, Marthe Macintyre, Ros Morpeth and Shirley Prendergast, 'A Daughter: A Thing To Be Given Away', in Cambridge Women's Studies Group, *Women in Society*, Virago Press, 1981, pp. 127–45.
21. Raymond Williams, *The Country and the City*, Paladin, St. Albans, 1975, p. 17.
22. Carby, op. cit., p. 69. 'A white woman teacher . . . may care about the position of black women and want to learn about them, understand them, teach them. Nevertheless, it would be important that she should recognise the implications of what womanhood means for black womanhood, clarify what are the social relations with those she teaches. . . . The conflict-ridden duality in the pedagogic role will remain unperceived if teachers . . . are too comfortable or complacent about their own anti-racism.'
23. Maureen Stone, *The Education of the Black Child in Britain: The Myth of Multiracial Education*, Fontana, 1981, pp. 61–2; p. 135. See also Ken Worpole and Dave Morley, *The Republic of Letters: Working Class Writing and Local Publishing*, Comedia, 1982, p. 104.
24. For a contemporary example of prescriptive multiculturalism, see Louis Cohen and Lawrence Manion, *Multicultural Classrooms*, Croom Helm, 1983.
25. Stone, op. cit., p. 69. Stuart Hall, 'Education and the Crisis of the Urban School', in John Raynor and Elizabeth Harris (eds), *Schooling in the City*, Ward Lock, 1979.
26. Alan James, 'The "Multicultural" Curriculum', in Alan James and Robert Jeffcoate (eds), *The School in the Multicultural Society*, Harper and Row, 1981, p. 23.
27. John and Elizabeth Newson, *Patterns of Infant Care in an Urban Community*, Penguin, Harmondsworth, 1965, p. 262.
28. Gordon Wells, *Learning Through Interaction: The Study of Language Development*, Cambridge University Press, Cambridge, 1981, p. 5. See also J. W. B. Douglas, *The Home and the School*, MacGibbon and Kee, Glasgow, 1964; R. Davie, N. Butler and H. Goldstein, *From Birth to Seven*, Longman, 1972; K. Fogelman, *Britain's Sixteen Year Olds*, National Children's Bureau, 1976; J. Essen and M. Ghodsian, 'Children of Immigrants and School Performance', *New Community*, 7:3 (1979), pp. 422–9.
29. See Ronald King, *All Things Bright and Beautiful? The Sociology of Infants' Classrooms*, Wiley, Chichester, 1978, p. 102, pp. 110–26, pp. 89–95. See also Rachel Sharp and Anthony Green, *Education and Social Control: A Study in Progressive Primary Education*, Routledge and Kegan Paul, 1975, pp. 137–65, and passim.
30. Department of Education and Science, *Children and Their Primary Schools* ('The Plowden Report'), HMSO, 1967, vol.I, pp. 57–9.

31. A. H. Halsey, *Educational Priority* (4 vols), *EPA Problems and Policies*, vol. 1, HMSO, 1972, pp. 43-53.
32. Audrey Curtis and Peter Blatchford, *Meeting the Needs of Socially Handicapped Children*, Nelson, Walton-on-Thames, 1981, p. 16.
33. Wallace E. Lambert, 'The Effects of Bilingualism on the Individual: Cognitive and Sociocultural Consequences', in Peter A. Hornby (ed.), *Bilingualism: Psychological, Social and Educational Implications*, Academic Press, New York, 1977. Jane Miller, 'How Do You Spell Gujerati, Sir?' in L. Michaels and C. Ricks (eds), *The State of the Language*, University of California Press, Berkeley, 1980, pp. 140-51.
34. Brian Jackson, *Starting School*, Croom Helm, 1979, p. 100, p. 136.

▪ True Romances

1. This is a shortened version of a chapter originally published in Raphael Samuel (ed.), *Patriotism: The Making and Unmaking of English National Identity*, (3 volumes), Vol. 1, Routledge, 1989, pp. 26-35.
2. *Observer*, 12 June 1983.
3. Christopher Hill, 'History is a matter of taking liberties', *Guardian*, 30 July, 1983. 'What is History? The Great Debate', *History Today*, 34 (May 1984), pp. 10-11.
4. For the text of Joseph's speech to the Historical Association of 16 February 1984, in which he revealed that history was to be a component of the core curriculum, see *The Times Educational Supplement*, 17 February, 1984, p. 32.
5. Sigmund Freud, 'Family Romances' (1908), *Standard Edition of the Complete Works*, vol.9, Hogarth Press, 1959, pp. 234-41.
6. Bruno Bettelheim, *The Uses of Enchantment: The Meaning and Importance of Fairy Tales*, Penguin, Harmondsworth, 1978, pp. 37-41.
7. ibid., p. 40.
8. Freud, op. cit., pp. 238-9.
9. Bettelheim, op. cit., pp. 35-41.
10. Henry Mayhew, *London Labour and the London Poor* (1861-1862), Vol. 2, Cass, 1967, pp. 66-9.

▪ Kathleen Woodward's *Jipping Street*

1. 'Introduction', Kathleen Woodward, *Jipping Street* (1928), Virago, 1983.
2. Jean McCrindle and Sheila Rowbotham, *Dutiful Daughters*, Penguin, Harmondsworth, 1979, p. 4, p. 116.
3. Joy Parr, *Labouring Children*, Croom Helm, 1980, pp. 14-26. James Walvin, *A Child's World*, Penguin, Harmondsworth, 1982, pp. 61-9. Carol Dyhouse, *Girls Growing Up in Late Victorian and Edwardian England*, Routledge and Kegan Paul, 1981, pp. 104-5.

4. T. A. Jackson, *Solo Trumpet*, Lawrence and Wishart, 1953. Guy A. Aldred, *No Traitor's Gait* (3 vols), Strickland Press, Glasgow, 1955–63. R. M. Fox, *Smoky Crusade*, Hogarth Press, 1937. Edward Royle, *Radicals, Secularists and Republicans: Popular Freethought in Britain, 1866–1915*, Manchester University Press, Manchester, 1982.

5. Gareth Stedman Jones, 'Working Class Culture and Working Class Politics in London, 1870–1900', *Journal of Social History*, 7 (1974), pp. 460–508.

6. Rupert E. Davies *John Scott Lidgett*, Epworth Press, 1957, p. 54.

7. Alexander Paterson, *Across the Bridges*, Edward Arnold, London, 1911.

8. Arthur Morrison, *Tales of Mean Streets* (1894), Methuen, 1903, 'Introduction'.

9. Kathleen Woodward, *Queen Mary: A Life and Intimate Study*, Hutchinson, 1927.

10. *Daily Mail*, 20 September, 1927.

11. Fenner Brockway, *Bermondsey Story: The Life of Alfred Salter*, Allen and Unwin, 1949, pp. 46–8.

12. Mary Agnes Hamilton, *Mary Macarthur: A Biographical Sketch*, Leonard Parsons, 1925, pp. 101–7; pp. 120–1.

13. *Daily Mail, Daily Express, Daily Sketch*, 20 September 1927. *World's Children*, November 1928. Records of the National Union of Journalists.

14. Cover copy, Longman edition, 1928. *Adelaide Register*, 17 November, 1928.

15. *Jipping Street* was simultaneously published in the USA, by Harper and Row.

16. Arthur Morrison, *Child of the Jago* (1896), Methuen, 1897.

17. Nancy Chodorow, *The Reproduction of Mothering: Psychoanalysis and the Sociology of Gender*, University of California Press, Berkeley, 1978.

18. Margaret Llewelyn Davies, *Maternity: Letters from Working Women* (1915), Virago, 1978.

19. William Labov, *Language in the Inner City*, University of Pennsylvania Press, Philadelphia, 1974, pp. 364–93.

20. Jonathan Culler, *The Pursuit of Signs*, Routledge and Kegan Paul, 1981, pp. 128–81.

21. Sigmund Freud, *Case Histories II* (Volume 9 of the Pelican Freud Library), Penguin, Harmondsworth, 1979, pp.287-90.

22. Anna Pollert, *Girls, Wives, Factory Lives*, Macmillan, 1980, pp. 121–22.

■ Written Children

1. I gave versions of this paper — originally called 'Theorising the Child-Figure, 1880–1920' — to Sheffield Polytechnic Cultural Studies Seminar in November 1988, to Liverpool University Education Department in May 1989, and to Warwick University Faculty of Educational Studies Cross-Disciplinary Seminar in October 1989. Above is the text of the

paper I gave to the Strathclyde University English Department Staff Seminar, in March 1989.

2. For a biographical outline of McMillan's life, see below, pp. 158–9.
3. For 'sacralisation' see Viviana A. Zelizer, *Pricing the Priceless Child: The Changing Social Value of Children*, Basic Books, New York, 1985.
4. Margaret McMillan, 'The Half Time System', *Clarion*, 12 September, 1896.
5. John Ruskin, 'Fairyland', from 'The Art of England' (1884), *The Library Edition of the Works of John Ruskin*, Vol. 33, Allen and Unwin, 1908, pp. 338–42, pp. 327–49. See also 'Design in the German School', from 'Ariadne Florentia' (1874), *The Library Edition of the Works of John Ruskin*, Vol. 22, Allen and Unwin, 1906, pp. 390–421.
6. John Ruskin, 'Humility', from 'Time and Tide' (1867), *The Library Edition of the Works of John Ruskin*, Vol. 17, Allen and Unwin, 1906, p. 406.
7. Ruskin, 'Fairyland', op. cit., p. 341.
8. Margaret McMillan, *Infant Mortality*, Independent Labour Party, 1906.
9. Peter Coveney, *The Image of Childhood, The Individual and Society: A Study of the Theme in English Literature* (first published as *Poor Monkey*, Rockliff, 1957), Penguin, Harmondsworth, 1967.
10. Robert Pattison, *The Child Figure in English Literature*, University of Georgia Press, Athens, 1978, pp. 47–75.
11. See David Armstrong, *The Political Anatomy of the Body*, Cambridge University Press, Cambridge, 1983, pp. 54–72 for the development of a psychology of childhood. See Robin Campbell and Roger Wales, 'The Study of Language Acquisition', in John Lyons (ed.), *New Horizons in Linguistics*, Penguin, 1970, pp. 242–260 for a brief but thorough mapping of the history of linguistic attention to children's speech.
12. Couze Venn, 'The Subject of Psycholgy', in Henriques, Jules et al (eds), *Changing the Subject*, Methuen, 1984.
13. Margaret McMillan, 'Gutterella: A Woman of the Age of Gold', *Weekly Times and Echo*, 28 December, 1895.
14. Margaret McMillan, 'In Holy Isle', *Highway*, October 1911.
15. Margaret McMillan, 'Lola', 'Lola: Conclusion', *Clarion*, 21 February, 3 March, 1897.
16. I have been unable to trace the source of this quotation. When McMillan used it again, years later, she called it a Russian proverb. See Carolyn Steedman, *Childhood Culture and Class in Britain, Margaret McMillan, 1860–1931*, Virago, 1990, p. 275, n.30.
17. Margaret McMillan, 'A la Salpetrière', *Clarion*, 29 April 1897.
18. Henri F. Ellenberger, *The Discovery of the Unconscious: The History and Evolution of Dynamic Psychiatry*, Allen Lane, 1970. Lancelot Law Whyte, *The Unconscious Before Freud*, Julian Friedman, 1979.
19. Concerning for instance, the reluctance of a six-year-old girl she had encountered through school visiting to take a bath, and how the child had revealed, in a matter-of-fact way, scarcely remembering, that her mother had drowned herself in the local dam. Margaret McMillan,

'School Board Notes', *Labour Echo*, 18 September, 1897. The same point about the paucity of memory and its repression in poor children was also frequently made by McMillan in her non-fiction writing. In an ILP pamphlet of 1902, she described another girl recounting her mother's death, in the same off-hand way.

> Not at all; the memory of that poor mother was already growing dim; but not because the child was unatural. The very poor *cannot afford to remember*. Your fidelity, your tender thoughts of those who are no longer with you, cost something to the organism. . . . Memory, more than any other faculty, is directly dependent on the blood supply, that is to say, on the food supply. Margaret McMillan, *The Beginnings of Education* (City Branch Pamphlet No. 8), City of London Branch of the ILP, 1902 (1903).

20. Margaret McMillan, 'Education in the Primary School', *Labour Leader*, April 27, 1899.
21. Rachel McMillan College Library, McMillan Collection, Letters, A1/1, Margaret McMillan to Sallie Blatchford, 22 February, 1895.
22. In *Socialism and the Home*, Katharine Bruce Glasier wrote 'Those who are familiar with the biographical writing of the brothers Reclus and Kropotkin, gathered into a wonderfully suggestive form by Drummond in his "Ascent of Man", will recognise the form of the argument that it has been the helplessness of little children more than any other influence that has led us up as a human race to the possibilities of the Socialist state'. Henry Drummond, *Lowell Lectures on the Ascent of Man*, Hodder and Stoughton, 1894. Katharine Bruce Glasier, *Socialism and the Home*, ILP Press, 1911, p. 7.
23. Drummond, op. cit., p. 282.
24. ibid., p. 288.
25. ibid., pp. 346–7.
26. ibid., p. 338.
27. Franco Moretti, 'Kindergarten', in *Signs Taken for Wonders*, Verso, 1983, pp. 157–81.
28. ibid., p. 162.
29. Margaret McMillan, 'In a Garden' *Highway*, June 1911; 'In Our Garden', *Highway*, July, 1911; 'In Our Garden: Marigold, An English Mignon', *Highway*, September, 1911; 'In Our Garden, I–V', *Highway*, April — September, 1912. See a reprint of 'Marigold, An English Mignon', *Christian Commonwealth*, 3 January, 1912.
30. Johann Wolfgang von Goethe, *Wilhelm Meister's Years of Apprenticeship*, (trans. H. M. Wardson), 6 vols., John Calder, 1977. For the song, Vol. 1, Book III, pp. 167–8. For the musical arrangement, 'Mignons Gesang', *Schubert-Lieder*, Band III, C. F. Peters, Frankfurt, n.d., pp. 221–4.
31. See *The Times*, 22, 28, February, 22 April, 1910. *The Times Literary Supplement*, 14 April, 1910. *Wilhelm Meisters Theatralische Sedung*, Von Goethe, Rascher, Zurich, 1910. *Wilhelm Meisters Theatralische Sedung*,

Stuttgart, 1911. *Wilhelm Meister's Theatrical Mission* (translated by Gregory A. Page), Heinemann, 1913. In reviewing the earlier version, the *TLS* noted that in the first version of Mignon's song the laurel tree stretched high with more ecstasy (*hoch* having later replaced the first choice of *froh*) — in a manner reminiscent of Mignon's bodily movements?

32. Goethe (1977), op. cit., p. 87, pp. 88–9.
33. ibid., p. 87, p. 89.
34. ibid., Vol 1, Book III, pp. 139–40; Vol. 2, Book V, pp. 110–11.
35. ibid., Vol. 4, Book VIII, pp. 89–90.
36. ibid., p. 105.
37. William Gilby, 'The Structural Significance of Mignon in *Wilhelm Meisters Lehrjahre*', *Seminar*, 26 (1980), pp. 136–50.
38. ibid., Vol. 1, Book II, p. 95, p. 98.
39. McMillan, 'Marigold' (1911), op. cit.
40. ibid. For Mignon's impulsiveness, Goethe (1977), Vol. 1, Book II, pp. 124–5, Book III, pp. 167–8.
41. Franco Moretti, *The Way of the World: the Bildungsroman in European Culture*, Verso, 1987, p. 47.
42. Goethe (1977), op. cit., Vol. 3, Book VIII, pp. 130–1.
43. Steve Neale, 'Melodrama and Tears', *Screen*, 27:6 (November/ December 1986), pp. 6–22.
44. Pattison, op. cit., p. 58.
45. Gilby, op. cit., p. 149.
46. For another writing of this moment, see Margaret McMillan, *The Nursery School*, Dent, 1919, p. 182; and for Marigold's fate, see Margaret McMillan, *The Camp School*, Allen and Unwin, 1917, pp. 82–3.

■ The Radical Policeman's Tale

1. I gave versions of this paper to the MA in Victorian Studies Seminar at Keele University in November 1986, to the Social History Seminar, Kings College, Cambridge in May 1987, and at the University of Sussex Graduate Seminar in June 1987. This version was given at Portsmouth Polytechnic in November, 1988.
2. Marquess of Anglesey, *Sergeant Pearman's Memoirs*, Cape, 1968, pp. 14–15.
3. ibid., p. 14.
4. ibid., pp. 17–18.
5. Linda H. Peterson, *Victorian Autobiography: The Tradition of Self-Interpretation*, Yale University Press, New Haven, 1986.
6. Carlo Ginzburg, *The Cheese and the Worms*, Routledge and Kegan Paul, 1980.
7. Carolyn Steedman, *Policing the Victorian Community: The Formation of*

English Provincial Police Forces, 1856–1880, Routledge and Kegan Paul, 1984.

8. James Gilling, *The Life of a Lancer in the Wars of the Punjab*, Simpkin Marshall, 1855.

9. William Hall, *The Diary of William Hall*, privately printed, Penryn, n.d. (1848).

10. Margaret Spufford, *Small Books and Pleasant Histories: Popular Fiction and its Readership in Seventeenth Century England*, Cambridge University Press, Cambridge, 1981, pp. 45–82; pp. 156–93. Bruno Bettelheim, *The Uses of Enchantment:The Meaning and Importance of Fairy Tales*, Penguin, 1978.

■ Forms of History, Histories of Form

1. This is the text of a paper I gave at the Institute of Contemporary Arts in 1988. A slightly different version was published in Helen Carr (ed.), *From My Guy to Sci-Fi: Genre and Women's Writing in the Postmodern World*, Pandora, 1989, pp. 98–111.

2. Margaret McMillan, *Life of Rachel McMillan*, Dent, 1927.

3. Albert Mansbridge, *Margaret McMillan, Prophet and Pioneer: Her Life and Work*, Dent, 1932. D'Arcy Cresswell, *Margaret McMillan, A Memoir*, Hutchinson, 1948. G.A.N. Lowndes, *Margaret McMillan, The Children's Champion*, Museum Press, 1960. Elizabeth Bradburn, *Margaret Mcmillan, Framework and Expansion of Nursery Education*, Denholm Press, Redhill, 1976.

4. The myth of Corinne is a myth of a woman's oratical powers as when the eponymous heroine of Mme de Staël's novel holds huge crowds in thrall at the Capitol in Rome with her extemporisations. See Germaine de Staël, *Corinne, or, Italy* (1807), translated and edited by Avriel H. Goldberger, Rutgers University Press, New Brunswick, 1987, pp. 26–31. Ellen Moers discussed the myth of the female orator in *Literary Women*, Women's Press, 1978, pp. 145–8.

5. Raymond Williams, *Marxism and Literature*, Oxford University Press, Oxford, 1977, pp. 145–8.

6. Percy Redfern, *Journey to Understanding*, Allen and Unwin, 1946, pp. 18–19.

7. M. M. Bakhtin, *The Dialogic Imagination: Four Essays* (Michael Holquist [ed.]) University of Texas Press, Austin, 1981, pp. 130–46.

8. Linda H. Peterson, *Victorian Autobiography: The Tradition of Self Interpretation*, Yale University Press, New Haven, 1986.

9. Virginia Woolf, *Three Guineas* (1938), Hogarth Press, 1984, p.177. I owe this reference to Kathryn Dodd. See Note 10.

10. Kathryn Dodd, 'Historians, Texts and Ray Strachey's *The Cause*', unpublished paper, 1986. Ray Strachey, *The Cause* (1928), Virago, 1988. Kathryn Dodd, 'Cultural Politics and Women's Historical Writing: The

Case of Ray Strachey's *The Cause*, *Women's Studies International Forum*, 13: 1–2 (1990), pp. 127–37.

Horsemen

1. First published as 'Horsemen' in the *London Review of Books*, 10:3 (4 February, 1988).
2. Marjorie Shostak, *Nisa: The Life and Words of a ¡Kung Woman*, Allen Lane, 1982.
3. Robert Roberts, *The Classic Slum*, Manchester University Press, 1971.

The Mother Made Conscious

1. This is a shortened version of the piece originally published under the same title in *History Workshop*, 20 (Autumn 1985), pp. 149–63, and reprinted in M. Woodhouse and A. McGrath (eds), *Family, School and Society*, Hodder and Stoughton, 1988, pp. 82–95.
2. Tamara K. Hareven, *Family Time and Industrial Time*, Cambridge University Press, New York, 1982, pp. 355–82.
3. Carolyn Steedman, *The Tidy House*, Virago, 1982, op. cit., pp. 85–8.
4. ibid., pp. 69–84.
5. Catherine Stanley, 'Journal of Her Five Children, 1811–1819', Cheshire Record Office, DSA 75.
6. Elizabeth Cleghorn Gaskell, *My Diary*, Clement Shorter (ed.), privately printed, San Francisco, 1923. Diary keeping like this was not restricted to literary families. In the 1850s Isabella Stevenson was able to set down little Louis's childhood in one of the blank 'Baby Books' then available. Margaret Isabella Stevenson, *Stevenson's Baby Book*, printed by John Howell for John Henry Nash, San Francisco, 1922. See Steedman (1982), op. cit., pp. 256–7.
7. Lilian G. Katz, 'Contemporary Perspectives on the Roles of Mothers and Teachers', *Australian Journal of Early Childhood Education*, 7:1 (March 1982), pp. 4–15.
8. Hippolyte Taine, 'The Acquisition of Language in Children', *Mind*, 2:6 (April 1877), pp. 252–9. James Mark Baldwin, *Mental Development in the Child and the Race*, Macmillan, New York, 1894. James Sully, *Studies of Childhood*, Longman, 1896. W. Preyer, *The Mind of the Child*, 2 vols, Appleton, New York, 1888–1890.
9. Charles Darwin, 'A Biographical Sketch of an Infant', *Mind*, 2:7 (July 1877), pp. 252–9. Jules Ronjat, *Le Développement du langage observé chez un enfant bilingue*, Champion, Paris, 1913.
10. Steedman (1982), op. cit., pp. 86–7.
11. Asher Tropp, *The School Teachers*, Heinemann, 1957, pp. 23–4. Frances Widdowson, *Going Up Into the Next Class: Women and Elementary Teacher Training*, Heinemann, 1983. Francesca M. Wilson, *Rebel*

Daughter of a Country House: The Life of Eglantine Jebb, Allen and Unwin, 1967, pp. 80–96.

12. Bertha Maria von Marenholtz-Buelow, *Women's Educational Mission: Being an Explanation of Friederich Froebel's System of Infant Gardens*, Dalton, 1855, p. 22. For an account of a 'professionalisation of the maternal role' among German middle-class women, and through the agency of the kindergarten, see Ann Taylor Allen, 'Spiritual Motherhood: German Feminists and the Kindergarten Movement, 1848–1911', *History of Education Quarterly*, 22:3 (Fall 1982), pp. 319–39.

13. W. H. Herford, *The Student's Froebel*, Isbister, 1899, pp. 34–5.

14. Johann Heinrich Pestalozzi, *How Gertrude Teaches Her Children* (1801), Allen and Unwin, 1900. Jane Roland Martin, 'Excluding Women from the Educational Realm', *Harvard Educational Review*, 52:2 (May 1982). pp. 133–48.

15. Friedrich Froebel, *Autobiography of Friedrich Froebel*, Swan Sonnenschein, 1906.

16. Marenholtz-Buelow, op.cit., pp. 6–7.

17. T. G. Rooper, *School and Home Life*, Brown, n.d., pp. 336–7.

18. Peter Coveney, *Poor Monkey: The Child in Literature*, Rockliff, 1957, pp. 280–1. Nanette Whitbread, *The Evolution of the Nursery-Infant School: A History of Infant and Nursery Education in Britain, 1800–1970*, Routledge and Kegan Paul, 1972, p. 34. Henry Morley, 'Infant Gardens', *Household Words*, 21 July 1855, pp. 577–82.

19. Roland Martin, op. cit., p. 135.

20. William Taylor, *Society and the Education of Teachers*, Faber and Faber, 1969, p. 12.

21. P. Woodham-Smith, 'History of the Froebel Movement in England', in Evelyn Lawrence (ed.), *Friederich Froebel and English Education*, Routledge and Kegan Paul, 1952, pp. 34–94. Maurice Galton, Brian Simon, Paul Croll, *Inside the Primary Classroom*, 1980, Routledge and Kegan Paul, pp. 33–4.

22. Raymond Williams, *The Country and the City*, Paladin, St. Albans, 1979, p. 9. Edmond Holmes, *What Is and What Might Be*, Constable, 1911, p. 154.

23. Margaret McMillan, *The Nursery School*, Dent, 1919, p. 182.

24. Margaret McMillan, *1901–1926: Twenty-Fifth Anniversary Celebrations*, Bradford Froebel and Child Study Association, Bradford, 1926, p. 2.

25. Margaret McMillan, *What the Nursery School Is*, Labour Party, London, 1923, p. 5.

26. Allen, op. cit., pp. 321–2.

27. Lesley Webb, *Modern Practice in the Infant School*, Blackwell, Oxford, 1976, p. 10. See also Lorna Ridgeway, *The Task of the Teacher in the Primary School*, Ward Lock, 1976, and King, op. cit., p. 72.

28. Johann and Bertha Ronge, *A Practical Guide to the English Kindergarten, For the Use of Mothers, Governesses and Infant Teachers*, Myers, 1884. Lileen Hardy, *The Diary of a Free Kindergarten*, Gay and Hancock, Edinburgh, 1912.

29. Margaret McMillan, *Life of Rachel McMillan*, Dent, 1927, pp. 170–201.

30. D. W. Winnicott, *The Child, the Family and the Outside World*, Penguin, Harmondsworth, 1964. For an account of Winnicott's 'ordinary devoted mother' see Madeleine Davies and David Wallbridge, *Boundary and Space: An Introduction to the Work of D.W. Winnicott*, Penguin, Harmondsworth, 1983, pp. 129-3.
31. ibid., pp. 189-90.
32. ibid., p. 203.
33. ibid., pp. 201-2.
34. Eli Zaretsky, *Capitalism, the Family and Personal Life*, Pluto, 176, pp. 27-8, pp. 54-5.
35. Dale Spender, *Invisible Women*, Women's Press, 1982, pp. 56-7. Dale Spender and Elizabeth Sarah (eds), *Learning to Lose*, Women's Press, 1980, pp. 69-89.
36. Roland Martin, op. cit., p. 137.
37. Denise Riley, *War in the Nursery*, Virago, 1983, pp. 80-108.
38. Davis and Wallbridge, op. cit., pp. 19-39.
39. Lawrence, op. cit., pp. 126-7, pp. 190-3.
40. Philip McCann and Francis A. Young, *Samuel Wilderspin and the Infant School Movement*, Croom Helm, 1982, pp. 172-4.
41. ibid., p. 175.
42. ibid., p. 42.
43. Widdowson, op. cit., p.42. The same dramatic shift can be seen in Scotland, where in 1851 women composed 35 per cent of the teaching population, a figure which had grown to 70 per cent by 1911. Helen Corr, 'The Sexual Division of Labour in the Scottish Teaching Profession, 1872-1914', in (eds) Walter M. Humes and Hamish M. Paterson, *Scottish Culture and Scottish Education, 1800-1980*, John Donald, Edinburgh, 1983, p. 137.
44. Widdowson, op. cit., p. 8. David, op. cit., pp. 125-6.
45. Clara E. Grant, *Farthing Bundles*, privately printed, 1931, pp. 34-5. Tropp, op. cit., pp. 10-11. Widdowson, op. cit., passim.
46. Grant, op. cit., p. 33.
47. Galton et al, op. cit., p. 35.
48. Brian and Sonia Jackson, *Childminder*, Penguin, Harmondsworth, 1979, pp. 22-3.
49. Margaret McMillan, *Schools of Tomorrow*, J. P. Steel Shelton, Stoke-on-Trent, 1908, pp. 15-16.
50. Alexander Paterson, *Across the Bridges*, Arnold, 1911, p. 58.
51. Whitbread, op. cit., pp. 1-15; pp. 81-99. Report of the Commissioners Appointed to Inquire into Popular Education, PP 1866, xxi (Part I), p. 28, p. 114, p. 539.
52. John R. Edwards, *Language and Disadvantage*, Arnold, 1979, p. 19.
53. Elena Giannini Belotti, *Little Girls*, Writers and Readers, 1975, pp. 106-158. See also Winnicott, op. cit., pp. 189-90: 'fortunately she [the teacher] need not know everything'. Tropp, op. cit., describes a mid-nineteenth century keeping of teachers in their intellectual place.
54. Elizabeth Fox Genovese, 'Placing Women in History', *New Left Review*, 133 (May-June 1982), p. 14.

55. ibid., p. 29.

◼ The Watercress Seller

1. I gave a longer version of this paper to Birmingham Polytechnic English Faculty Lecture in March 1987, under the title of 'Images of Childhood'. This is the text of an earlier and shorter version, given under the title 'Henry Mayhew and the Problem of Transference' to a Conference on the Ethnography of Childhood at Kings College, Cambridge, in July 1986.
2. Deborah Gorham, 'The "Maiden Tribute of Modern Babylon" Re-examined: Child Prostitution and the Idea of Childhood in Late Victorian England', *Victorian Studies*, 21:3 (Spring 1978), pp. 353–79.
3. Reports of the Commissioners on the Employment of Children in Trades and Manufactures Not Already Regulated by Law, PP 1863, xviii; 1864, xxii; 1865, xx; 1866, xxiv; 1867, xvi. Report of the Commissioners of Inquiry into the Employment of Women and Children in Agriculture, PP 1867–8, xvii.
4. John Ruskin, 'Humility', from 'Time and Tide' (1867), *The Library Edition of the Works of John Ruskin*, vol. 17, Allen and Unwin, 1906, pp. 405–9.
5. Elizabeth Gaskell, *Mary Barton* (1848), Penguin, Harmondsworth, 1970, pp. 49–53.
6. Richard Hoggart, *The Uses of Literacy*, Chatto and Windus, 1957, pp. 32–8.
7. Steven Marcus, 'Freud and Dora: Story, History, Case-History', in *Representation: Essays on Literature and Society*, Random House, New York, 1976, pp. 247–310.
8. Gorham, op. cit., p. 365.
9. See above, pp. 84–7.
10. See 'Dudley Street, Seven Dials' (facing p. 158) and 'The Organ in the Court' (facing p. 176), Gustave Doré and Blanchard Jerrold, *London: A Pilgrimage* (1872), Dover, New York, 1970.
11. John Thomson, and Adolphe Smith, *Street Life in London*, privately printed, London, 1877.
12. The source-book for all the photographs now discussed is Graham Ovenden and Robert Melville, *Victorian Children*, Academy Editions, 1972; on which, see below.
13. Jacqueline Rose, *The Case of Peter Pan, Or, The Impossibility of Children's Fiction*, Macmillan, 1984, p. 30. M. Linklater, "Victorian" Photos Faked', *Sunday Times*, 19 November, 1979.
14. Dominick LaCapra, *History and Criticism*, Cornell University Press, Ithaca, 1985, pp. 71–94.

Index